West

Side

Predators

The Indigenous Shifter Superhero
Series(Book One)

This is a work of fiction. Names, characters, businesses, places, events, and incidents are either the product of the author's imagination or used in a fictitious manner. Any resemblance to actual persons, living or dead, or actual events is purely coincidental.

West Side Predators

The Indigenous Shifter Superhero Series(Book One)

Copyright © 2023 Dwight Salaam

ISBN: 979-8218348731

This book is dedicated to my late friend John Kahionhes Fadden who patiently took my hand, guided me, and blew away the fog of misinformation and miseducation. He showed me the beautiful and advanced Haudenosaunee culture. But it wasn't all work. We listened and laughed at each other's wry humor. Peace!

Chapter One

In the city that never sleeps, rookie NYPD Homicide Detective Sunny McGraw jogged on the sidewalk under the glowing streetlights. She ran along cozy West Twenty-second Street through the lower west Manhattan neighborhood of Chelsea, with its abundance of sycamore and dogwood trees, rose gardens, three- and four-story red brick apartments, townhouses, and condos. She veered around a plump, floppy-eared beagle and then a fluffy white poodle, both on leashes out to do their last business of the night. Moments later, she sidestepped residents dragging large black plastic garbage bags to the curb for morning pickup. A half block more, Sunny momentarily swerved into the street as movers lugged a tan leather sofa across the sidewalk and into an apartment. She soon tired of all the disruptions and, ignoring brief apprehension, decided to head to her usual daytime running path. She craved the endorphin release.

The Job consumed much of her life, and that last case was a real gut punch. Crimes against children could push all her stress buttons. In the interrogation room, the suspect probably thought she had lost her mind, but she was able to extract a confession from a heartless infant killer.

At Ninth Avenue, next to the Rite Aid drugstore, Sunny ran in place while waiting for the traffic light to change. On the left side of the drugstore, Bill's Bakery

1

beckoned. She could almost smell the lemon cupcakes. She would grab one on the way home—no, two...one for her sister. Sunny pulled up her turquoise jogger hoodie against the cool night summer breeze from the Hudson River three avenues away.

"Lookin' good!" A brash young man with long brown hair, about twenty-five, appreciated Sunny's physique as he cruised by in his loud muffler Toyota Camry with Jersey plates, a Rutgers University decal on the back window. Detectives paid attention to the little things. Little things could solve big cases.

At thirty-one, Sunny still had her college basketball forward body and her Oklahoma high school homecoming queen good looks. But tonight, she was all business. She ignored Mr. Hoped-To-Get-Lucky.

The traffic light changed bright green in the night. Her shapely, long legs took her faster and farther west, then across Tenth Avenue in no time. Her taut muscles gratefully warmed, obliterating her troubles and clearing her head as she pounded the pavement. People strolled above on the High Line—an abandoned, one-and-a-half-mile, elevated, train-track-turned-urban park of sprawling greenery.

She jogged several more minutes, building up a sweat before crossing Eleventh Avenue and the busy West Side Highway using the pedestrian crosswalk. Mingled with the fretful car horns, somewhere on the Hudson River, she heard the occasional rumbling ferry boat motor and its groaning foghorn.

At the north side of the Chelsea Piers Sports Complex, Sunny stopped under a lighted section of the Hudson River Greenway—an asphalt path for running, walking, and cycling. She had only jogged here one time at night in her nine years in New York City. A fellow runner, a man in quite tight running shorts, approached, jogging from the opposite direction. Good. Maybe more people were on the path. She hadn't run in a week. She would make it quick.

2

Sunny debated whether to tie her jogger jacket around her waist now or later when she was in full sweat. *Leave it on*, she decided. She pulled down the hoodie and tightened the elastic hair tie around her brunette ponytail before starting the run. On her iPhone, she chose shuffle mode, allowing the device to select the tunes, pop, country, R&B, Hip Hop. In Sunny's ears, Alicia Keys' silky piano commenced "If I ain't got you."

The shadowy tree-lined running trail ran the north and south length of Manhattan through a number of individual parks alongside the peaceful, sparkling Hudson River. This mental release was the medicine the doctor ordered against the inhumanity Sunny encountered on a daily basis. In a spiritual zone now, she increased her pace. Alicia crooned her love song. Sunny flashed to the handsome assistant district attorney who worked with her on the infant case. He attempted to convince her to have at least lunch with him. For the time being, she put him off, although she contemplated saying *yes* tomorrow. Life as a detective had taken a severe toll on her personal life. Alicia's piano notes floated.

A brilliant white light exploded in Sunny's head, and her ears rang loudly. She briefly saw a shadow in the dark, but it was too late to stop the blow to the side of her head. She toppled sideways, her consciousness quickly fading.

In a paralyzed daze, Sunny felt herself being dragged off the asphalt path. The back of her sneakers scraped, then quieted on the grass. The leaves of brush swiped the side of her face as she was dragged deeper off the path. She heard a number of hushed, distant-sounding male voices in the darkness.

"Me first!" a husky voice blurted.

"Hurry!" another attacker muttered breathlessly.

Now pinned on her back to the cool ground, strong hands grasped her arms and legs. Grunting and heavy breathing surrounded her. Then, another powerful set of hands wrapped around Sunny's neck, strangling her. She gagged helplessly. Her turquoise sweatpants slid down, and the crisp breeze from the Hudson River washed over her moist bare skin. Another attacker straddled her waist from above.

The nightmare of every woman. The nightmare not only in New York City but in every city, every state, every country. Sunny's last reserve of oxygen was running out fast as she weakly squirmed for freedom from the pack of wolves.

Her shocked consciousness struggled to recover from the head blow, but depleted oxygen from the stranglehold conspired to take her life. Confused, whimpering, trembling, in one last adrenaline-powered gasp, she twisted her right arm, popping it free from the muscular hand. She moaned, flailing wildly at the hulk atop her. Finally, she clawed him as her strength failed. Exhausted, life draining, she started spinning toward nothingness.

Floating…somewhere.

Then, with the powerful strangling fingers still around her neck, her head suddenly jerked from the ground and then slammed back into the grass. The strong fingers were no longer squeezing the life out of her. She gulped a huge breath of fresh air. Shadows swirled above her. She strained to scream but was caught in a fit of coughing.

As her mind attempted to climb out of the depths of panic, darkness, and disorientation, the man sitting on her waist groping at her pink thong was posthaste lifted, his crushing weight no longer pinning her down. Her mental haze and terror, combined with the darkness, made it difficult to focus on the shadowy images. Her vision was swimming. But she could hear guttural growling.

Animal growling! Snarling!

The attacker straddling her waist yelled, "Whadda fuck!" His voice faded as if sailing through the air then landing with a great groan as the wind was knocked out of him. There was more growling and grunting in the night.

"Let's get outta here!" another man hissed in alarm. Running, scattering footsteps filled the gloomy night.

But there still remained heavy breathing and grunts from…something…in the murky park. She had escaped the predators. But was something far worse out here? Saving her for what? Her stunned, oxygen-deprived brain was trying to locate its wits as she lay flat on her back, gagging, with no strength. Her turquoise sweatpants were pulled down around her ankles.

In the distance to her left, Sunny heard cars along the West Side Highway. Even at night, impatient New Yorkers laid on their car horns, urgent, blaring. Car horns that never sounded so welcoming. If she could only muster a burst of energy, she could run to safety and flag down a driver. She lay in the darkness, eyes closed, willing her muddled mind to overcome the head blow that had knocked her off her feet.

Sunny flinched as one enormous leathery hand slid behind her naked knees, and another large hand scooped under her back. She rose from the ground with a levitating sensation, her arms and head dangling, lolling. Instinctively, she reached up and wrapped her arms around his hairy—no…furry—neck. Her heart nearly stopped. Her chest heaved with loud panting breaths as *it* cradled her.

In one fluid motion, it flung Sunny over a furry mountain of the shoulder. It snorted triumphantly before bounding to a nearby tree, up, up, up, hand over hand, jostling Sunny's dazed mind. She whimpered weakly, helplessly. Dangling upside down, through half-closed eyes, she glimpsed the starry sky and the Hudson River reflecting the sparkling city lights. The cool river breeze washed over her naked legs where the immense fur-covered arm left them exposed.

"Who...are...you?" Sunny begged raggedly, bouncing off its furry back. "What are...you...going to...do to me?" She could barely keep her eyes open.

Gently, it set Sunny on the birch tree limb and propped her back against the tree trunk. Squirming, still trying to catch her breath and clear her head, she finally pulled up her jogging pants. She took the opportunity to groggily extract her cell phone from her jogging jacket to see what was panting so heavily in the black night. Without her wits to access the flashlight feature, she used the dim display light of the phone as illumination.

Sunny gasped!

They held each other's gaze, studying. She sat face-to-face with a massive...gorilla...a gorilla in a sweat-soaked, grass-stained, gray sweat suit, a sweat suit stretched and pulled tight over an enormous body, the fabric torn by rippling, bulging, well-defined muscles. His massive chest rose and fell from exertion. Sunny squeezed her eyes shut and vigorously shook her head in a futile attempt to clear it. She reopened her eyes, stretching them wide for clarity. The ape was still there.

She was supposed to be scared...but as they gazed curiously...eye to eye...something...something in his soft, intelligent protective eyes, his gently flaring nostrils, his slightly curled upper lip said she wasn't in danger. She exhaled the tension.

The phone light glinted off a chain necklace and pendant around the great ape's neck as he grunted softly and curiously cocked his head, observing her. Where had she seen those symbols? A row of four purple and white squares with a spearhead-like design in the center dangled from the gold chain, nearly hidden in his thick, shiny black fur.

Now, she remembered where she'd seen the design. A weekend trip. The Native American casino in upstate New York. The Haudenosaunee. The Iroquois.

But why was a gorilla wearing it? More important, why was she face-to-face with a gorilla in the first place? She pressed her eyes shut again, then popped them open. The ape appeared amused, throwing his huge head back, his eyes curious.

From a squatting position on the large, high tree limb, the huge ape suddenly stood some six feet tall, towering above her. The birch limb shook, rustling leaves. He pounded his enormous glistening chest with both fists, bared his long white canines, and grunted contentedly. He dove with ease to an adjacent branch, rocking the tree, slid down the thick birch tree trunk, and bounded to the ground. The animal disappeared into the New York City night.

Her mind clearing, Sunny rested the back of her head against the tree trunk and dialed police dispatch with her location and condition.

"And bring a ladder." She massaged her aching head and took one big, relaxing breath. What had just happened?

Chapter Two

The bumpy cobblestone streets of the Meatpacking District made for rough and unsteady jogging. Camille Smoke always used the stones as a marker to start the cooldown following a clandestine night run along the Hudson River Greenway. Just south of the neighborhood of Chelsea in Manhattan, the Meatpacking District, with its few remaining butcher shops, still earned its name despite all the new trendy restaurants and fashionable clubs that sprang up. Trains filled with livestock once lumbered south down the west side of Manhattan along the present-day High Line to the Meatpacking District.

Clubgoers hung out on the dimly lit sidewalks, talking, laughing, smoking cigarettes, and passing around blunts. Camille took shortcuts, past the U-Haul depot, ducked into dark alleys and backways to avoid being seen. One more minute to MH Construction Company. He would quietly go upstairs to his bedroom so he didn't wake Marshall.

"Perfect timing," Marshall Hall shouted as Camille opened the front door of the construction company. "Hand me a flathead screwdriver from the toolbox."

Following a strenuous day at a construction site, Marshall could usually barely keep his eyes open in the evenings, but not tonight. Camille's short, stout business partner and childhood friend sat on a backhoe tractor bucket as a seat while he leaned toward a broken cement mixer. A dark blue work cap sat high and twisted on a head of disheveled hair. Night news blared from the wall-mounted TV. He raised his head from his work as Camille closed the shop's front door. A faint cleaning solvent, oil, gasoline, and soil odor permeated the shop. The air compressor motor kicked in, whirring, refilling the air storage tank.

Their eyes met, and shock immediately crossed Marshall's face. "What happened to you? Why is your sweat suit all torn up? Looks like you were in a fight with a tiger." Grunting, he quickly rose from the tractor bucket. He grabbed the remote to turn down the TV volume.

Camille didn't want to answer. Didn't want this argument…again. He removed his beige cap, allowing his single braid to fall down the center of his back. He tossed the cap like a frisbee to the company's workbench.

"You said flathead screwdriver, not Phillips, right?" he repeated to avoid answering the questions. By this time, Marshall was right behind him, curiously looking Camille up and down.

"Dude, what happened?" Marshall stressed, eyeing Camille.

Camille handed the flathead screwdriver over his shoulder without turning around to face Marshall. The argument was going to be heated. They always were.

The TV news finished a piece about a four-alarm fire in Staten Island, the night sky orange from the intense flames. The next news story was familiar to Camille. Very familiar. He negotiated his way through the shop around the

9

air compressor and some scaffolding in a trailer to reach the TV set to turn the volume back up. Marshall was right on his heels, still demanding answers, but Camille's attention was riveted to the nightly news.

An on-site NY5 night news team was reporting a sexual assault on the Hudson River Greenway. The reporter, a young redhead, said: *"A female NYPD detective in a turquoise jogging suit—name withheld for now—was sexually assaulted by a gang of men tonight as she jogged along the Hudson River Greenway just west of Chelsea."*

"What's this?" Marshall insisted, pointing at the TV. Camille was still focused on the broadcast. He raised a hand to silence his partner. Marshall sighed in frustration.

The NY5 reporter, restrained by yellow crime scene tape, continued: *"How she got way up in that tree, we don't know. Police are mum at the moment. She appears to have bruises on her neck, we assume from the attack. Stay tuned. We'll bring you more as we get it."*

Standing shoulder to shoulder with Camille, Marshall slowly looked down from the TV to stare at Camille from the side and slightly upward. Camille stood six foot one. Marshall pointed at the TV, his eyes burning into the side of Camille's head. He interrupted again.

"Isn't that where you run at night?" It really wasn't a question. He knew Camille ran up and down the length of Manhattan along the HRG, mostly at night, to avoid being seen, unless he absolutely grew too stir-crazy, in which case, he risked daytime jogging.

"Yeah." Camille wasn't in the mood for a lecture. He walked away toward the shop stairs, which led to the upstairs bedrooms, the shop office, and his makeshift gym slash art studio.

"Yeah!" Marshall shot back and quickly stepped after Camille. "Just *yeah*?" he shouted up the stairs at Camille's back.

Camille heard footfalls behind him as he made it to the second story. He spun to put an end to the discussion. "What was I supposed to do?" he angrily yelled and spread his arms in resignation. Marshall was now in his face.

"Camille, this is not only about *you*, remember?"

"Again! What was I supposed to do?" Camille shrugged his broad shoulders.

"You"—Marshall jabbed his index finger into the chest of Camille's dirty, ripped sweatshirt—"are going to get *us* caught...and then it's over. We can't draw attention to ourselves." He sighed heavily.

"Answer me!" Camille slammed his fist on his hips, leaning forward, looking down at Marshall. "What was I supposed to do? Let that gang rape and kill her?"

Marshall took a step back, shook his head, and took a huge, deflated breath. "So, what did you shift into? Your clothes are a mess." He waved his hand up and down at his buddy's tattered sweat suit.

They finally smiled at one another. They never could stay angry at each other for long. They'd known each other since boys on their upstate New York, Haudenosaunee— pronounced *Ho-den-no-sho-nee*—territory. Marshall had bought the downstate construction company. When his homeboy needed a job and a place to lay low, Marshall didn't hesitate.

Camille laughed. "I shifted into a gorilla." He threw his arms out, balled his fist, growled, beat his chest. "Didn't have time to get out of my sweat suit." He tugged at his ripped clothes.

Shaking his head, Marshall nervously wiped his mouth on his shirt sleeve. "Okay. We have to follow that story to make certain it doesn't make its way to us." He clapped his buddy on the shoulder and returned downstairs to his repairs.

Chapter Three

The morning after her assault, Sunny—sore head and all—climbed the stairs to the third floor of Manhattan South Homicide on East Twenty-first Street. MSH worked homicide cases from Fifty-Ninth Street—which runs along the south of Central Park—to the southern tip of New York City, the Battery. Manhattan North Homicide solved cases above Fifty-Ninth to the northern tip of New York City. The chorus of fifteen detectives talking to each other or talking on the phone spilled out the door as she stepped onto the third-floor landing. She pulled her collar high to hide the neck bruises.

Sunny's partner, Kevin "KD" Douglass was already at his desk writing on a yellow legal pad. His ever-present *New York Times* and *Wall Street Journal* were pushed aside, awaiting a lull in their multiple caseload of investigations. KD looked up as she approached, but before she could greet her partner, the lieutenant of Manhattan South Homicide leaned halfway out his door and called them to his office.

"Douglass. McGraw. My office. Now!" his gruff voice boomed above the precinct din.

Still standing, Sunny pushed her chair back under her desk. "Loo, can I get a coffee first?"

"No. Drink during your drive," Lieutenant Sanchez said bluntly and pivoted back into his office.

The detectives exchanged a quizzical look. KD offered his cup of joe to Sunny. She wrinkled her nose. "I don't want your backwashed coffee."

"Hey!" KD feigned hurt feelings but then suddenly smiled with perfect white teeth framed by his—what did he call it?—mocha complexion. The squad room's florescent lights reflected off his clean-shaven brown scalp. A well-groomed goatee surrounded his mouth. "I'll have you know my backwash can boost your immune system, lady."

At forty, KD kissed his athletic, college football bicep through his expensive, crisp, baby blue shirtsleeve. KD, like most of the famed Homicide, dressed well but didn't go so far as facials and manicures.

As the two walked to the Loo's windowed office off the squad room, Sunny's hair fell back, exposing her reddened temple bruise.

"What happened to you?" KD asked, squinting at the injury, true concern for his partner. She waved a dismissive hand as they entered Lieutenant Sanchez's office.

Stocky, in his mid-fifties with salt and pepper slicked back hair and a large head, Lieutenant Sanchez beckoned them in while he spoke in rapid Spanish on his desk phone. He reminded Sunny of the comedian George Lopez, but minus the humor. On the credenza behind him lay his great-grandfather's tattered cowboy hat—its origin inspired by the Mexican vaquero, or rancher. Above the hat hung a large map of the early Americas when the western third of the United States was part of Mexico. A large red circle encompassed the Mexican state of Zacatecas in Central Mexico. Another red circle was drawn around Albuquerque,

New Mexico. KD had told Sunny that Lieutenant Sanchez could trace his Indigenous lineage from his Albuquerque birth town down to Zacatecas, Mexico. The border had later *crossed* his family, the lieutenant always clarified.

Lieutenant Sanchez leaned back in his squeaky chair and closed his eyes, rubbing them with his free hand while listening to the person on the other end of the phone. Something wasn't going so well. A few seconds later, he slammed the receiver down.

"My grown ass son," he groused, pointing at the dead phone, "got his car towed. Alternate side of the street parking bit him in the ass again." He shook his large head. "Wants to borrow mine." He guffawed. "I don't think so." His head was still shaking. "Cut the cord with offspring," he said, and gestured scissoring his fingers.

The lieutenant leaned forward, elbows on his desk, and directed his attention to Sunny. "Morning reports say you were assaulted last night along the Hudson River Greenway. A blow to the head and strangled."

KD turned to re-examine the red spot on Sunny's temple as she pulled back her shoulder-length brunette hair. She tilted her head to expose a red ring of bruises around her neck.

"It's nothing," she said, rubbing her neck. She woke up this morning with a low-grade headache, but that was also partly due to her older sister keeping her up late last night all fuss and feathers about the dangers of police work…again.

From across his desk, The Loo eyed the bruises. "Do you need some time off? I can partner Douglass with someone else for a few days."

Sunny assured Lieutenant Sanchez she was good to go. She felt worse than this when she was fifteen, learning to ride Thunder, her uncle's horse. She had tumbled from the saddle a number of times. She suspected the men in MSH would actually have to break a bone before they took off.

14

"Okay then. It's you and KD next on the board. The local precinct on the West Side will work your assault case, McGraw. Homicide has a new case." The lieutenant leaned back in his oil-deprived chair. "We have a female DOA near the West Side Highway." He glanced at Sunny.

Near the West Side Highway? Too close for comfort. Sunny shifted anxiously in her chair. Could it be the same gang? Could it have been her lying dead? Sunny swallowed hard.

"We're on it," KD assured him as they rose from the chairs and headed for the office door.

"Detective McGraw," the lieutenant called behind her. She turned. The Loo rarely smiled, but smile he did. "One day, tell me how you got your ass up in that tall tree last night."

"Tree?" KD repeated, surprised, studying his partner anew.

"I'll explain on the ride over." She slapped her partner on the back. "But first, I need some *un*-backwashed coffee."

Chapter Four

With the black unmarked Ford Fusion double parked, Sunny hopped out, rushing into the deli for coffee. She sipped at each stop in the morning traffic. KD finally broached the subject.

"Fill me in on what happened to you last night."

She took another sip of the hot brew at the traffic light at Forty-Second and Tenth. "Went for a jog to unwind. I was just hitting my running stride when *wham*." She massaged her sore temple. "Don't remember much after that except there was a gang of them."

Sunny remembered much more. But she hadn't even shared those parts of the harrowing night with her sister, Jennifer. That, for all appearances, a gorilla…had come out of nowhere. Sunny still wasn't sure what she saw. It all still felt like a horrible nightmare. But how had she shimmied up the wide tree trunk to that high branch? That was real! She didn't think she could manage such an athletic feat, not even on her best day.

In the warm summer morning, their fleet car was stuck behind a parked, sparkling brown UPS truck, the driver unloading boxes onto a two-wheeler. Her headache eased as the caffeine went to work. She vaguely remembered a firefighter climbing a ladder to retrieve her from the high birch tree branch, a look of bewilderment on his face as fire truck floodlights illuminated every inch of the area. In the FDNY EMT ambulance, the technician tended to her bruises and monitored her blood pressure and heart rate. Sunny refused to be transported to the hospital. She declined a rape test. The predators hadn't made it that far. The apparent gorilla in the ripped sweat suit wearing a necklace had rescued her before anything worse happened to her. Inside the ambulance, a woman Crime Scene Unit analyst had scraped under Sunny's fingernails and commandeered her turquoise sweat suit for trace evidence: hair, fiber, saliva. Sunny had stepped out of the ambulance donning a borrowed white crime scene, one-piece suit replete with foot booties.

When traffic cleared, Sunny held onto her coffee cup as KD nimbly wheeled the car around the huge UPS truck. "And what was The Loo talking about you up some tree?" KD asked with disbelief in his voice.

If she told the whole truth, the entire Manhattan South Homicide squad would think she'd lost her mind, a King Kong ribbing not far behind. Quick on her feet so she didn't sound as though she were crazy, Sunny told her partner that extreme adrenaline must have kicked in giving her extra strength. KD shook his head at the bizarre explanation.

Sunny changed the subject before KD's head stopped shaking. They were driving north on the West Side Highway, the Hudson River Greenway to the left, almost at the DOA crime scene.

"I wonder if this is the same gang that attacked me," she said angrily, pointing to her favorite running path, now a second crime scene. Sunny would stop at nothing to bring justice to those who took the life of this innocent woman…and those who nearly took her life.

Across the opposing traffic along the West Side Highway, NYPD police cruisers, a blue and white Crime Scene Unit van, an FDNY EMT ambulance, and an NYPD Medical Examiner van were parked along the Hudson River Greenway. At the next traffic light, KD hit the car's emergency lights to stop opposing traffic for his severe, tire-squealing U-turn. Sunny barely held on to her coffee. Several impatient New Yorkers didn't heed the emergency. He yelped a few quick bursts from the siren. *Whooop! Whooop! Whooop!*

KD hollered out the window at an offending silver Jaguar driver who forced the detectives to wait for *her* to pass. "You betta be glad I have bigger fish to fry!" He shook his head in frustration. "What is it with New York drivers?" he grumbled.

He completed the turn, approached the crime scene, and drove up on the park grass. Sunny emptied the remainder of her coffee onto the ground and dropped the cup on the backseat floorboard. She stepped out into the bright, warm, sunny day.

A middle-aged woman held a yapping, yapping, yapping brown and white cocker spaniel on a taut leash. The dog's long, floppy ears bounced with each annoying bark. A uniform officer, pen and pad in hand, was interviewing to the dog owner. Another officer beckoned KD and Sunny over.

"KD, haven't seen you in many moons, man. Your old partner, Evelyn Jordan, retired to North Carolina, I hear. Is she your new partner?" the uni asked, pointing his chin at Sunny.

"Sunny. Carl Sanders," KD said as an introduction. "Sunny McGraw."

The tall, husky officer extended his hand to Sunny. "Word is, KD, you requested another female partner." Officer Sanders made a suggestive face.

Slightly over a month now in Homicide and this was the second time Sunny had heard such a specific request. She would have to see what was behind KD's decision. *Yap, yap, yap* the dog continued its irritating barks intruding on Sunny's attention.

KD pursed his lips, ignoring his uniformed friend. "Carl, what do we have here so far?" he asked, scanning the scene.

Officer Sanders introduced the detectives to the lady with the noisy cocker spaniel. During their morning walk, her dog, Petunia, took a leak off the trail and caught the scent of a dead body. The detectives thanked the lady for her 911 call, lifted the yellow crime scene tape, and made their way through the grass and down a gentle slope behind a stand of bushes. The Hudson River was a stone's throw away.

Sunny recognized Associate Medical Examiner Sheila Choi. Sheila had performed the autopsy on the infant in their last homicide investigation. Sunny had only witnessed an occasional death. God only knew how medical examiners like Sheila Choi dealt with death on a daily basis. Sunny still hadn't gotten over the child's death. Would she ever?

"Detectives." Sheila acknowledged their presence and snapped off her blue latex gloves. "A brutal one here. Looks like she was attacked by animals of the human type." The medical examiner pointed out the strangulation finger marks around the DOA's neck. "The perp strangled the poor woman from the front as she was pinned to the ground." The nude white woman lay on her back, paper towels covering her breasts and genital areas like fig leaves.

"Any TOD estimate?" KD asked. He got down on his haunches for a closer look, shaking his head in disgust.

"Time of death? Judging from the lack of rigor mortis, I'd say just after"—ME Sheila Choi thoughtfully poked her pen into her chin—"dark yesterday." She nodded. "As you know, dead bodies stiffen a few hours after death, then relax as the muscle chemistry changes.

Sunny's mind did the calculations. Sunny must have been their second target. Something in the back of her mind was working. Voices. Voices in the night. That terrible night. What had those bastards said? She was having a hard time remembering. The blow to her head had left her dazed. Her strong suspicion was that this was the same gang that assaulted her…nearly killed her.

Sunny suddenly felt her anger building. She involuntarily massaged her neck, a neck with finger marks and bruises like this woman, only less noticeable because…*he* saved her!

"Any identification, clothes, purse?" KD asked, looking around the crime scene.

"Crime Scene bagged a bracelet, and there are some clothes scattered over there." The ME pointed twenty feet away at the CSU techs. "Harbor Patrol scuba divers," she pointed at the river, "will search the river for a purse and anything else."

A gawking crowd was growing around the yellow crime scene tape perimeter—parents and nannies with babies in strollers, more dog walkers, and those out for a morning run on the brilliant, sunny day.

Sunny caught the sun's glint off a man's necklace. Tall, very fit. He wore exercise sweats, dark shades, and a cap brim pulled very low over his brow. The necklace he wore sparkled in the sun as he rubbernecked with the growing crowd for a better view of the crime scene.

Sunny's mind commenced rapid associations. The necklace design resembled the one revealed by her cell phone light last night high in the birch tree. But this man at today's crime scene perimeter was only a gawker, not an animal. Her memory was of a necklace buried in thick black fur.

KD was asking more questions. "Can you tell if she was raped?" he directed at Sheila Choi.

The ME related that the dead woman's severe vaginal bruising indicated rape. Her office would thoroughly test once the DOA was in the lab. After KD sent a few uniform officers to canvass local clubs and businesses, he glanced at Sunny and took the opportunity to school the rookie homicide detective.

"These footprints in the dirt? I'm counting about four different prints." KD ordered Crime Scene to make footprint molds if they could, and then he directed Photo Unit to get pictures from all angles.

Sunny bent close to where her partner was pointing, but her mind was back on the necklace again. As soon as her partner had finished his field class, she quickly stood up straight, searching for the man with the purple and white Haudenosaunee necklace.

She nearly did a three-sixty before catching sight of the man jogging south some distance down the asphalt path. She took off at full gallop after him. The necklace coincidence was just too much for her. Same design. Same location.

Her arms swinging, hands chopping the air, she ran as fast as she could in her police boots along the asphalt path. The same boots had splintered and kicked in a few doors and threatened to kick the shit out of any perp who dared to attack her. The necklace man was far ahead of her, but she kept him in sight as he jogged across the West Side Highway at the pedestrian crossing.

If she wasn't a runner, there was no way she could have closed the gap. He disappeared into the Meatpacking District. Flashing her detective shield around her neck, Sunny risked crossing the busy West Side Highway against the light—a dangerous decision with New York drivers, horns blaring at the nut running through traffic.

She finally caught sight of the man as he passed a U-Haul depot and disappeared into a nearby building with an MH Construction sign hanging over the sidewalk. She didn't pursue him any further now that she knew where he was. He had run past all the other businesses to enter the construction company like it was familiar to him. He wasn't a suspect, and she wasn't ready for any gorilla conversation with the NYPD. She would come back later. She jogged back to the crime scene.

"Where the hell were you?" KD shouted as she approached the crime scene, huffing and puffing. "Shit! One minute, I'm talking to you...the next, I'm talking to my damn self," KD bellowed, his brow deeply furrowed.

"Criminals always return to the scene of the crime, and I thought I saw someone suspicious." She shrugged apologetically to complete the excuse.

KD stood there staring, sighing, mouth agape at his new partner.

Chapter Five

In addition to the woman detective, Camille desperately wished he could have somehow saved the second woman along the jogging path last night. He would find a secret way to help apprehend those responsible for the gruesome crime. That thought finally released his troubled mind to continue his day.

Late afternoon now, and the Native American drum recording blared upstairs at MH Construction in the Meatpacking District.

"Listen to the ball!" Camille "Teeyeehogrow" Smoke shouted, meaning keep the *tewaraton*—lacrosse—stick near his ear, ready to pass or shoot. He cut left and right, weaving against an invisible opponent, his eye on the goal.

During the Naming Ceremony when Camille was eight years old, his parents chose the Indigenous name Teeyeehogrow—Double Life—for he lived in the Sunadaga's ancient territory in upstate New York near the Canadian border, and also lived in the United States. His

Indigenous name took on a new meaning later in life. And to hide his true identity, Camille never uttered his Native name these days. He desperately missed his family, his late mother, and his father, Ariwiio Smoke—president of the Sunadaga Nation, and not to mention his activist sister, Amanda Smoke. He and his younger sister were once inseparable. He thought of how she now traveled the United States without him in pursuit of Native American justice and recognition.

Bare-chested, in dark blue sweatpants and sneakers, Camille had pushed the office furniture and his art studio equipment against the walls to give himself plenty of room to simulate a lacrosse field. A lacrosse goal with netting was at the far end of the large space. Tewaraton was a medicine game given to the Haudenosaunee—the Sunadaga being one of the Federation Nations—by the Creator hundreds of years ago. The medicine game was once played over miles and days to heal, strengthen, dissolve ill feelings, and resolve disputes. No score was kept.

After a half hour of exertion, Camille paused for a drink of cold bottled water. His head bobbed rhythmically to the recording of the thundering drumsticks crashing—never faster than the human heartbeat—on the taut deer skin. The hypnotic chants of the warbling singers he felt deep in his soul. It reminded him of social singing and dancing in the rotating powwow circle of friends and family. He ached to go home to his people. So close, but yet so far.

He grabbed the tewaraton stick again and exploded toward the goal, the thirty-three-year-old's six-foot-one, athletic frame glistening with sweat. His long, shiny, jet-black braid bounced on his back. He whipped the stick to generate speed on the ball, just as he had done leading his upstate high school to a championship. He had also coached children in the Sunadaga territory to play lacrosse. The ball found the crease, fluttering the back of the net. He scored.

Camille threw his arms up in triumph. "Yay!" he celebrated. Again, he bobbed his head to the hard downbeat of the drum. He chanted along with the singers. But then he froze.

The accident years ago had left Camille with powers no other human possessed. Long before he saw her, her pleasurable perfume wafted into the upstairs open space. His keen nose analyzed each scent molecule. It was the same sweet lavender he'd smelled in her hair on the night of her assault, the same sweet scent as at today's murder scene along the Hudson River Greenway. And with his ultra-human hearing, he heard the downstairs door knob twist, then the shop door open and close.

"Hello!" the detective called out. "Hello!"

He had to think fast. If the detective got a good look at him, she might recognize him from police mugshots. An idea hit him. Shift into a bird, an eagle… No, eagles shouldn't be in a construction shop. Maybe a small brown sparrow that somehow got stuck in the shop. Or…maybe a cat. Many shops had cats to catch mice. But the rumbling drum music? She was an NYPD detective. She knew someone was here and would keep returning until she caught up with him.

Camille didn't have to decide. The detective climbed the stairs without much hesitation. First, he caught sight of the top of her head—brunette, shoulder-length hair. As she climbed, the two locked eyes. His acute eyesight discerned brown eyes with green flecks. She stepped or rather agilely leaped over the final step into the loft.

Standing there glistening, sweat rolling down his chest over muscular pecs, thanks to boxing, bench pressing, and pushups, Camille couldn't find words. This was a nightmare come true. He was going back to the slammer for an even longer sentence. Probably for life this time.

The roaring drum recording echoed in the expanse of the loft. She hadn't said a single word, studying him. Her eyes fell on Camille's chain necklace, its Haudenosaunee design, purple and white. He swallowed hard, rubbing his moist palms on his sweatpants.

But then something in her expression changed. Her knitted brow smoothed, relaxed. She was tall and took several cautious steps closer, never taking her eyes off his chain necklace as though it had hypnotized her. Finally, her gaze shifted to the large burn scar on Camille's shoulder, part of his childhood accident.

Unsure and lowering his tewaraton stick to the floor with his long braid falling forward, Camille stepped to the CD player and turned off the blaring powwow recording. The room fell tomb silent as they studied each other.

Still not sure of her intentions, Camille took no chances. "Do you need construction work done?" he asked tentatively.

The attractive detective didn't answer his question but rather extended her hand for an introduction. "I'm NYPD Homicide Detective Sunny McGraw."

Camille finally took a deep breath. He again wiped his hands on his sweatpants before shaking her soft but firm hand. "Camille," he simply said. He quickly turned, grabbed his sweatshirt, and slipped it on. When his head popped out the top, she was already looking around, being a detective.

"No. I don't need construction work done, Camille." She sounded suspicious and relieved.

"Okay," he replied skeptically. *Then what?* His mind was racing as the detective looked over his things: his office manager desk, his painting supplies, and his exercise equipment. On the wall hung a corkboard, myriad business cards, Post-its…and three news clippings that grabbed her attention. She moved closer, reading and studying the articles. Camille didn't know what to say to her. He wrung his hands nervously.

"I remember these," she finally said while pointing at the articles. She twisted to look at Camille, her eyes asking questions before her mouth did. "May I ask why you're keeping these?" She turned back to the articles.

Good, he thought. She missed his momentary shock. Or had she?

In one news clipping, a toddler had somehow squeezed between the window bars of a fourth-floor Queens apartment and crawled onto the ledge, a red pacifier in his mouth. Oblivious to the danger, giggling, the baby inched farther from the window and his distraught mother's outstretched pleading arms. Fire truck sirens were in the distance but would probably arrive too late.

Camille had darted into the alley, ditched his clothes, and transformed into a huge golden eagle, not a second to spare. The baby slipped and went into freefall, the red pacifier trailing.

In a dead-stoop power-dive, Camille tucked his wings in and back to get as aerodynamic as possible. The airborne toddler flipped and tumbled past the second floor, the cement sidewalk looming larger and larger. Horrified onlookers screamed and shouted, slapping their hands to their mouths.

Near the first floor, Camille focused his keen eagle's eyesight on the toddler's Winnie the Pooh diaper as the kid spun in terror. He needed a place to sink his four-inch talons without tearing the child's flesh to bloody ribbons. With an eagle's acute eyes powered by human intelligence, he timed the tumbling child just right and safely released the screaming toddler into the soft grass with only two rolls.

In the second news clipping on the corkboard, he had shifted into a bottlenose dolphin to rescue sightseeing tourists from a capsized boat on the Hudson River. He couldn't resist a few joyous breaches out of the river spinning in the air. In the last article, he lifted a taxi that had accidentally jumped the curb, pinning a senior citizen's yellow Labrador under the taxi's undercarriage. A crowd formed. Struggling to lift the heavy yellow taxi, Camille feigned straining, grunting loudly. He actually did ninety-five percent of the lifting. He disappeared before people did the math and started asking questions.

"I keep those news clips because I love animals," Camille said, thinking on his feet. "And the incredible things they're capable of." His culture taught him to help all living things.

"Uh-huh," the pretty detective responded incredulously. Her phone rang.

"Hey, Lieutenant, what's up?" she asked and listened for a moment. Camille listened to her side of the conversation. "Now?—Boss, get to Forensics in Queens ASAP in evening rush hour traffic?—but KD and I were going to do some more canvassing of bars and restaurants in the area where the body was found." She listened with a frown. "Let KD go by himself?"

Camille watched her start toward the staircase, the phone still to her ear. *Close call.* The detective didn't have time to snoop around.

At the garbage can next to his boxing heavy bag, she halted. "I know," she said to her lieutenant. "We must uncover evidence to clear these cases *and* keep your closed case numbers up." Her half-attention was drawn to the contents in the garbage can.

She placed her hand over the mouthpiece and quickly spun to ask Camille, "Are these your grass-stained, ripped-up sweats?" She immediately apologized to the caller for the interruption. "Yes, I'm listening, boss."

She mouthed "*I'll be back*" to Camille and left MH Construction talking animatedly, phone glued to her ear.

Chapter Six

He killed his brother. He killed his wife. He shot them both in *his* bed. The bitch thought he had gone to work, but he circled back an hour later.

Sergey Karolev escaped Russia into Belarus. He made his way through Poland and finally to Germany. After several years, a work visa landed him in New York City as a cab driver chasing the American dream. New York City's Russian mob helped supplement Sergey's income. He later jettisoned the taxi, along with its obnoxious passengers, for full-time mob muscle and contract hits. Money was so easy to make in America.

Out Sergey's sixteenth-floor Yorkville apartment window, afternoon traffic on the FDR Drive was waning. He sipped a steaming cup of coffee. The telescope at Sergey's side allowed him to view water traffic along the East River and look out over Queens—one of four outer boroughs. His high Slavic cheekbones, round head, and lazy left eye reflected back in the window as he lifted the cup to his lips.

From a poor farming village outside of St. Petersburg, Russia, to a fashionable high-rise apartment in the Big Apple, Sergey had done well. Killing came easily. The mob contracts came regularly now. He rose quickly in the crime organization as an efficient killer.

Coffee finished, Sergey placed the cup and saucer on the kitchen counter and walked to his second bedroom. He opened the door. Sergey had never used the space as a bedroom. The models he had assembled over the years greeted him.

In his farming village in Russia, the soil was tilled each year in preparation for planting. Planting was a must to stave off starvation in Mother Russia. One bad planting season, and the family had to seek out soup kitchens to survive. Turning the soil churned up not only worthless stones but also ancient artifacts: buttons, ladles, and a few coins. To nine-year-old Sergey, all those artifacts paled to the bone fragments he found one chilly spring day as he and his older brother walked behind their father's old smoke-belching tractor collecting the unwanted debris. His brother threw chunks of dirt at Sergey, demanding he remove the bone fragments from his pocket. His brother was constantly picking on him, blaming him for the death of their mother, giving birth to Sergey. What a burden for a child to bear. Sergey refused to drop the bones despite the pelting. He suspected the bone fragments belonged to no human or farm animal.

Sergey stepped into his Yorkville apartment's second bedroom. The dinosaur bone fragments unearthed on the family's subsistence farm still fueled his imagination all these years later. The predators, especially Tyrannosaurus Rex—the tyrant lizard king—captured his fantasy. A killing machine, fifteen feet tall, forty feet long, with six-inch serrated teeth, the animal was a nightmare for any in its sights. Sergey identified with the creature. It ate and did as

30

it pleased. All feared it. He tightened his robe straps as he admired his collection of dinosaur models.

His cell phone rang in the living room. The preprogrammed ringtone suggested the need for a professional hit. His heart quickened as he padded to reach the phone, the ominous *Jaws* theme song filling the air. He clicked to answer and waited the full agreed upon ten seconds before speaking. The ten seconds felt like an hour. He was eager to make more easy money.

"What do you have for me?" Sergey asked, breaking the seeming interminable silence.

"The boss has a job for you in far upstate New York on some Indian reservation."

Rush hour *anywhere* in Manhattan was an absolute nightmare. Sunny had long ceased complaining about the traffic jams back in Oklahoma City. She hopped into the unmarked and allowed GPS to guide her path from the lower west side Meatpacking District. Her apartment, her dinner, and a cold Heineken were only fifteen minutes north of where she was now…but, oh well.

She caught Fourteenth Street headed east. Her Loo, and all the brass and higher-ups for that matter, stressed over case clearance rates. Promptly closing cases put feathers in their caps and increased their chances of promotion. Sunny understood it all, but the numbers game surely put unwelcome pressure on the detective in the street. At the village of Gramercy Park, she made her way north to her destination, the Queens Midtown Tunnel.

She resolved to get through the forensics of her assault to remove at least one of the three weighty matters she was juggling. She sat fully back into the car seat, no longer leaning impatiently forward. There was no moving this traffic faster. Using the car's emergency lights would buy little time and only increase her stress. The second matter on her mind was this afternoon's DOA along the Hudson River Greenway. It would require her complete attention once the Crime Scene Unit completed its investigation for evidence and the medical examiner finished the autopsy. Uniform officers had completed a canvass of local businesses and residents. KD was currently combing through the officer's reports and preparing to hit the streets for more interviews.

That poor woman. Sunny shook her head dolefully. Sunny could have met the same deadly fate were it not for…it…him. She needed to clear up this third matter by returning to MH Construction.

She was still wrestling with the harrowing night in the tree. She prided herself as a logical, reasonable, scientific, left-brained person. There had to be a logical explanation. It must have been the blow to the head…. But the trip to MH Construction? The chain necklace? The ripped sweat suit in the garbage can?

She drove through the Manhattan village of Kips Bay and into Murray Hill, still headed north. The traffic crawled as she crept her way to NYPD Forensics. Angry horns blared as her car approached the entrance to the Queens Midtown Tunnel to drive under the East River. Exiting the claustrophobic tunnel, she wound her way to her destination.

NYPD's Jamaica Queens Forensics office stood five stories. A virtual square, the nondescript edifice was white with windows in clusters of three. Sunny pictured a forensic scientist as PhD-looking, prim, conservative, bookish, button-down, not the pink-haired youngster with a nose ring, who led her through the halls.

"No. I'm not a forensics analyst. I'm Katie Miller," the woman giggled. "I'm part of the intern program. Mr. Searle sent me to show you in." But Sunny wasn't too far off in her central casting when introduced to Forensic Scientist

Michael Searle. Wire-rimmed glasses, in his mid-fifties, heavyset, he got right to work after the introductions.

As Michael Searle led Sunny toward a powerful electron microscope, his question came out left field.

"Detective McGraw, have you recently visited some kind of petting zoo?" The skeptical lilt in his voice chilled Sunny. He lifted a large transparent evidence bag containing Sunny's turquoise jogging suit from the night of her assault. It was one of her favorites, and she wanted it back.

"No," she stammered, unprepared for a question about a zoo. But then her mind raced ahead, making connections, tenuous, but nonetheless connections of the near-fatal, horrific night in the park...and now MH Construction.

The forensic scientist lifted the evidence bag up toward the ceiling florescent lights, studying its contents as though for the first time.

"Been near anyone with exotic pets?" he continued, his face a picture of doubt. Still holding the bag high, his curious eyes dropped to Sunny, searching her for a reaction.

Sunny slowly started shaking her head no. More pieces to the puzzle. She needed to get to the bottom of this—*on her own.*

"Katie, get me those photos off the desk, please," Michael Searle said firmly. The intern did as she was told.

He shared the photos with Sunny. They were enlarged photos of the zipper on Sunny's turquoise jogging suit.

"See this?" Michael Searle pointed to the spot on the photo where the zipper sides were joined.

Sunny moved closer, squinting to see. Something stringy was stuck in the zipper. "What am I looking at?" she asked, not sure she wanted to know judging from the suspicious eyes of the scientist.

"It's fur," he said flatly, not mincing his words.

33

Sunny batted her eyes several times, uncomprehending. "Okay," she drawled, waiting for him to drop the other shoe. "I have a cat." She'd held Tuffy before she went for the jog. The cat wanted to go out a second time that night.

"It's not just *any* fur," the forensic scientist said, studying her. Sunny now knew what it felt like to be interrogated by a detective. And she was one of those suspects who pleaded ignorance.

She puffed out her cheeks and exhaled. What was he getting at?

Michael Searle handed Sunny another picture. To Sunny, she was viewing four tree trunks—one pink. But there were no such things as pink trees.

Pointing at the high powered, electron microscope behind him, Michael Searle explained, "The pink hair strand on the left is Katie's, my intern. The second is an African-American hair strand found inside your sweat suit hoodie from someone in obvious close proximity to you. The next one is mine." He paused and looked up from the photo at Sunny. "The last is fur. Fur...from a...gorilla."

Sunny's expression immediately fell to one of concern. Her mind was racing. She started shaking her head faster and faster. "Must be some mistake." She thrust the photo back into his hand.

She flashed to the night in the birch tree, not wanting to believe what was happening to her. But the evidence was mounting.

Michael Searle wasn't finished. This time, he pointed to a huge machine against the back wall of the lab. "We went further and analyzed the...*fur*...using our mass spectrometer." He explained how the extremely sophisticated piece of equipment determined the *molecular* makeup of any material: toxic substances in human skin tissue or body fluids, trace evidence—paint, glass, carpet fibers from crime scenes, arson and explosive residue, and...*distinct* animal furs.

"It has to be some kind of mistake," she maintained. "Or evidence contamination, or faulty equipment." She pointed an accusing finger at the mass spectrometer.

"Okay, detective, here's what I'll do." He sounded slightly peeved. "I'll run the test on a mass spectrometer at another location. And as for the human skin cell DNA scraped from beneath your fingernails, it's still being processed."

Sunny couldn't get out of there fast enough. Matter number three—get back to MH Construction—burned in her consciousness.

Chapter Seven

"As we speak, I'm leaving Forensics," Sunny said to KD, phone pressed to her ear. She stepped out onto busy Jamaica Avenue, encountering speeders, horns, and cabbies. The sun had just set. Her black department Ford was parked across the street from NYPD Forensics in Queens. She timed the irritable drivers—walk, stop, walk, stop—weaving herself to the unmarked.

"Get anything useful from the bar and restaurant canvass?" she asked, unlocking the car with the click of the locks.

"Nah. But I found this fabulous Thai restaurant where I can get some Tom Yum Goong. If I weren't on duty, I would have gotten myself a big bowl of that spicy shrimp soup. Did Forensics help us along with some evidence?"

She turned the ignition key to start the car. "The forensics technician found African-American hair stuck in my sweat suit hoodie."

"Okay. That's something, but we'll need much

more."

"Yep. The DNA results from under my fingernails will take more time." She wasn't going to get into the gorilla fur findings. "You want me to head your way to do more canvassing?" Sunny searched the side view mirror's reflection of the swift-moving traffic.

"Let's call it a night. I'll see you at the precinct tomorrow morning."

The reverse drive from the Queens Forensics office flowed much to Sunny's liking. With people home from work now, the next problem was parking near her Chelsea apartment. She circled the block twice, waiting for someone to exit a spot. A green Volvo pulled out a half block away. She gunned the engine to reach the open spot in no time.

After climbing the stoop and unlocking the vestibule door, Sunny checked apartment 3A's mail. Most of it was her sister's mail. Sunny received some junk mail credit card applications, which she ripped on the spot. She had enough trouble paying her current credit cards. She entered the apartment building hall, climbed the stairs of the three-story walkup, and entered her apartment.

Within minutes after kicking off her boots and storing her service weapon, she had a cold Heineken in hand. She switched on the TV news. Tuffy finally made his grand entrance, rubbing against her ankles before hopping onto the sofa. One day, several summers ago, the black feline materialized on her apartment's fire escape. He wouldn't stop meowing into the screened window. Sunny, an animal person—unlike her sister—couldn't resist the tenacity of the tough city tom living on the streets in the big city. The black cat gave her superstitious sister the heebie-jeebies. Sunny had always been well-grounded in science and loved her golden-eyed furry friend.

Another gulp of the cold brew, and she was finally starting to relax after a hectic day. She channel surfed until she hit upon her objective. On the TV set was the news of her and KD's new case—the DOA along the Hudson River Greenway: *"The nude body of an unidentified young white woman was found by a lady walking her dog along the Hudson River Greenway, the same park off-duty NYPD Homicide Detective Sunny McGraw was assaulted. Police investigations are ongoing. Are women safe in the Big Apple? With tourism a multi-billion dollar industry in New York City, certainly there is tremendous pressure for a resolution of these horrific crimes."*

Sunny massaged her sore temple again, still unable to fathom that the nude DOA could have easily been her. She didn't want her mind to go there. And if she even broached what she thought she saw in the park that night, the department would require her to visit Psych Services, probably ending the career she had coveted since listening to her police officer father recount how he saved the world from the bad guys. Oh, how she missed him. He'd lost his life in the line of duty.

Tuffy leaped from the sofa and padded to the window. He wanted out for his nightly wherever he went, whatever he did. Sunny obliged the feline before pulling open the kitchen drawer of take-out menus. She texted Jennifer about Chinese food and received a thumbs-up emoji.

Down the McGraw sister's apartment hall, two bedrooms were on the right. Sunny's was the farthest. Sitting at her three-mirror dresser, she pulled back her hair to observe the fading neck bruises of last night. She would love to get her hands on her attackers…and likely the murderers of the young woman. Once the ME autopsy was complete, notification of next of kin was next, and then Sunny planned to exact justice.

Attached to the large left side dresser mirror were pictures of Sunny and her family: thirteen-year-old Sunny riding her uncle's horse, Thunder, at his Tulsa, Oklahoma farm; ten-year-old Sunny sitting on her father's lap behind the steering wheel of his patrol car, her head swallowed under his patrolman's hat; a family summer picnic photo at Lake Eufaula in Oklahoma City; her college graduation picture.

She took a quick shower to wash away the troubling day. While toweling off, she heard the apartment front door unlock, open, and close.

"Food here yet?" Jennifer called out.

"I'm fine. And you?" Sunny cracked on her older sister for thinking about her stomach first.

Jennifer was the first of the McGraw sisters to arrive in New York City a decade ago, pursuing a career in fashion. She and a friend split the rent, but her friend had moved to Chicago. When Sunny finished college in Oklahoma City, she moved to New York City and worked a multitude of waitress jobs before taking the civil service test. In her father's footsteps, she joined the police force as a patrol officer. She later earned a degree in Criminal Justice, was promoted to local precinct NYPD detective, and then later to the prestigious rank of homicide detective. Her promotion track was fast, which didn't go unnoticed. There were whispers of female affirmative action.

Sunny exited the bathroom and stepped into the hall. She saw her sister—even taller than her—in the dinette, rifling through the mail. Sunny's college basketball team could have used that height, but Jennifer never gravitated to athletics as Sunny had.

And the differences went further. Some would never have placed the two women as sisters. Jennifer took their mother's Irish red hair. The dissimilarities didn't stop at external characteristics, either. As a young girl, Jennifer learned to sew at her mother's side, no doubt propelling her into the world of fashion. Both sisters participated in Toddler and Tiara-style baby beauty pageants until four-year-old Sunny tossed her tiara on the backstage floor, refusing to enter any more shows. What she wanted on her head was her father's patrol hat. She admired her courageous dad, who caught the bad guys. After her father was killed, her uncle stepped up. Young Sunny couldn't wait for the days she would visit her uncle's farm a few counties away to tend to the animals, especially his horses, which she rode and cared for. Uncle Joe even taught her how to fly the crop dusting airplane for his extermination side business. Sunny enjoyed barrel-rolling the single-engine Cessna at the end of each row of corn.

"Food should be here any minute," Sunny shouted before disappearing into her bedroom. Almost on cue, there was a knock at the apartment front door. Dinner had arrived. She crawled into a pair of comfortable sweats. She had crisp egg rolls and a second frosty Heineken on the brain.

As Sunny walked to the dinette table and took a stool, her sister suggestively asked, "Who's Greg?" She held Sunny's cell phone in her hand, viewing the screen.

"Gimme that!" Sunny snatched the phone from her nosy sister who was standing there with a huge smirk on her face.

"New man in your life?" Jennifer dramatically threw her fist to her hips. "It's about time."

Several months ago, Sunny broke up with Donald, her real estate boyfriend. He lived in a condo on the Upper East Side. The couple attended many social events and parties. He had entrée into much of New York society. But as time went on, Sunny realized that Donald wanted her as some trophy, and by extension, she presumed, a trophy wife one day. Sunny marched out of a Long Island art gallery grand opening when Donald kept cutting her off midsentence among a circle of his friends. She was having trouble adjusting to the whole "society" thing anyway. Before her dad landed the police job, the family had lived in a trailer park. And although Sunny was only six years old when they moved into their small, two-bedroom house, the kids at school were already calling her names like "trailer trash." Jennifer came home in tears many a day. Sunny told the bullies where they could go: H-E-double hockey sticks!

Munching on an egg roll while reading the text message on her cell phone, Sunny smiled and then revealed who Greg was. "He's the assistant district attorney I worked with on my last case." *And he's intelligent...and handsome.* But Jennifer didn't need to know all this yet.

"Uh-huh," Jennifer grunted, her voice still questioning.

"He wants to have lunch tomorrow."

"And are you?"

"That's for me to know"—Sunny stuck her tongue out, egg roll and all—"and for you to find out." She stuffed her phone into her pocket, away from her busybody sister.

"Invite him over," Jennifer persisted. "I'll have Jeffrey over too." Jeffrey was her investment banker boyfriend.

To change the subject, Sunny asked, "Last night, did you tell Mom about my assault?"

"No way! But now I really see why Mom is so afraid for us here, with the attack on you and all. And that other woman…. Are you sure you're okay?"

The sisters alternated calling their mother in Oklahoma City. Law enforcement was the last occupation Margarette McGraw wanted for either of her daughters. Revealing the assault would only reinforce their mother's opposition. Losing her husband in the line of duty had soured their mother against the risky, dangerous profession.

"I'm fine, and I won't tell her about last night either." Sunny popped a chunk of orange chicken into her mouth. After a few bites, she continued, "And what does Mom ask every time we call?" Sunny playfully pointed her plastic fork at Jennifer to prompt the answer.

Jennifer theatrically cleared her throat. *Ahem!* "When are you two getting married?" Jennifer mimicked her mother's high-pitched whine. "I'm not getting any younger, and you aren't either," she continued mimicking. The sisters burst out laughing, with Sunny nearly spitting out her chicken chunk.

A half-hour later, beer in hand, Sunny sat quietly at the foot of her bed. *Maybe it was someone in an elaborate gorilla costume*, she mused hopefully. But the scientific part of her brain wasn't satisfied. Forensics had identified that it was *real* gorilla fur tangled in her sweat suit jacket zipper. She took a long swig from the bottle. Tomorrow, she needed to get back to MH Construction.

Chapter Eight

The summer morning promised an exceptionally warm day as Sunny made her way up the steps of Manhattan South Homicide on East Twenty-first Street. No matter what time she arrived in the squad room, KD was already there. She sensed his punctuality trait helped propel him to first-grade detective, a station she aspired to one day. The *New York Times* and *Wall Street Journal* lay in front of him on his desk, but his brown bald head bobbed affirmative to someone on the other end of his desk telephone. He looked up at Sunny, his eyes saying the call had something to do with her.

"The medical examiner wants us to come down in two hours," KD said as he hung up. "She has some information on our dead Jane Doe."

"That was quick," Sunny replied. Usually, the detectives had to hound and cajole the ME to move autopsies to the front of the line.

"I betcha the mayor's office has something to do with it." KD pushed the newspapers next to a picture of his daughter and his fiancé, Angela, with her daughter. They both had one child. Layla, KD's daughter, was four. Angela's daughter was five. KD's wife had been killed by a drunk driver on the Long Island Expressway.

Lieutenant Sanchez stood in his office behind the glass. He was on the phone. He peered through the glass into the squad room and caught Sunny's eye. He maintained eye contact a beat too long. Did that call also have something to do with her? She wasn't going to wait around to find out.

"You want more coffee?" Sunny asked KD, picking up her cup.

"Nah. I'm good. Anymore and my eyeballs will start to float."

Sunny rushed over to the coffee pot. The person who poured the last cup of coffee left just enough for half a cup. *Piece of shit!* Too trifling to make a new pot? It reminded Sunny of being a young girl in Oklahoma City on a blistering hot day only to find that Jennifer had left a single ice cube in the ice tray, too lazy to fill the tray. Sunny sipped on the half cup of hot brew while she made a fresh pot.

She realized she was correct about the look on the Loo's face. When she returned, he was sitting on the edge of her desk discussing the DOA in the morgue with KD.

"So you two give me an update immediately upon leaving the ME's office," Lieutenant Sanchez said gruffly, now standing. The detectives agreed. Sunny pulled back her desk chair, took a seat, and sipped her coffee.

The Loo directed his next question to her. He held his amused expression for several seconds before talking.

"The morning reports show little progress in your assault case." He clicked his tongue as he gazed down at her. "First, you're up some huge tree, no explanation." Then he turned his palms up in resignation. "Gorilla fur?" He stood and grinned, turned on his heels to head back to his office.

Oh boy. Sunny didn't want to go into this subject with anyone, let alone the entire detective squad, including

KD. She could have sworn the entire room went quiet, waiting for her response. Seated at the desk behind her, chubby Andrew Rizzo had certainly heard the Loo. He twirled in his desk chair to face Sunny.

"McGraw, is King Kong back in New York City rescuing damsels in distress?" Detective Rizzo snorted. He mimicked a gorilla pounding its chest.

Most of the squad went easy on Andrew Rizzo. His father was an NYPD captain in Queens. If she didn't want to end up on the wrong side of the brass, she should take a pass on Andrew. But Sunny never cared about office politics. She figured her audacity would slow her career only a tad. She had never been good at holding her tongue.

Looking down at his newspaper to conceal his face, KD snickered. "I think he has the hots for you," he whispered. Sunny threw an ink pen at him and turned back to the Pillsbury Doughboy.

She sniffed the air a couple times in Andrew's direction. His amused expression evaporated, replaced by confusion. "Rizzo, I smell gorilla." Andrew sniffed the air, baffled, before twisting back to his Dunkin Donut French cruller and coffee.

But Sunny wasn't done with the teacher's pet. "Did it hurt when you pounded your tits?" The entire squad room erupted in raucous laughter. She had not only sent a message to Rizzo that she was no shrinking violet but also to the rest of the squad that she would give as good as she got. That was how respect was won in the NYPD.

Sunny rolled her chair back under her desk. "You're really funny, dude," she said to KD. "The hots for me. You'll get yours. I promise."

KD stifled a laugh. He glanced at the wall clock. "We have an hour and a half before we need to be at the ME's office." He pulled open his desk drawer and removed a case folder along with an evidence bag. "I caught this case in Murray Hill just before you came to Homicide. I need to close it. We juggle multiple cases in Homicide. I could use a new set of eyes."

"I have a lunch…uh…uh…luncheon engagement this afternoon," Sunny stumbled to explain her lunch "date" with ADA Greg Ross. She also wanted to drop by MH Construction for a few minutes.

"Your lunch engagement is safe. This shouldn't take long." KD grinned and winked at her, giving her a thumbs up. She feigned, throwing another ink pen at her partner.

KD grabbed a portable police radio, and they descended the precinct stairs. Just as they exited the precinct onto the sidewalk, the portable crackled to life. It was a Be On The Look Out, a BOLO: *"Prisoner escaped from a Corrections van in Queens. Be on the lookout for Timothy Wong…"*

KD and Sunny both stopped dead in their tracks. KD lifted the radio to ear level. With a deeply creased brow, Sunny leaned in to hear above the street traffic. The radio transmission was repeated.

"You gotta be shittin' me!" Sunny blurted.

The detectives had recently put Timothy Wong away for the infant's death. Sunny had played *bad cop* entering the interrogation room noisily kicking over a chair, waking and startling the snoozing Timothy, so relaxed. Fifteen minutes into the interrogation she feigned, taking a swing at the child killer's jaw, knowing that KD would grab her arm.

Sunny stood on the sidewalk outside the precinct, hands on her hips, looking into the sky with frustration. "We *must* find him."

"No! No *we!* There's a BOLO out," KD responded. He held up his palm as Sunny started to object. "We got other work to do. He won't get far. We can check the laptop later for the details."

To simultaneously read the details on the Murray Hill case and Timothy Wong on the lamb, Sunny powered up the laptop on the drive over. She studied the Murray Hill murder file before she turned to the prisoner escape. Twenty, barely talking, fuming minutes later, Detectives Douglass and McGraw ducked under crime scene tape across the door of the Murray Hill apartment on East Fortieth Street. The neighborhood was located just west of the Queens Midtown Tunnel.

"It feels like we just locked his ass up a few days ago," Sunny groused and bellyached over Timothy Wong's escape. She stood in the apartment living room, taking in the layout.

The one-bedroom apartment was frozen in time. A coffee cup still sat on the living room coffee table, which had one side pushed against the sofa, just as Sunny had read in the case file on the drive over.

"So, how did Wong fly the coop?" KD asked.

Sunny shook her head in dismay. "He was being escorted to his mother's funeral in Brooklyn. At a stoplight, he somehow slipped his cuffs, opened the Corrections van's side door, and disappeared into the hustle and bustle."

KD laughed. "I guess he didn't make it to his *mother's* funeral. Like I said, there's a BOLO out. They'll catch him."

At trial, Sunny recalled that smug bastard sat there stoic while his girlfriend, Sheryl Chen, cried so hysterically she had to be removed from the court. Sunny turned back to the matter at hand.

"So, there was no sign of forced entry here," Sunny noted, examining a perfect doorjamb. KD nodded, confirming her observation. "And Oleksandra Zakharov was found dead here?" She pointed near the kitchen sink and glanced back at the awry coffee table where the struggle possibly started.

"Yep. And the bouquet of flowers lay here." KD pointed to a spot on the carpet near the door. "No card, no receipt, nothing with the bouquet. We checked flower shops.

Nothing."

"And her husband, Liev Zakharov, just vanished like smoke in the wind," Sunny muttered.

"Yeah. No phone calls, no texts, no credit card usage," KD replied. "Maurice and I canvassed neighbors who said they heard and saw nothing." KD's longtime partner, Evelyn Jordan, had already retired, leaving him with Maurice Michaels, a young man, first week as a detective. The fresh detective was soon transferred to Queens, and KD snatched up Sunny.

"In the case file, it says this place doesn't warrant a doorman or security cameras," Sunny remarked, easing toward the bedroom. A doorman and cameras would have provided an abundance of leads. The bed was made, bedspread tight. The woman was meticulous. Sunny only pulled the sheets up on her bed each day.

A picture of Oleksandra and Liev adorned the left side of the woman's dresser. A huge oak jewelry box dominated the right side. Sunny slid open each jewelry box drawer. Real diamonds, pearls, and rubies sparkled back at her, unlike all the costume jewelry she was forced to wear in her child beauty pageants. Sunny wasn't much of a jewelry wearer—a chain necklace, a ring here and there.

She strode into the hall and back to the living room. "Let me see that photo again of Mrs. Zakharov." KD finger through the file folder and handed Sunny the NYPD Photo Unit snapshot of the dead woman.

Mrs. Zakharov lay splayed on the kitchen tile floor. She was strangled to death.

"Now let me see the necklace again that's in the evidence bag," Sunny requested, hand extended.

KD obliged and said, "Forensics says it's not a human bone, thank God. Some kind of animal. The dishwater contaminated the piece of bone too much. We found the necklace in the sink dishwater. We speculated that in the struggle to strangle her, this necklace popped loose from Mrs. Zakharov's neck and landed in the sink."

Sunny was already shaking her head. She glanced at the photo again. Sunny held the evidence bag high, rotating and examining the necklace. In the bag, a suede string was strung through a hole in a piece of bone. Through the plastic bag, her fingers isolated the piece of bone.

"No *woman* would wear this shit, this piece of bone." She dangled the evidence bag like something that stunk. "Especially when she has diamonds and pearls like I just saw in her jewelry box." She pointed down the hall. She fanned the photo in her other hand. "Ain't happening."

KD was nodding his head in approval. "Good point, partner," he conceded the revelation. "We dudes didn't catch that."

"So that means Mrs. Zakharov snatched the *bone* necklace from the perp's neck during the struggle," Sunny concluded. "But unfortunately, the dishwater has washed away any trace DNA, so your DD-5 says."

"True. I was of the mind to turn this over to Cold Case or OC as maybe a Russian organized crime turf war," KD said. "But maybe now *we* can investigate it a little longer."

"I know you want to solve cases on your own, so let me take the case file and sealed evidence bag home with me to study before you make a final decision."

"Cool. I'll notify Property that you're now in possession of the case evidence."

Sunny tucked the file folder under her arm and stuffed the sealed evidence bag into her pants pocket. They left for the ME appointment.

Chapter Nine

The Chief Medical Examiner Office of New York City was located just north of Manhattan South Homicide's East Twenty-first Street precinct. Sunny had been there before during the murdered infant investigation. The baby wasn't his. Sunny still thought murderous Timothy Wong got off easy with a prison stint upstate at Green Haven Correctional Facility. Now the piece of shit was on the loose!

The ME's office at First Avenue and East Thirtieth Street was near Bellevue Hospital. Sunny eyed the hospital as they drove past. As a patrol officer, on Sunny's first trip to Bellevue, all she could think about was "sounds like somebody escaped from Bellevue," a phrase teenage Sunny had used in Oklahoma referring to someone acting crazy and stupid. Although, at the time, she had no idea where Bellevue was. Back then, she envisioned wild-haired patients on the sidewalks surrounding the hospital, rambling to themselves, all their business exposed out the rear of their hospital gowns. Once she moved to New York City, she learned that Bellevue Hospital was one of New York State's leading hospitals.

KD circled the block looking for a parking spot, lucking out on the second loop around. He switched off the ignition but didn't immediately unlatch his seatbelt. He turned to Sunny.

"McGraw, you okay? You were awfully quiet on the ride over. Sure you want to go in?" He took a deep breath himself. "Remember, I was the lead on that baby case *and* lead on this new Hudson River Greenway DOA case. This is what homicide detectives do day in and day out. Get used to it. Shit happens. We did *our* part. This ain't the movies where everyone gets their just dessert." He unsnapped his seatbelt. "Wong's escape is weighing on your mind, but we have other work in front of us now. His mugshot was sent to forty thousand cops."

Sunny begrudgingly unlatched her seat belt, a small sign she was ready to forge ahead. She peered out the passenger window at the ME's building, then swung her head to KD.

"I know. Thanks for keeping me focused." She sighed, clearing her head now, thinking only of last night's murder. *That could've been me in there*, she again thought glumly. She started nodding progressively faster and faster. "I want these bastards who took that woman's life!" Grabbing the handle, she angrily swung the car door open. "Let's do it!"

The detectives entered the well-lit autopsy room, its walls constructed of glossy tan blocks. The ceramic tile floor underfoot lent itself to easy washing into floor drains. The thermostat was low to preserve the bodies resting on the stainless-steel tables. The place had a supermarket meat counter smell. Sunny scrunched her nose at the odor. She still remembered the very table the baby had laid on. She had a difficult time looking at that particular table. She stifled a shudder.

A woman a few tables away had her head down with her hands inside the chest cavity of a huge, hairy, white male.

"Maria," KD called out to her. The woman looked up, viewing them through a clear plastic face shield. On the ride over, KD had informed Sunny that the senior pathologist was Maria Bhadelia. KD seemed to know all nine million people in the five boroughs. Sunny had worked with a different pathologist on her one and only visit here.

Sunny hung back a bit as KD peeked inside the chest of the whale of a man. "That's ripe!" he said, now leaning away. He introduced the two women.

Sunny placed the senior pathologist at around forty-five. A few strands of gray added character and maturity to the woman's black hair. She wasn't slim but moved agilely on her feet.

"Kate, close this one up, please." Maria directed the request to an assistant as the senior pathologist pulled off elbow-high blue surgical gloves. She tossed the bloody gloves into a medical waste bin lined with a bright red garbage bag. Dr. Bhadelia strolled to a table against the wall. Using a white plastic fork, she stabbed a glazed Munchkin doughnut and popped it in her mouth. Sunny felt nauseated at the juxtaposition of doughnuts and ripe dead bodies.

"Over here," the pathologist said through a muffled mouthful of Munchkin, pointing to a covered body on table 7. "KD, you still have that Corvette?" she said over her shoulder while making her way to table 7.

Corvette? Sunny pondered. He never told her he had a Corvette. Sunny wished she had the money for a damn Corvette. Must be nice.

"You bet." KD mimicked shifting car gears. "Nineteen-sixty-nine," he said out the side of his mouth to Sunny, and then to Maria, he said, "Steve still have that sixty-six Mustang?" The ME confirmed her husband still had the car. KD quickly filled Sunny in that he and Steve met at a weekend car show. KD had recognized the name Bhadelia, and the rest was history.

Maria Bhadelia pulled back the sheet of a white woman on table 7. The senior pathologist swallowed the Munchkin. "Didn't have to do a prolonged DNA or dental record search to identify her."

"Why is that?" Sunny responded, taking in the pretty face of the DOA.

Dr. Bhadelia leaned close and gazed into the face of the young woman on the stainless-steel table. The pathologist went quiet for a moment as if she didn't want to wake a peacefully sleeping person. "She's military." Dr. Bhadelia lovingly straightened the white sheet over the woman's breasts, though it didn't need straightening. She raised the dead woman's right arm to reveal a tattoo. "An Army tattoo. I was immediately able to identify her through military records."

"What's her name?" KD said, an angry edge in his voice.

"Christine…Christine Lowry." Dr. Bhadelia exhaled heavily.

Sunny inched closer to the *sleeping* woman. She couldn't tear her eyes away from the deep crimson bruises around Christine's perfect neck. Sunny swallowed hard. Her neck bruising had nearly faded away. She had been rescued in the nick of time. *This could have been her lying here*, her mind kept repeating. She vowed to bring the murdering lowlifes to justice, she silently promised Christine.

Sunny looked back up at Dr. Bhadelia. "The Army," Sunny reflected. Her late police officer father was in the Army.

"She did tours in Afghanistan *and* Iraq," the pathologist said.

53

Sunny bristled. Christine risked her life abroad for her country only to be treated like a piece of garbage back home. The monsters!

Pointing with her ink pen, the medical examiner directed the detective's attention to bruises around Christine's slender neck.

"Whoever strangled the poor woman had huge, *very* strong hands." Maria Bhadelia bent to point around the back of Christine's neck. "His fingers nearly met back here."

Sunny observed where Maria pointed. She involuntarily reached for her own neck but caught herself. She momentarily flashed to the park that night, and the viselike fingers around her neck attempting to strangle the life from her.

The pathologist slid the pen into her white lab coat top pocket. "Strangulation. Definitely the cause of death."

KD stroked his goatee in thought. "Maria, we're trying to determine why Christine was in the park in the first place. Maybe we can backtrack from there. Can you tell if the murder positively happened in the park, or was she murdered someplace else and then dumped there?"

The senior pathologist rolled the dead woman slightly over on her side. With a small flashlight, she illuminated Christine's back.

"See this purplish Jell-O coloration up and down her back?" The detectives acknowledged the purple color. The doctor now shone the light on Christine's legs. "It's here, too." She raised Christine's right arm. "But not on the back of her arm." She placed the woman's arm back down. "Photo Unit pictures from the crime scene show her right arm draped over her abdomen—off the ground."

"Un-huh," KD grunted knowingly. Sunny nodded. She also knew where the pathologist was going with this.

Maria carefully rolled the body back flat. "As you know, heartbeats keep blood components mixed and moving. When the heart stops, gravity takes over and forces red blood cells to pool at the lowest points. She was found on her back. The right arm wasn't at a low point, so we can reasonably assume Christine was killed in the park."

"Okay, so the struggle and murder happened in the park." Sunny was in the park jogging that same fateful night. What decision put Christine in the park? "Any signs of drinking...or drugs?" Sunny blurted.

The medical examiner turned on her heels to retrieve a folder from a desk against the wall. She returned, thumbing through sheets of paper until she found what she needed.

"BAC of point-oh-three," the pathologist read.

"One glass of wine," KD interjected. "A blood alcohol content of point-oh-eight is considered too drunk to drive. She wasn't drunk."

"And what about drugs?" Sunny chimed in.

"Tox screen shows no drugs," the pathologist said flatly.

Again, rifling through pages in her folder, Dr. Bhadelia studied a new page for just a moment until recognition crossed her face.

"Judging from the lack of rigor mortis at the crime scene, my office puts TOD at about several hours after sunset yesterday." Three to four hours after time of death, a dead body stiffens, then relaxes. Christine's body had already experienced rigor mortis.

Sunny calculated that Christine was murdered shortly before she herself was assaulted. She nervously wiped at her mouth. She wasn't supposed to be standing here today. She was supposed to be lying on a sparkling stainless-steel ME table. She wrung her hands.

"Was Christine raped?" KD finally asked, almost whispering as he gazed down at the woman on the table.

Maria nodded, inhaling hugely in renewed disgust. "Multiple times." She hung her head. "A large amount of vaginal tears and semen."

Sunny was shaking her head in revulsion. "I know it's early, but has any suspect DNA or trace evidence been identified yet?" Sunny asked, her gears turning. With the DNA from under her own fingernails and these semen samples, the investigation could take a huge leap forward in identifying the animals who assaulted her and murdered Christine.

Dr. Maria Bhadelia composed herself enough to leaf through the folder again. She found a page, studied it for a moment, and looked up at Detective McGraw. She held up her hand to slow Sunny's questioning. "Regarding the semen, we're working as fast as we can to ID the DNA."

KD blew out his cheeks in frustration. "Okay. Maria, let us know immediately, please. We don't care what time of day or night. Call immediately."

"Will do," Dr. Bhadelia said stoically. She crossed her arms and glanced at both detectives.

"Anything else?" KD asked.

"This may or may not be helpful. It appears Christine had recently eaten. Her meal was still in the gastric phase. It was still in her stomach."

"So the food hadn't transitioned to the duodenum?" KD interjected. Sunny glanced at her partner, impressed.

"Correct." Maria agreed, nodding.

Maria stepped to the wall table again and came back with a clear jar of brown swooshing stuff. Sunny felt a surge of nausea at what she presumed was stomach contents.

Maria continued. "My parents immigrated from India. I was born in Queens—native New Yorker," she proclaimed with pride. "They taught me to cook traditional Indian dishes." She pointed at Christine's stomach under the sheet. "I'm certain that she ate biryani for dinner. It's essentially two dishes, the first being a veal curry and the second a fragrant rice called basmati. *Bas* is Hindu for 'aroma,' and *mati* means 'full of.'" Dr. Bhadelia stopped and

56

raised her eyebrows at the detectives. "Either Christine cooks Indian cuisine—"

"Or she had recently eaten at an Indian restaurant," Sunny finished the sentence as she and KD glanced knowingly at each other.

"We'll increase our canvass radius to include Indian restaurants and post a uniform at Christine's apartment now that we know who she is." KD held up the portable radio, indicating he would use it soon to dispatch the uni. "As usual, you've been most helpful, Maria," KD said, getting ready to leave.

"Glad to meet you, Maria," Sunny said.

The doctor held up her index finger to halt the detectives in their tracks.

"One last thing." The doctor paused with severe concern in her eyes. "Christine was pregnant," she revealed, shaking her head. "She may not have even known it."

The detectives returned to the precinct and parked the unmarked in a diagonal parking spot out front. As they got out of the car, KD agreed to grab a sandwich to eat at his desk while writing up the ME DD-5 and updating Lieutenant Sanchez as promised. He would do preliminary research on Christine Lowry to bring with them to her apartment. Sunny would join him following her lunch. Her sister had already texted her for the juicy skinny of her *date*. Two minutes later, Greg drove up in his Lexus.

Chapter Ten

"Greg, can you grab us a table while I make a quick run over there?" They stood outside Sally's Deli in the Meatpacking District. "Order me ham and Swiss on Italian…Dijon mustard, please. I promise I'll be right back." She needed to do this on her own.

Sunny had chosen Sally's Deli for its particular location. She was pointing at MH Construction across the street as she stepped off the curb, leaving Greg perplexed and speechless.

She held up a palm to halt an approaching green Nissan Altima as she quickly jaywalked to the other side of the street. The driver angrily laid into his horn. Greg was saying something as he chirped his Lexus' car alarm, but Sunny couldn't understand him over the traffic noise. With one stone, she sought to get two birds today—start a new relationship with Greg and find out who Camille was. Something about the man looked familiar…and it had nothing to do with the events surrounding the night in the park.

Sunny entered MH Construction. The faint gasoline and construction equipment odor met her nose again. It was quiet this time, no rumbling drum recording, no chanting, no one grunting and wielding a lacrosse stick. But she heard a noise up the staircase. It sounded like something dropped to the wooden floor with two soft thuds. She weaved her way around a large post-hole digger similar to the one used on her uncle's farm to erect wooden posts for a barbwire fence.

The stairs creaked as she ascended. She didn't call out this time to alert anyone. Her nagging mind was working overtime on what was familiar about this guy. Then it hit her!

Her partner, KD, was forever alert, studying faces. He impressed on his partner to memorize peculiarities in mugshots, which she eagerly did.

She had a strong suspicion now that the man at the top of these stairs was in one of those mugshots. The last time she was here, the man had said his name was Camille. She couldn't remember Camille's last name. Did he tell her? She had gotten interrupted by a call from her boss to immediately head to Forensics.

Sunny withdrew her 9mm and aimed the Glock up the staircase. She hadn't expected to be dealing with a fugitive. She should call for backup, but now ambivalence hit her. Her first visit here was nonthreatening, so she delayed. Something just wasn't adding up, and she needed some answers. But just in case, she wasn't putting the gun away.

"I know who you are!" she yelled aggressively as she climbed enough steps to put her eyesight at floor level of the second-story office...art studio...gym. Whatever!

Sunny carefully stepped to the second floor. She listened intently as she spun three-sixty, her elbows locked, ready for the Glock's recoil, if need be.

"I know you're here. I heard you when I opened the front door. I have a gun, and I'll use it. Come out now!" She listened for a response. There was none.

Suddenly, a white cat with a large copper spot on its back calmly and quietly padded from behind a partition wall. Sunny jerked her weapon, aiming at the feline. She nearly pulled the trigger. The man who called himself Camille must be on the other side of that wall.

Sunny raised the nine to eye level again. She attempted to step closer to see around the wall, but the cat entwined himself around her ankles, rubbing and meowing affectionately. She was having trouble moving without tripping over the animal. Tuffy did this very thing when he wanted to be held. There was no way around this persistent cat.

Without taking her eyes off the partition wall, Sunny quickly squatted and lifted the amorous cat with her left hand, tucking it under her armpit. She took another tentative step closer to the wall. This doting cat had to be with someone…someone on the other side of this wall.

"You killed a man," Sunny continued. "You went to prison, and then you broke out. Come from behind that wall. I know who you are!"

Her hands and arms were full. She leaned to her left to peek behind the wall.

"I didn't kill anyone," a voice said smoothly…somewhere to Sunny's left. With the cat underarm, she immediately twisted to her left…but saw no one, her eyes wide, unblinking. She spun back to the right, doing a three-sixty. "I'll shoot! Where are you?" she shouted, jabbing the gun forward with each word for emphasis.

The voice again came from her left…close…as if in her ear.

"I'm right here."

She suddenly looked down at the cat clutched under her arm. *Did I just hear a cat talking?* The white cat peered up at her, piercing yellow eyes.

"I didn't kill anyone," the feline repeated.

"What the hell!"

Sunny dropped the cat to the floor and trained her weapon for a headshot. Her trigger finger removed the slack, ready for the deadly shot. Her hands shook slightly, but she was close enough not to miss. Plus, with twelve rounds, one was bound to tear through the target.

A talking cat! Had she woke up this morning? Yes...she toasted a bagel for breakfast, went to the morgue, and had lunch with Greg. The cat seized her attention again.

"Watch this," the cat said. The feline casually strolled, tail high, and disappeared behind the partition wall. Sunny firmly gripped the nine, ready to kill. She heard rumbling and several moments later got another bizarre surprise.

"It's me."

Stumbling backward, Sunny was nonetheless able to aim her Glock squarely between his huge pink eyes. What's going on? She felt as though she were losing her mind, seeing things. She was having difficulty catching her breath. On her uncle's farm, she had encountered many animals: chickens, pigs, cows, horses, and even rabbits. But none of the animals could speak.

The white rabbit before her said, "Can you lower the gun, please?" The creature's ears rotated like radar dishes. His nose full of whiskers twitched from side to side.

Stunned by a second talking animal, a speechless Sunny shook her head in advanced disbelief. She vigorously rubbed her forehead but won't lower the weapon. This was so confusing.

"I don't think I'll lower my gun," she warned, now adjusting her sweaty, shaky, two-handed grip on her only means of safety.

The rabbit sat back on his haunches. His nostrils flared, sniffing the air. "You remember me from that night up in the tree? If I wanted to harm you, I would have already." The rabbit raised a brow as if to say think about that.

Sunny held the weapon level as she pondered his words. Licking her dry lips, she finally and slowly lowered the gun barrel but maintained a firm grip just in case.

Preoccupied with the abnormal circumstances, she muttered, "That was *you* in the tree that night?" The rabbit nodded in response. She couldn't believe she was talking to a rabbit. Though Sunny was having a tough time processing it all, she forged ahead.

"Thank you," somehow escaped her lips. She lowered the weapon further, one hand, barrel aimed at the floor, finger off the trigger. "You saved my life," she said quietly.

She hesitantly looked around the room with renewed interest. She pointed at the news clippings pinned to the corkboard of the eagle saving the falling child, the dolphin that rescued sightseeing tourists from their capsized boat on the choppy Hudson River, the unknown man who lifted the car off the yellow Labrador.

She turned back to the rabbit. "That's you in the news clippings saving all those people and animals?"

The rabbit smiled.

"But...but how?" Sunny slowly holstered her Glock.

"It's a long story. But let's just say, for now, that it was a bit of my misfortune as a child." The rabbit paused and twitched his whiskers, pink eyes studying her. "I'm a shifter."

Sunny swallowed hard. "A what?"

"A *shifter*," he enunciated.

"You mean like I see on TV? People turning into wolves, bears, and stuff?"

62

The rabbit shook his head, his ears flopping, his eyes smiling. "And much, much more."

Downstairs, they heard the front door open. The rabbit twitched his nose, sampling the air. "It's Marshall," he told Sunny. At her uncomprehending frown of how-did-he-know-who-was-at-the-door look, the rabbit tapped his nose twice. "And I also can smell something of T-Rex in your pocket."

Sunny was thoroughly confused. *T-Rex?* she thought as she touched her pocket. *What is he talking about?*

"Camille, do you have that contract ready," the man shouted from downstairs, his heavy footfalls coming up the steps. When he made it to the top, he froze. "What's going on?" he asked unsurely.

"Marshall, meet NYPD Detective Sunny McGraw," the rabbit said.

Marshal was a short, stocky man with short hair spurting from under his work cap. His coveralls were covered with grime. His eyes darted several times from Sunny to the rabbit, then back. He didn't seem surprised by the talking rabbit, but he looked as though he were ready to bolt right back down the stairs. Marshall finally glared at the rabbit in anger.

"Camille, have you lost your freakin' mind?!" he railed. "A detective?"

"She knows," Camille said, his voice even. He hopped back behind the wall, leaving Marshall and Sunny alone.

The two held an uncomfortable gaze for a long moment. Some of the fear had dissipated from the man's face, replaced by simple unease. He shifted his weight from one foot to the other. He swallowed hard, his Adam's apple bouncing.

Marshall closed his eyes and slowly massaged his temples with both hands. "Are we going to prison?" His words were pained. He opened his eyes and looked at something over Sunny's shoulder. She turned, following his gaze.

Camille had stepped from behind the wall, barefoot, wearing blue jeans, buttoning his shirt across his broad chest. He appeared nonchalant about all that had transpired. In fact, he wore a small smile. "I miss anything?" he jested.

Sunny found herself on the dilemma's horns. Something told her this man wasn't a murderer. He had actually saved her life. But then, she was law enforcement— one to uphold the law, not interpret it. She pointed a reprimanding index finger at Camille, but then her phone rang. It was Greg.

"Is that you I see up there in that window?" he asked.

She peered through the window down at Sally's Deli. Camille peaked down with her. Sunny waved at Greg. "Yeah, it's me. I'll be right there." She ended the call, not wanting to describe or explain the bizarre events up here.

"I *have to* go now," she said to Camille. "I'll be back after work. You be *here!*" she demanded, jabbing her index finger at the floor.

Sally sliced her ham paper-thin. Her fresh-baked Italian bread had no rival in Sunny's opinion. Their small table draped with a red and white checkered tablecloth afforded a front window view of the Meatpacking District's cobblestone streets. The deli buzzed in full swing with a customer line nearly to the front door. A wall-mounted TV added its part to the cacophony.

"Who's he?" Greg asked, looking out the window and up at the second floor of MH Construction. He ran his fingers through his sandy-blond, curly hair.

Did something in his tone relay jealousy? "Oh, just someone who frequented the Hudson River Greenway," Sunny stammered slightly. "As part of the investigation, Homicide is interviewing as many as we can to puzzle the murder together."

She had left MH Construction with more questions than answers. And, of course, many of the questions related to the man named Camille—and his transformation. What did he call it?

Shifting? He was a shifter. Camille the Shifter.

She still couldn't talk to a single soul about the bizarre events she'd recently experienced. Plus, Camille was a fugitive. But one who had saved her life. What did she owe him? The day was making little sense... She was glad when Greg didn't ask any more questions about the construction company.

"You detectives save the world," he said and then chomped down on the turkey sandwich. "How is the new case coming along?"

From anyone else, Sunny would have been insulted by the seeming dig about saving the world. The Job. Law enforcement never took a rest. Sunny and her ilk solved cases and then turned the matters over to Greg's legal team. Greg understood the demands of the law, unlike her ex-boyfriend.

Tossing a couple potato chips in her mouth behind a bite of ham and cheese sandwich, Sunny responded between chews. "The case is"—*crunch, crunch*—"inching along." She kept furtively glancing out the window at the MH Construction building across the street.

"You seem unusually preoccupied," Greg observed, his tone one of concern, his gray eyes fixed on her. "Does it have anything to do with Timothy Wong's escape? I got the alert." Everyone attached to the case received an alert: judges, prosecutors, patrol, detectives. Retribution from prisoners unfortunately occurred.

One of Greg's strongest traits was his empathy, which Sunny found attractive. He could turn it on and off like a light switch. In the courtroom of their last case, mild-mannered, non-athletic Greg went for the jugular of Timothy Wong. Sunny was so pissed that the scumbag killer attempted to blame the death of his girlfriend's infant girl on a goodhearted elderly neighbor. She nearly got herself removed from the case for feigning that swing at the POS in the precinct interrogation room. With the baby's mother at work, the kindhearted elderly woman had agreed to babysit the already *sleeping* child while the boyfriend lied that he had to immediately go to DMV to renew his license. In the courtroom, Greg was in pit bull mode, unlike now.

"Are you?" he asked again about her preoccupation.

She snapped out of her distraction. "Sorry. So much going on."

"No need to apologize. Guess who just got assigned as your riding ADA." He flashed a crooked knowing smile. "Yours truly." He poked his thumb into his chest. "Bring me up to speed when you and KD have time."

Sunny promised she would. But she wasn't ready to tell all until she understood and didn't sound off her rocker trying to explain. She glanced out the window again at the construction company.

They enjoyed their lunch while watching the world go by out the front window. Greg's shifted gears on the subject.

"So what's it like working in a male-dominated profession?"

Sunny took a swig from the Coke can, then another. "There's still some knuckle-dragging Neanderthals out there." She glanced out the window again. Across the street, a cat padded to the curb, took a seat, and stared lazily toward the deli. *Customers must feed him on their way out*, she thought.

She turned back to Greg. "They think I should be barefoot, pregnant, and in the kitchen."

"When will it ever end?" Greg sympathized.

"Really!" she wholeheartedly agreed. "Fortunately, KD is different. He sought out a female partner. I'm still trying to find out why."

"And I'm sure KD has some juicy stories he can tell," Greg continued.

Sunny nodded confirmation while chomping on the ham sandwich. She was still getting to know her new partner. He garnered respect in MSH with the highest clearance rate, and she wanted to help him keep it that way. She would continue to work the Murray Hill case, the one with the bone necklace. Her phone chimed with a text message—speaking of KD.

When you and lover boy finish your lunch, I'm ready to take that ride down to

Alphabet City to Christine Lowry's apartment.

"The Job?" Greg asked, pointing at her cell phone. She smiled, not wanting to hurry the lunch along. She enjoyed his company. But she had a case to solve for Christine.

Out the window, the cat continued to stare. Recognition suddenly struck Sunny. She stopped chewing. This cat had the same copper-colored, saddle shape patch on its back as the one at the construction company. Greg must have seen the change in Sunny's expression from enjoyment to one of disquiet. He followed her gaze out the window.

"Do you have a cat phobia?" he asked in jest.

Sunny brought her attention back to the deli. "Actually, I have a cat. Tuffy."

"I'm not really a cat person. My family had dogs my entire life out on Long Island. Maybe Tuffy would like a friend," Greg said, nodding toward the alley cat sitting on the curb staring at the deli.

"No," she said as the cat walked away. "Tuffy doesn't like sharing."

Chapter Eleven

"Pop, is that cat still coming around? I see you left out a can of cat food on the porch," Amber Smoke observed as she and her father, Ariwiio Smoke, climbed the steps to his house on Sunadaga territory in upstate New York.

Ariwiio was pronounced *A-lee-wio* because there were no *R* in the Haudenosaunee language. As a child, Ariwiio was forbidden to use his Native name. The "savages" were stripped of everything: their names, their hair, their clothes, their culture, their dignity. The forced assimilation policy had gone from "The only good Indian is a dead Indian" to "Kill the Indian to save the man."

On old knees, Ariwiio grunted on each step up the porch. The Vietnam War injury to his shin didn't help matters either. He was left with a permanent limp.

He ran his finger through his snow-white mop of hair. "That cat and Rex act like they know each other," Ariwiio said of Camille's dog, Rex, and the cat with the huge copper patch on his back. Ariwiio had cared for his son's chocolate lab since the incarceration. His son was missing, and Ariwiio had a lawsuit lodged against the Department of Corrections.

He inserted the key into the door, and they entered. Amber gasped!

His daughter stopped short in the living room. "Pop, when are you going to store some of these books? Mom would be appalled."

Amber was the image of her mother with the way her glossy black hair fell over her shoulders and the way she defiantly pursed her lips when challenged. True, his late wife would have gone up one side of Ariwiio and down the other for making such a mess. This bad habit crept up on him. He stood there with a look of half embarrassment on his face. He gave a lame shrug.

Ariwiio pitched in to help his daughter stack loose textbooks and magazines. His passion was reading history, business, economics, psychology, sociology, whodunnit mysteries, sci-fi, and thriller novels. Anything but fashion. Jeans and sneakers were just fine. And he was particularly adept at math and statistics. He liked to believe that Amber, an accountant, was a chip off the old numbers block. As for statistics, it was an acquired skill for the Sunadaga president. The fight and struggle for Native American rights ended up in the courts many times. With his keen memory of numerical facts, he helped the legal teams put slippery opposing parties back on their heels, stammering.

It was Angel Smoke who had kept family life functioning as a well-oiled machine. And though the mother and wife was all business, Amber and Camille never wanted for love and affection from her. Angel's patience for details complemented Ariwiio's desire for the big picture. Since Angel's sudden and suspicious death, Ariwiio found himself floundering at home and struggling as the Sunadaga Nation president.

A half-hour later, the clutter was in its proper place. Amber and Ariwiio enjoyed tea at the kitchen table while they caught up on the last month.

"North Carolina reminded me so much of upstate New York—forest, mountains, wildlife," Amber started. "Principal Chief Jesse Running Deer of the Eastern Band of the Cherokee Nation is receptive to forming a 527 among the Indigenous nations and tribes."

Ariwiio blew on the hot cup of liquid and then slurped a small amount. "That's fantastic. And thanks for stepping up into your brother's place." His voice trailed off in anguish.

Ariwiio had been grooming Camille, his oldest child, to one day climb to the Sunadaga Nation presidency. Their proposed 527 PAC, a political action committee of Indigenous people, was formed to influence federal, state, and local candidates. The PAC was first headed by Camille with his younger sister as PAC vice president. Ariwiio now groomed Amber for the Sunadaga presidency one day.

Amber added a teaspoon of sugar to her tea. "Before I talked business with Chief Running Deer, he invited me to the Cherokee Mountainside Theater. You should have seen this place, Pop," she said excitedly. "In the middle of a pine forest, the Cherokee built a twenty-one-hundred-seat amphitheater. The production was called *Unto These Hills*, the Cherokee story. Once gold was discovered, the Cherokee were forced into concentration camps and then along the deadly Trail of Tears. We all know the story, but to see it…"

Ariwiio listened intently, watching his daughter's excitement. In addition to the Cherokee, forced along their separate hellish Trail of Tears were the Choctaw, Creek, Chickasaw, and Seminole—the so-called Five Civilized Tribes. The elderly, women, children, men, all freezing, starving, exhausted, forced to trudge a thousand miles through *their* country to Oklahoma, practically emptying the south of Native people. Nearly a quarter died. Yes, he knew the history of Native forced migration out of their homes, off their properties rich in farmland, timber, gold, silver, coal, oil, and iron ore. Location, location, location, Natives retaining next to nothing of the over two billion acres, today supporting a twenty-five-trillion-dollar-a-year US economy, the world's largest. He knew the numbers and many other Trails of Tears. *We want our wealth returned*, he finished the thought.

"Principal Chief Running Deer is all for the PAC. He's bringing the idea before the Tribal Council," Amber concluded, then sipped her tea. She clacked the cup noisily into the saucer and gazed at her dad.

"What's wrong?" Ariwiio asked.

"The strangest things are happening as I travel promoting the 527 idea." She took a deep breath, caressing her teacup with both hands. "I could just swear there's an eagle following me around the country," she said with a perplexed look.

Ariwiio chuckled at her spooky declaration. "There are eagles all over the United States."

Amber was shaking her head. "No. Something's different."

Ariwiio turned serious. "You know as well as I do that in Haudenosaunee culture, an eagle watching over you is a *good* sign. Means you're protected."

"I know," she said, her tone unconvinced. She lifted the teacup to her lips and sipped. She exhaled heavily and then switched subjects. "I need to do some repairs to the beadwork on my overdress for the upcoming powwow." The velvet and cotton dress was made of hundreds of beads laced into the traditional outfit. The colorful beads snapped and hissed to the beat of the powwow drum as the dancer circled. "And I'm going to change into mom's dress halfway through the powwow to honor her." Amber looked away, her emotions flaring. Ariwiio placed his hand over hers.

"We all miss her, sweetie," he said consolingly.

Chapter Twelve

A, B, C, D. The avenues of Alphabet City, part of the East Village in lower Manhattan, Tompkins Square Park at its center. The neighborhood was not always a tourist destination. Its grit and grime were now transformed by cookie-cutter gentrification, but its rough edge character was never quite subdued.

The NYPD unmarked Ford rolled down Avenue B. Sidewalk vendors hawked their wares, nostalgic vinyl records, clothes, and jewelry. Sunny slammed the butt of her fist into her chest to dislodge a belch.

"Too much Dijon mustard on Sally's ham and cheese," she quipped from the passenger side, her other arm resting on the open windowsill, allowing in the warm sunny day.

"Woman, were you born in a barn?" KD said with a smirk.

"Close. I've cleaned one out." She belched a second time, which got a laugh out of her partner.

They stopped at the Fourth Street light. KD quickly dug in his pocket and pulled out a ten-dollar bill. He handed it to Sunny and told her to pass it to a homeless man sitting cross-legged against a laundromat building on her side of the car. The tattered-clothed man sprung to his feet and thanked Sunny. The light changed to green.

"Some of us are fortunate, privileged," KD explained. "Christine's apartment is near Third Street and Avenue B." They found a parking spot and threw the official NYPD parking card on the dashboard to prevent towing or theft.

KD pressed the doorbell labeled *Super* from among the thirty or so doorbells. After three tries, a heavily accented voice answered. Sunny guested the Middle East, but there was something else there.

"Can this hold until after prayer?" the building superintendent asked.

"No!" KD barely allowed the man to finish. "NYPD detectives. Buzz us in. Now." There was a huge sigh in the speaker, and then the door buzzed and clicked.

A sixty-ish, rawboned man in a white prayer cap awaited the detectives at the top of the stairs leading to the first floor. With Southeast Asian features, he apologized for asking the detectives to wait.

KD and Sunny flashed their shields and introduced themselves to Mr. Sutan Ali.

"We saw Lowry on one of the doorbells, Mr. Ali," Sunny said. She stood a head taller than the super. Sutan Ali gazed up, blinking his eyes excessively. Sunny had run across persons whose second language was English who blinked like that. Maybe it was the stress of the translation process.

"She pays on time. Good tenant," Mr. Ali offered without prompting.

"When was the last time you saw her?" KD asked.

There was a pause. His gears were turning. He shook his head vigorously. "Oh, I don't... how you say...keep track of these tenants," he said, waving his arm down the hall.

"Good enough," KD responded. "We're going to need to get into Miss Lowry's apartment."

Sutan Ali looked stunned. "She okay?" He pointed up the staircase. "The officer guarding the door won't tell me anything."

"She's dead, Mr. Ali," Sunny said without preamble.

The super's mouth fell open, and he turned on his heels to enter his apartment. Moments later, he returned, jiggling a huge ring of keys. "She's on the fourth floor. 4B. I can't believe this." He bound up the stairs like someone half his age.

"Where's the accent from?" KD asked at the second-floor landing. The staircase wound through the center of the old walkup apartment building.

"Indonesia," the spry old man replied, stepping to the third floor.

"Which of the seventeen thousand islands?" KD followed up. Sunny gave her partner a where-did-you-get-that-shit-from look. He winked at her and then said, "If you ate meals at the table with my father, Ronald Douglass, you'd understand." Sunny nodded, not totally understanding. *Later.*

"Java," Sutan Ali said over his shoulder.

When they arrived at 4B, Sunny heard KD breathing hard. "My, my, Mr. Douglass, do we need more exercise?" He rolled his eyes and wiped his glistening, shaved brown scalp with his hand. KD straightened up and caught his breathe. The uni at the door to preserve evidence in the criminal investigation logged the detectives into his notepad.

Sutan Ali searched the massive ring of keys for 4B. It sounded like windchimes in the tight hall. He unlocked and opened the door. He started to step in, but Sunny caught him by the shoulder to stop him.

"We can take it from here, Mr. Ali," Sunny interjected. "You can finish your prayers now," she continued. The polite man bowed slightly and swiftly left.

The tiny studio apartment was barely a few steps in any direction. The fold-down bed would have dominated the living room/bedroom. The kitchenette, like the bathroom, could barely accommodate one person.

"I'll start in the bathroom," KD said, pointing. He took one step up into the cramped space.

"I'll check this chest of drawers." Sunny slid open the top of four drawers, a mirror sat atop the chest. Cosmetics filled the topmost drawer.

Sunny was still learning her partner after a little over a month together. Just before the detectives were interrupted by an officer needs assistance call over their police radio a few weeks ago, she was telling KD more details about how her police officer father was killed in the line of duty. That day, they were the closest law enforcement. Outside Grand Center Terminal, the detectives helped uniform patrol officers subdue a pickpocketing duo. They never got to finish the talk about his father.

"Again, I'm sorry to hear about your father," Sunny empathized. She heard him rummaging through the medicine cabinet.

"Thanks. Pop was a middle school history teacher, and I was a captive audience. That's how I knew Indonesia was comprised of seventeen thousand islands. It's also the most populated Muslim nation. You name any country, and I can probably tell you a lot of its history. Been hearing it since I could talk." KD chuckled, but there was a sad quality mixed with the mirth. The metal medicine cabinet door slapped closed. "Nothing of interest in the medicine cabinet," he said.

Sunny opened the second chest drawer. She sensed KD had more to say. And he did.

"It happened at the school," KD continued. Sunny pulled her hands from the underwear drawer and closed it. "A stroke left him paralyzed." She heard KD jerk open the plastic shower curtain with a swish.

"KD, I'm sorry."

"Thank you. I'm not finding anything of value in the bathroom. How 'bout you?" He stepped down and out of the bathroom and headed for the kitchenette.

The third chest drawer appeared to be a miscellaneous, catch-all drawer. Sunny found pay stubs, takeout menus, and a glossy picture of Christine Lowry in her Army uniform. She served her country in war-torn, dangerous Iraq and Afghanistan. Sunny fumed. Christine's life was snuffed out on American soil. Sunny vowed to get justice for this hero.

"I have a paystub here. Appears she worked at a veterinary facility," Sunny noted.

KD leaned out the kitchenette to view the paystub. "This office is in the Upper West Side," he observed. "Hang onto that paystub. We may need to head up there next."

"Here's her laptop. Maybe we can get some local leads," Sunny said after opening the bottom drawer. "Christine's cell phone and purse are probably at the bottom of the Hudson River. Harbor Unit still has divers in the water," Sunny said, thinking of the NYPD specialized Aquatic Unit that patrolled the waterways of the city surrounded by water.

KD opened and shut cabinets in the cramped kitchenette. "I'll call Christine's parents. I got their names from her military records while you were on your *date*." He spun one-eighty to examine the refrigerator contents. "Yogurt, cold pizza, diet soda. Yuck."

Sunny's cell phone rang. "McGraw here."

"Detective McGraw, this is Michael Searle from Forensics." Sonny's blood ran cold for a moment. The gorilla fur. "Two things," he continued. "First, a second spectrometer confirmed gorilla fur, but we're going to prioritize other evidence first and come back to the fur later." Sunny finally released the breath she was holding. She would visit the construction company after work. "Second, regarding your Christine Lowry case…"

Sunny interrupted, "Wait a second. Let me turn on my speakerphone so my partner can hear. It's just the two of us here. Talk freely."

KD closed the barren refrigerator and stepped next to Sunny. The forensic scientist spoke.

"We got a hit on some fingerprints on Christine's bracelet. Male. African American. Jonathon Williams. His fingerprints were in our system from priors. Accessory to robbery. Seems Mr. Williams doesn't watch any of the CSI-type TV shows like normal people. Eight years ago, he was the watch out for a gang robbing a bodega." What Sunny called a convenience store in Oklahoma was nuanced in NYC, like so many other things. *Bodega* was Spanish for "storeroom." "Mr. Williams must have gotten the munchies during his lookout. Caught on surveillance cameras, and his fingerprints were lifted from a crumpled candy wrapper and compared to earlier priors. He now works at a fitness gym on the Upper West Side."

"Good work," KD said into the speaker. "Maybe this is our big break. Send us a pic and his work address." The scientist promised to do so right away.

Before the detectives left, KD sat in a chair, phone to ear, eyes closed, head down, massaging his temple. He delivered the tragic news to Christine's parents. From his gentle, measured tone, Sunny could tell that her partner had been there many times. She observed the way he delivered the devastating news to loved ones.

Chapter Thirteen

At the driver's side of their department car parked outside Christine's apartment, Sunny beckoned, hands cupped above the car's roof, for KD to toss her the keys. He did no such thing.

"McGraw, slow down. I know you think this guy Jonathon Williams was part of the gang that assaulted and nearly killed you in the park, but we have to go by the book if we want to collar this vicious gang."

Sunny stood frozen, her nostrils flaring, her chest heaving, glaring at KD. She placed both palms flat on the sun-warmed car roof to compose herself. A large box truck with vegetables painted on its side zipped behind her. The box truck's strong wind wake blew her brunette hair. Sunny exasperatingly blew the wind-whipped strands from her face.

KD dangled the keys above the roof, just out of reach. "I'm not going to bail your ass out. Get a grip on it. I want justice as much as you." He paused and raised his eyebrows for her to think about it.

She nodded approvingly. "I hear ya. Now throw me the keys."

"What's the magic word?"

Sunny pursed her lips and exhaled hard. "Please," she grudgingly offered.

KD's face split into a wide smile of pearly whites. He waited another beat, then did a basketball three-point shot into her hands. He lifted his chin, pointing down the street. "There're some cool eateries here in Alphabet City," KD suggested to a calmer Sunny. "If you like German beer and German sausage, Latin or Jamaican, it's all here."

"I'll have to come back," she replied distractedly, peering through the side view mirror from the driver's seat. She threw the car into drive and weaved out onto Avenue B, did a U-turn, and headed north. KD grabbed the dashboard to secure himself. A few minutes later, they turned west onto Fourteenth Street. Her tense partner had momentarily halted the conversation, keeping his eyes glued on the road. His leg moved, applying imaginary brakes. None of it stopped Sunny from talking.

"You never told me why you chose me as your partner," Sunny said as she executed a right and turned north onto Eighth Avenue. The car's tires squealed for traction.

KD ignored the question. "Where did you learn to drive?" he asked, leaning deeply to the right to counterbalance the sharp turn. "I drive a hot ass Vette." His tongue made a clicking sound. "But I don't drive this wild."

"I drove off-road using my uncle's farm truck to round up stray cows and goats." She glanced over at KD, whose eyes were riveted straight ahead. "Now," Sunny repeated, "why did you choose me?"

"I keep my ear to the ground. You had a sterling NYPD patrol and precinct detective record. Your father was law enforcement. If your father losing his life as a cop didn't dissuade you, then you have the right stuff." KD suddenly pointed to a bicycle courier weaving through traffic ahead.

"I see him. Continue," Sunny asserted.

"Evelyn and I went incognito on some surveillance situations." Evelyn was his former retired partner. "The bad guys took us for just another hand-holding couple, allowing us to get close." KD suddenly twisted in the seat to face her. "And don't get any ideas about holding my hand and cuddling, McGraw." He smirked. "I'm taken!"

"Pleaseeeee!" She noticed he was relaxing a bit. He wasn't wiping his glistening head as much. "And?"

"And I wanted to snatch you up before some slug got to you. I didn't want you to end up with some lazy lard ass guiding you wrong. I think you have potential. If..." He let the word hang for a few moments. "...if we can control that damn temper of yours."

Sunny guffawed and slapped the steering wheel. "I don't have a temper," she said in a faux-innocent voice. "I'm just...passionate." She extended a fist to bump. They were true partners.

For half the drive, Sunny strategically used the siren and emergency lights to veer in and out of her lane. At Fifty-ninth Street, Eighth Avenue's name changed to Central Park West as the detectives continued rolling north to West Eighty-second Street. Absolute Fitness lay between Eighth and Ninth Avenues.

KD's phone rang. "It's the Loo. I was going to update him with something of substance after we left Absolute Fitness. Oh well." He turned on the speakerphone. "Hey, Loo."

"Are you two having fun?" His voice didn't relay joviality. "I need an update. The mayor's up my ass! The city is frightened. And you know which way shit rolls, eh, KD?"

"Yes, sir. From the mayor, to the police commissioner, to the chief of detectives, to you, and then to us." KD looked over at Sunny, an eyebrow raised. "Did I get it right, sir?"

"Despite KD being a wise ass, did you hear that, McGraw?" he barked.

Without taking her eyes off the insane New York City traffic, she leaned closer to the phone. "Got it, sir." She stuck out her tongue at the phone. "Shit rolls downhill on me."

KD informed their Loo about the crime lab's fingerprint findings on the bracelet, which could be a substantial break in the case. Christine's distraught parents were also flying in from Illinois to identify her body. KD would let the Lieutenant know more after Absolute Fitness.

Sunny located a parking spot near the fitness center. A perky receptionist greeted the homicide detectives as they entered. Sunny leaned on the counter and flashed her tin. The receptionist's name was Erica.

"Erica, I'm NYPD Detective Sunny McGraw, and this is Detective Kevin Douglass." She intentionally left out *homicide*. People tended to freak out at the ominous word. They needed to keep this low-key, although Sunny was fuming to get at this murderous son of a bitch. Even with *homicide* deleted, Erica still hadn't batted an eyelid yet. She escorted them to Jonathan Williams as requested.

"Wow! This place puts my basement workout room to shame," KD commented as they entered the fitness center's expansive workout area. Weight benches were filled with sweating, grunting fitness center members. Others jumped rope while more lifted kettlebells from the rubber floor.

"At least you have a workout room," Sunny remarked. *And a Vette.* Sunny lifted weights in her bedroom and drove her sister's or the department's car.

"You're welcome to use my workout room. In fact, I'll have you over for a Sunday dinner one day. You can check out the room then." She took him up on the invitation.

The picture of Jonathan Williams sent by Forensics was eight years old, a mugshot. The detectives weren't ready for the man Erica pointed to in the treadmill area of the fitness center.

Jonathan Williams walked the aisle of fifty or so treadmills, motivating reluctant members. He leaned and pressed a button on a struggling member's machine.

"We're going from three-point-five miles per hour to five miles per hour," the trainer shouted above pounding sneakers and whirring treadmills. The smell of sweat permeated the air.

Jonathan Williams, a mountain of a man in a maroon warmup suit and brilliant white sneakers, stood six-three and about two hundred and thirty pounds. He strolled the aisle, increasing treadmill speeds, barking instructions to sweaty, panting members.

"Man! I hope he doesn't cause a stink," KD warned as he tapped his gun holster, ready for trouble.

Sunny pictured Jonathon's huge, strong hands around her neck, strangling the life from her. Forensics had his fingerprints on Christine's bracelet. She didn't care how big he was. This was personal. They approached the man from behind.

"Jonathan Williams! NYPD. Got some questions for you," KD shouted authoritatively.

Sunny pulled back both sides of her jacket, simultaneously revealing her shield and nine. She quickly scanned around Jonathan, judging the proper angle to avoid collateral damage if bullets flew. The big man spun around agilely, his eyes wide with shock.

"I didn't do anything wrong. What do you want with me?" he demanded, his frowned eyebrows nearly touching.

Sunny noticed a bulge at the man's left inner ankle. She knew that shape from her own ankle. "Gun!" she yelled. The room abruptly fell quiet—no pounding treadmill feet, no grunting weight lifters. She drew her service weapon. "Hands high!"

His gun drawn, KD cautiously retrieved the man's gun from the ankle holster. "You have a carry permit for this, Mr. Williams?" KD asked as he whipped out his handcuffs. The huge man lowered his head, shaking it. KD borrowed Sunny's pair of handcuffs, linking them as he read Jonathan his rights.

Chapter Fourteen

On the ancient Sunadaga territory, the dropping orange sunset the Adirondack foothills in upstate New York ablaze. Ariwiio Smoke switched off the kitchen ceiling light after he and Amber finished putting away the washed dinner dishes into the cabinets.

"That was Camille's favorite meal," Amber reminisced.

"Wasn't it, though? He would hunt all day in those woods for rabbits." Ariwiio pointed at the window above the kitchen sink to the woods beyond. "And your mother's recipe had him licking his fingers." He laughed out loud. "Add the Three Sisters, and the man was in culinary heaven." The Haudenosaunee Confederacy—the Sunadaga being one of the nations—cultivated the Three Sisters: squash, beans, and corn.

Ariwiio and Amber grew quiet. They missed Camille and Angel. The family never believed that the car crash that took Angel's life on a road just off the territory was an accident. And their lawsuit against the Department of Corrections, which operated the prison where Camille somehow vanished into thin air, was meeting roadblocks.

The stray cat with the huge copper patch on his back relished the rabbit, too. The feline meowed loudly at Ariwiio's shin for more of the succulent dish.

Amber placed the last fork in the silverware drawer and shut it. She reached down and stroked the friendly cat. "Once you feed them, Pop, they're yours." The cat purred affectionately.

"Ain't that the truth? But this one disappears for long periods."

She continued to pet the cat. "I'm going to take some leftovers home for your granddaughter. She should be home from karate practice about now."

Done with the dinner dishes, they retired to the living room. Amber strode to the fireplace and counted the logs in the holder.

"Pop, you want me to bring in a few more logs and start the fire before I leave?"

"Nah. I'll pull up an extra blanket if it gets chilly tonight."

Amber absently straightened the family pictures on the fireplace mantle. Next to the pictures, she stroked the hair of her corn husk doll dressed in traditional Haudenosaunee regalia.

"How old were you when you and your mother made that doll?"

Amber had to think for a moment. She lifted the faceless doll to examine it more closely. "Around ten, I believe. Twenty years ago." The faceless dolls were made of discarded corn husk from the fall harvest. The story was that a girl once thought she was the most beautiful in the world, and she flaunted it. The Creator couldn't convince her that she was no better than anyone else, so her face was removed as a lesson of arrogance to Haudenosaunee children.

Amber walked over to where her father was seated in his favorite chair. She kissed the top of his snowy white head. "I'm going to leave now. I have an early flight to Wounded Knee tomorrow to pitch the PAC to the Oglala Sioux."

"The Sunadaga Nation really appreciates you carrying your brother's load of the PAC." Camille had spearheaded the effort before he was sentenced to prison.

The cat meowed at the screen door. Amber let him out. Crickets sang their songs in the fresh early evening.

"Pop, will you be opening the cultural center soon for the summer crowd?"

"Almost done. Lyle is there now supervising the cleaning." Lyle was the plainspoken vice president of the Sunadaga Nation.

"Lyle! What a character. I'll stop by to lend a hand when I return from Wounded Knee."

As Amber opened the screen door to leave, Ariwiio called out. "Don't plan any trips close to the powwow date. Wouldn't want you to get delayed somewhere and miss it."

"Not for the world," Amber said as she shut the screen behind her.

Ariwiio soaked up the quiet for a few minutes, allowing the rabbit and Three Sisters to digest. Finally, he rose from his chair to get a last look at nature before checking his e-mails. Something outside riveted his attention.

What did he just see? He rubbed his eyes for clarity. Were the evening shadows playing tricks on his old eyes? He rubbed them again. Did he just see that cat turn into a swan and then take flight? Must be the fading light. He shook his head. He latched the screen door and went to power up his laptop.

The old man would be easy money. *Easy to dispose of,* Sergey Korolev observed as he switched on the car's headlights to follow the woman. For twenty minutes, her Subaru wound its way through dark roads, finally pulling into the driveway of a raised ranch house.

Sergey passed the house and pulled off the road to hide again. Unlike his urban hit jobs, where the streets were illuminated and people were everywhere, making his job more difficult, this place—How do Americans call it? Fish in a bowl...maybe barrel. Whatever.

From his car's trunk, he removed a telephoto lens Nikon camera, a parabolic microphone, and his favorite silencer-lengthened sniper rifle. After a short trek through the woods, he was at its edge listening, aiming the small dish of the high-power microphone at an open window.

The woman matched the pictures Sergey was given by his handler. *Amber Smoke.* The man in the house had to be her husband, and the little girl, about six years old, her daughter. Sergey focused the camera and snapped a few family photos. The man and the kid might one day be his next targets. He placed the camera back on the ground and re-aimed the microphone.

"I'll be flying out tomorrow to Wounded Knee," she said to the man.

Wounded Knee? What is that? Sergey asked himself, and then he remembered from reading his American history textbook. American's behavior was so confusing to him that he bought used textbooks off Amazon for three bucks. He also downloaded American history textbooks to his smartphone.

Since arriving in the US, he'd had such a hard time understanding the tensions in his adopted country—ethnicity, class, gender, age. He now remembered that Wounded Knee had something to do with a battle or massacre...some kind of killing. He would reread the chapter tonight in his hotel room.

The kid whined to travel with her mother. The little girl started bawling when she couldn't go. The mother removed several Tupperware of food from a paper bag. Sergey stored his equipment safely back in the car's trunk. He would kill no one tonight. Now he knew the lay of the land. He needed to arrange travel to Wounded Knee, wherever that was.

Manhattan South Homicide was located in the NYPD Thirteenth Precinct. Evenings at the precinct were normally subdued affairs with detectives, completing DD-5s before heading home. In the process, they recounted war stories of the day before deciding which law enforcement watering hole to congregate at for a few cold ones. But this gorgeous summer evening at the Thirteenth wasn't hushed or subdued.

Jonathan Williams protested to high heaven in the interrogation room down the hall from the Loo's office.

"Absolutely not!" From behind his office desk, Lieutenant Sanchez shot down Sunny's request to be the bad cop in the interrogation. "I want you to be *sunny*, as your name implies. I barely allowed you on this case, remember?" Sunny's assault could be tied to Christine Lowry's murder. "One slip up by a detective with an ax to grind, and we lose our chance to break open this case." Sunny threw herself into the back of her chair, seething, disappointed. "KD, you're the bad cop," the Loo commanded, pointing an index finger at the first-grade detective. "The ADA and I will be on the other side of the one-way window." District Attorneys present at an interrogation implied the extreme gravity of a case. "Let's go!" Lieutenant Sanchez directed. They all filed out of his office to an even louder Jonathan Williams.

A uniformed officer stood sentry outside the interrogation room. He swung the door open for Sunny and KD to enter...and hear Jonathon's loud mouth.

"Take these off!" the musclebound Jonathan Williams yelled, veins popping in his forehead, eyes ablaze.

Chained to the interrogation room table, he violently jerked the handcuffs, crashing them against the inescapable iron loop attached to the table. "Take these off, I said!"

KD calmly took a seat opposite the agitated man. "I don't think so," he teased nonchalantly, tapping the iron loop with his ink pen. Jonathan took another feeble jerk of the clanking chains.

As the reluctant "good" cop, Sunny stood leaning against the painted gray cinderblock wall next to the one-way window that concealed Lieutenant Sanchez and ADA Greg Ross, watching and listening from the observation room. She so wanted to jump across the table and beat the shit out of one of the SOBs she believed nearly killed her.

"Brother, you're going to let 'em put me in chains like this? Like some slave at auction?" Jonathon spat the words, his eyes fixed on KD.

The bad cop guffawed, throwing his head back. KD toyed with his goatee, an impish smile behind it. "It was *brother* here," KD poked his chest with his thumb, "who required the chains." Jonathon's expression dropped. His head steady, the incensed man allowed his eyes to slowly rise to Sunny, swing to the one-way window, and back to the Cheshire cat smiling KD. Jonathan was out of moves. He exhaled heavily.

"You really complicated things for yourself, Mr. Williams, with an illegal weapon in your possession," KD threw down, leaning toward the chained man. "Where'd you get it?"

Jonathan's heaving chest settled. He loosened his angry jaw. "Bought it at a gun show in another state," he answered flatly. "Look, several businesses in the area, including our fitness center, were jacked over the last few months by masked gunmen. I had a gun in my face, demanding my watch, phone, ring, and necklace. Our gym members were robbed." Jonathon gave a wry smile. "I was going to be ready if they thought about double dipping."

89

KD shook his head. "Okay. We're going to deal with this later." He retrieved papers from a folder. "You have a little record here," KD said, sliding Jonathon's arrest history to the other side of the table. "I see you and your gang did a little armed robbery."

The deflated man slowly reared back into his seat, his large, cuffed, Mr. Universe arms extended on the table.

"I was young and desperate," he replied, sneering. "There weren't many opportunities in the hood." He hurled the words. "Plus," he added confidently, "I paid my dues to society." He glanced again at Sunny and the window. The man was familiar with the setting. He knew someone was behind the glass. "So why do you *really* have me here?" he asked, now toying with the handcuffs, a smirk on his face.

"We ask the questions here," Sunny suddenly piped up, the response allowing her to release a little steam. Jonathan nodded.

"Do you know Christine Lowry?" KD asked, locking eyes with the man.

"Never heard of her," Jonathon said after a half beat of hesitation.

With one foot, Sunny pushed off the cinderblock wall. She clasped her hands in front, fingers interlocked to control her rage. She slowly marched to the table, her eyes fixed on Jonathan. It was time to play *half*-bad cop and make him sweat. Coming to a military-boot-knocking halt behind the predator, she stood ramrod straight. An uneasy Jonathan shifted from one side to the other to gauge her location. His handcuffs rattled.

From behind, Sunny leaned in uncomfortably close to Jonathan's right ear. He leaned away attempting to get some distance.

"Jonathon, you don't want to lie to us. It pisses us off. And we're not good company when we're pissed off," she whispered unnervingly in his ear, moving closer and closer. Sunny quickly shifted to his left ear, startling the chained man. She repeated the veiled threat again.

Now, KD took over the tag team. "Well, Jonathan. If you don't know Christine Lowry, how do you explain your fingerprints at the crime scene?" Latent Unit had lifted Jonathon's full prints from Christine's sterling silver cuff bracelet. Something clicked behind Jonathan's eyes, and KD pressed his advantage. "Admit that you and your gang killed her."

"Killed her?" the man snapped angrily, violently clattering the cuffs and chain.

"Yes, Jonathan. It sounds like you know her after all." KD slid a writing pad and pen across the table. "Give us the other names for your boys, and you can score some points with the ADA back there. KD thumbed behind himself to the window. "He may also make that illegal gun possession disappear."

Jonathan peered over KD's shoulder, a half-stunned, half-defiant scowl on his face. He started shaking his head vigorously. "What are you talking about," he finally shouted, suddenly sitting forward. "Christine's dead?"

Sunny walked back next to the window, leaned against the wall on one leg again, boot sole against the cinderblocks, arms defiantly crossed. She needed to see the expression on the lying sack of shit's face. He knew Christine. He was caught now.

Jonathan's broad, muscular shoulders now sagged. His eyes dropped to the table as he slowly shook his head. Eyes of fire earlier were now moistened with tears. "Tell me this ain't true," he pleaded, his head hanging.

"Where were you Monday night?" Sunny asked. Her assault was Monday night, the same night Christine was brutally raped and strangled to death on the Hudson River Greenway.

Jonathan's head rose ever so slowly. He wiped his wet cheeks with the back of his cuffed hands.

"We were intimate," he said out of the blue. He squeezed his eyes shut in pain. "I loved her. I would never hurt her." Jonathon choked up.

KD looked around at Sunny, then at the window.

Ahem. Sunny cleared her throat. The sobbing man's shoulders bounced as he broke down further.

"You two were in a relationship?" she asked in a surprised tone.

Jonathan only nodded, unable to talk for the moment. He blew out a stream of exasperated air. "I can't believe this." He suddenly looked back and forth at the two detectives. "Please, don't tell her parents about us...even now."

"Why is that, Jonathon?" Sunny asked, her arms still folded tightly against her chest. She braced herself for something small-minded, prejudiced, or racist.

"In my opinion, it was a long time ago, but her parents wouldn't approve of my criminal record."

"Where were you Monday night?" she probed again. The detectives weren't about to lie to the parents.

Jonathon sniffled. He leaned back, eyeing the ceiling, seeing that night. "We had dinner at Essence of India on the West Side." He composed himself a bit more. "Christine wanted to take a stroll on the Greenway along the Hudson after dinner. I was beat. I've been working mad hours to surprise her with a bigger apartment. I can barely turn around in her place without banging into the walls. My apartment isn't much larger."

"Why didn't you launch a Missing Person report?" KD snapped.

"Christine's done this before. She'll get mad at me and won't text or call. She shuts her phone off. Like I said, I've been working my ass off." His voice cracked again. "I can't believe this!"

Sunny wondered if Christine wanted to take a romantic stroll to tell Jonathon she was carrying his child.

The news was going to be a one-two blow for the man. He'd probably blame himself forever. They would hold that news off for the time being.

The intercom crackled. Lieutenant Sanchez's voice came through. "Uncuff him and meet me out in the hall."

While multitasking on his smartphone reading something, Lieutenant Sanchez said to check for a credit card payment at Essence of India and then street Jonathan Williams. While studying the smartphone, his expression darkened.

"Shit!" the Loo blurted. "E-mail from the chief of detectives. I'll send it to both of you. Read it. I have to call him ASAP." Lieutenant Sanchez sprinted to his office.

Chapter Fifteen

The investigation was back at square one. The detectives had a uniformed officer drive Jonathon Williams back to the fitness center, but the officer relayed back that Jonathan didn't enter. The distraught man walked down the street and sat on a park bench, his face buried in his hands.

At their desk in MSH, Sunny and KD read the stunning e-mail from the chief of detectives. An information leak from Forensics had hit the New York City newspapers with a splash. The African American hair found at Sunny's assault scene was sensationalized by right-leaning news outlets dredging up the Central Park Five case, stretching the similarities.

Sunny recalled discussing the Central Park Five case at the police academy. During wilin' or wilding one night, five Black and brown teens were wrongfully charged and imprisoned for the brutal beating and rape of a white female jogger in Central Park in 1989. The teens were later exonerated. A street was later named after them. Lesson learned: the NYPD was careful and transparent in the Hudson River Greenway homicide.

KD leaned over his desk and whispered, "I hear one of the interns blabbed at a keg party about the hair evidence." He exhaled heavily. "Where're we getting these folks? They sign documents to keep their mouths shut."

Sunny was distracted, picturing the four tree trunks—one pink—magnified by the electron microscope at Forensics. She hoped the leak wasn't the nice, helpful, pink-haired Katie Miller. Then she recalled Forensic Scientist Michael Serle walking her to the mass spectrometer that identified the gorilla fur. She hoped the gorilla fur information didn't also leak at the keg party.

Alone that evening in her apartment—except for Tuffy—Sunny fed her furry friend and then let him out onto the fire escape. She went and showered off the day's grime. Not bothering to eat, she later searched the internet for shifter information before she headed to MH Construction. She read about shifters like the ones on TV. Camille resembled them. The search engine expanded to include shapeshifter. There were Indigenous people who did *extra* things, for instance, transforming into another being, especially animals. Fully morphed, the animals even talked to each other. Somewhere between amazed and curious, Sunny stared at the different images on the laptop.

She jumped in her car before Jennifer got home to pump her for the juicy of the lunch date with ADA Ross. Sunny had earlier demanded Camille be at MH Construction. She had to know more about him. And now she had a second reason.

"You said it's a long story, but I have to know how you transform into animals," Sunny said as she wolfed down an Indian taco made from Camille's mother's secret recipe. "I need to know Camille the Shifter." Everything still felt like a dream, but she plowed ahead. "But first I... We... The city…needs your help in cracking this case before someone else is killed."

They sat at a tiny two-person table on the second floor of the construction company. Grated cheese fell from the side of his frybread—a simple fried flatbread mixture of milk and leavening—taco as he listened intently to Sunny's plea. His long hair was freshly braided, hanging forward over his left shoulder.

Sunny wiped taco sauce from her hand with her napkin. "I know it was extremely dark the night you saved me," she said as she reached across the table and placed her hand atop his. "But do you remember anything?"

Camille pondered the question for a moment, his dark eyes pools of mystery. He cocked his head to the right. Then slowly, he started nodding his head.

"Now that I think about it, I do remember something." He wiped his mouth with a napkin. "Many years after my accident, I noticed that I can remember smells long after the trail has gone cold, if you will."

Sunny leaned forward, peering deep into the man's eyes. He was reliving the night. "So you do remember them? I thought I heard four distinct voices that night."

"I remember the scent of four—five, including you that night."

"Camille, we need your help now!" she pleaded.

He paused, about to say something, thought again, then snapped his finger. "I know how I can help."

"Camille, that's wonderful," she exulted jubilantly. "Tell me."

"I can fly the street grid of Manhattan tonight."

"In an airpl—" she caught herself. He smiled knowingly.

"A turkey vulture. Shift into a turkey vulture. If I shifted into a bloodhound, it would take weeks to walk the dozen north/south avenues and over two hundred east/west cross streets. The island is thirteen miles long, two miles wide." His warm, crooked smile was still there. "But a turkey vulture can catch a scent a mile above gliding over the city. I can finish before sunrise." He explained that once he was done, he needed a quick nap before he flew off to Wounded Knee, South Dakota, to secretly be with his sister, Amber, who would be there promoting a PAC.

Sunny listened intently. He most certainlyly didn't strike her as a murderer. He wanted to help people. And now she sought to help him. "I want to help exonerate you of the murder charges."

His face brightened. "I badly want to come out of the shadows—hug my father and sister—but it's going to require you traveling to Sunadaga territory to understand the circumstances surrounding my murder conviction."

"I can do that." She would certainly need GPS to make her way around upstate New York.

Camille got up from the table and disappeared for a moment inside a closet about fifteen feet away. She heard him dragging something along the wood floor. He emerged with a black footlocker trunk with bright silver trim. Once he opened the trunk he pulled out...what?

Sunny left the table to join him. The odd-looking object was a saddle. Sunny had ridden horses on her uncle's farm, but none of the saddles resembled this one.

"For an ostrich?" she joked.

"Close," he said with a broad coy smile. "I made it." He turned the saddle this way, then that, displaying it. "When Marshall and I go home, upstate"—he sounded choked up—"I fly as a falcon if we're in a hurry. Falcons can fly faster than some airplanes." He paused. "Or cruise"—he slowly flapped his arms—"if there's no hurry. Swan. Owl." He shrugged his broad shoulders.

She studied the large, unconventional saddle. He must have read her mind.

"So as not to draw attention, I usually shift into a *normal*-size animal." He pointed to the wall news clippings.

"Normal eagle. Normal dolphin. But all I have to do is imagine larger." She nodded a small measure of understanding trying to grasp it all. There were more odd items in the trunk.

Sunny leaned, peering inside. "That's one beautiful and serious looking bow." A single feather dangled from the bow's top. Her uncle's store-bought compound hunting bow was a contraption of cables and pulleys. She was looking at art and craft here.

Camille laid the saddle on the floor and lifted the bow. "I carved it. Our father taught me and my sister woodwork." He flexed the string pulling it so far that Sunny stepped back and grimaced thinking the bow would snap in two.

Camille chuckled and released the string tension. "This string will *never* break. It's actually made of multiple strands of my hair when I was in *war mode* one day." With a smile he held up his hand to stop the questions. "I'll explain it all when we have more time."

Pointing into the trunk, she had never seen arrows quite like these. "What's going on at the end of those arrows?" Just behind the arrowheads someone had modified the shafts.

Camille lifted one arrow and unscrewed the arrowhead revealing an enlarged hollow compartment inside the shaft. He looked at Sunny for a moment, his eyebrows bouncing impishly. "It's where the payload goes," he said while screwing the arrowhead back on.

She closed her mouth and finally blinked. "I can see you're never going to cease to amaze me." It all felt surreal. This was all exquisite traditional handiwork, but the detectives still had cases to solve. *Payload?* She would come back to his myriad powers later. They returned to their taco at the table.

"My second reason for coming here was that today you said that what was in my pocket smelled like T-Rex."

She extracted the sealed evidence bag. She knew that bears could smell food no matter how hermetically sealed the package. And very little escaped the keen nose of a mouse. The evidence bag leaked molecules of T-Rex scent.

Between chews, Camille said, "Back to my childhood accident again." He touched his shoulder burn. "I'll tell you the complete story later. But it left me with above human senses of smell, sight—you name it. That's the same smell"—even with a two-handed frybread taco grip, he managed to point his little finger at the evidence bag—"that I recalled at the T-Rex exhibit at the American Museum of Natural History. Sometimes, I get so bored of being cooped up in here that I risk just a little quiet, solitary entertainment like the museum or a movie." Sunny made a mental note of the AMNH information.

He mentioned Marshall would be home soon from a long workday. Sunny and Camille exchanged phone numbers and bid each other good night. There was work to do, lives and a city to save.

Still energized, Sunny braved the traffic and drove up the West Side Highway looking for more leads, anything. She questioned doormen. She watched security video from apartment door cameras. She questioned more dogwalkers. Stuffing her notepad in her jacket pocket, she finally plopped her rear end into the car seat. She inched her way home, bumper to bumper, to review her findings.

Her apartment was quiet. Jennifer was out with some girlfriends from work for a few drinks. Tuffy was nowhere in sight. Unable to shut down just yet, she made a call then left the apartment again. She didn't feel like fighting traffic this time.

Sunny always stood. It was due partly to restless energy, partly to her always wanting to be ready for action if the situation arose. Her ass was not about to hit those orange and yellow plastic seats.

She held tightly to the handrail above. Tonight's energy she channeled into getting some of her partner's…correction…*their* multiple cases closed. The metrics of the NYPD demanded it.

Sunny's stance was slightly wider to maintain better balance as the C train rocked from side to side. The subway car was packed with expressionless New Yorkers headed home after another grueling day at work, some behind Covid masks, though it wasn't required anymore. Everyone avoided prolonged eye contact lest they were suspected of being up to no good.

It was 6 p.m. The museum closed at 5:45 p.m., but the director of the American Museum of Natural History was willing to assist in a police investigation any way he could. Sunny assured the director there wasn't a threat to museum visitors. He would have a tour guide escort Sunny and answer any of her questions.

The subway door slid open. One crowd exited, and another entered, shoulders bumping, the price to pay for the quickest commute in NYC. Sunny stepped above ground at West Eighty-first and Central Park West. The AMNH loomed. The statue was now gone as Sunny had seen on the news.

Not long ago, a statue of President Theodore Roosevelt was removed from the entrance to the museum. Today's sensibilities from diverse voices wouldn't tolerate the image and the message of Teddy atop a high-stepping horse while one Indigenous man and one African American walked at Teddy's horse's side.

Two at a time, Sunny bounded the steps to the museum entrance. Camille recognizing the scent in KD's evidence bag had given her an idea. She was still dumbfounded by Camille's super-human powers as a shifter. But if his abilities could solve cases and keep people alive, she would ride this horse until it bucked her.

She pulled on the museum door, but it was locked. A

young lady with a blue and white tour guide badge around her neck hurried to let Sunny in as she flashed her detective shield. The early twentyish guide wore a dark blue shirt and beige pants. She introduced herself as Jessica.

"We can start with the North American Mammal exhibit," Jessica suggested, her voice echoing in the cavernous Theodore Roosevelt Memorial Hall. She spun one-eighty to head for the first-floor exhibit.

"Jessica, thanks, but my interest tonight is only in the T-Rex."

The guide stood stunned. "Oh...okay." She pointed to the elevators. "Well, we need to go to the fourth floor." She led the way.

On the fourth floor, Sunny looked up into the gigantic mouth of a Tyrannosaurus Rex. Her only experience with the monstrous creature was from the *Jurassic Park* movies. The last one she saw was devouring a whole live goat. *Damn! Look at those teeth.*

Jessica was chattering something about millions of years ago, and the asteroid that wiped out the dinosaurs as Sunny's detective mind went to work. While she looked up at T-rex, her eyes scanned the hall for security cameras. Someone passionate enough to wear a dinosaur bone necklace would visit this place more than a few times, she suspected.

After ten minutes of T-Rex details, Sunny declined Jessica's offer to observe more dinosaur exhibits on the same floor.

"I really appreciated the tour. Let me catch the director before he leaves." She would request camera footage and visitor logs. It was like looking for the infamous needle in the haystack, but when your chances were slim and none, you went with slim every time.

Twenty minutes later, Sunny descended back into the subway tube. The approaching subway forced a blast of hot air before it.

Chapter Sixteen

At a pause in the HRG cases until Crime Scene's DNA work could finish processing, KD and Sunny spent the next morning at their desk formulating their next moves. With quick, acerbic wit, Sunny sent Pillsbury Doughboy Rizzo packing with his tail between his legs. She still couldn't care less that his father was an NYPD captain in Queens. He was one of those implying that Sunny was some sort of affirmative action hire.

"Yeah, well, I'm not plugged into the old boy network like you, Rizzo. *Daddy* didn't get me my job. I earned it." She was in no mood for banter, nor was KD.

"I'm setting up another meeting with Gang Unit," KD announced, talking to Sunny, but giving Rizzo the evil eye. "Now that we—and the rest of the world—know that this gang reasonably contains at least one African American, we can whittle down the list to those we need to drag in here for interrogation."

The Forensics department's leak was inadvertent. The NYPD suspended its forensics intern program. A little too much alcohol at a party had loosened the lips of pink-haired Katie Miller. She had apologized profusely, believing she had, if not derailed the case, certainly hampered it. In her short Crime Lab visit, Sunny had grown fond of the woman, but maintaining protocol was paramount in law enforcement.

Elbow on her desk, head resting in her palm, Sunny listened to KD lay out the plan. She pondered Camille's text about his flight over Manhattan last night, wondering how his findings could help the HRG case. In a wide radius, he detected strong scents last night on the West Side but *not* on the HRG. Her mind was also still processing yesterday's museum visit to help KD close the Murray Hill murder case. Multitasking was a detective's life.

"McGraw? McGraw? Are you listening?" KD broke into the thoughts of his musing partner.

"Of course." She sat up straight. But still multitasking, she briefly wondered if Camille had made it to Wounded Knee, South Dakota.

"I have a couple of CI's on the West Side," KD continued, "we can hit up." Confidential informants were valuable at providing street-level information in exchange for staying out of prison for their offenses.

KD's eyes suddenly peered over Sunny's shoulder. She turned to see Lieutenant Sanchez quickly stepping into the squad room, a severe look on his face. The Loo strode closer.

"You two. In my office," he barked as his fast-stepping breezy wake washed over Sunny. The two detectives looked quizzically at each other, then quickly rose and followed the lieutenant.

They entered just as Lieutenant Sanchez flopped down wearily in his squeaky chair.

"No need to sit," the Loo said. As if her hand was suddenly burned, Sunny released the chair she was sliding closer. "We believe we have another victim," Lieutenant Sanchez continued, sighing hugely.

Sunny felt her heart stop for a moment. KD grumbled and swiped at his goatee.

The Loo leaned forward, elbows on his desk. "Same general area. On the West Side, but in Hell's Kitchen, still not far from where we found Christine Lowry's body." Lieutenant Sanchez took a deep, relaxing breath. "The command structure is up my ass! I've been summoned to Headquarters. The chief of detectives wants to bring in the FBI and start a task force." He held up his palm for calm as KD launched into orbit.

"Loo, we don't need no damn FBI!" KD cried, the veins in his neck bulging.

Sunny had never worked with the FBI, but she always noticed the visceral reaction from NYPD when the fibbies were mentioned. The concern seemed to center on the FBI poaching NYPD choice cases and grabbing the limelight after much NYPD investigation.

Lieutenant Sanchez nervously wiped his mouth with his hand and gestured for KD to hold his horses. "KD, I know how you feel, but this is out of my hands. I know you two can solve this, but I hear Roland has a hand in this decision." Roland was Mayor Roland Myers.

"Politics," KD quietly conceded, shaking his bald head following the hit to his pride and abilities.

"Our vic is clinging to life at Saint Anthony Hospital. Get over there now to see if she can tell us anything."

Chapter Seventeen

On eagle wings high above Rapid City Regional Airport, Camille soared in lazy circles, taking advantage of the hot South Dakota air updrafts. Little energy was required, a wing flap here, a wing flap there to correct his westerly drift. He appreciated Nature's buoying assistance because he was quite fatigued from flying Manhattan's grid of streets last night. He hoped the scent trail information in the text helped Sunny and law enforcement apprehend those committing the grisly crimes before anyone else was killed. During his Manhattan grid flight he also picked up scents of bakeries, restaurants, grocery stores, and drug stash houses.

He wondered what Sunny was doing now. Was she handcuffing the suspects who assaulted her and killed Christine Lowry? He wanted to look into her warm, yet resolute, brown eyes again and see the green flecks.

With a wingspan fourteen feet tip to tip, Camille dipped right for a view of the eastern horizon. An eagle's binocular vision enabled the raptor to spot a rabbit three miles away. Couple keen animal senses with his human intelligence, Camille could distinguish over five miles away a rabbit's longer ears and a hare's longer legs. His chameleon accident as a youth had supercharged his senses.

A glint on the horizon. His sister's plane reflected the hot, brilliant sun off the passenger jet's fuselage. At a safe distance, he followed the plane's approach to the airport.

Camille wished that he could see his sister, hug her, tell her how much he loved her, missed her, and was proud of her. If Sunny could clear his name, maybe...

He opened his beak wide and screeched with glee as the plane touched down safely. Huge plumes of smoke from the plane's tires billowed as the Delta flight shed momentum and taxied to the terminal.

Morning rush hour complete, KD and Sunny made good time headed west on Forty-Second Street headed to the hospital where a new victim lay at death's door. On the right, train commuters flowed out of Grand Central Terminal. Sunny smiled each time someone called the structure Grand Central *Station*—the 60's music group, a mistake she made when she first arrived in the Big Apple.

When Sunny first rolled into New York City, a place called Hell's Kitchen gave her pause. The neighborhood was once gritty. Its name was changed to Clinton in a gentrification push. Realtors unsuccessfully pushed even further to rename the area Midtown West, a nod to pricey Midtown and Midtown East.

Simultaneously, their phones chimed with a new message. KD was driving so Sunny viewed her text first. *Harbor Unit found a soggy movie ticket stub near the Christine Lowry crime scene. CSU was trying to lift latent prints, but the theatre ticket's timestamp and location at the park made the ticket holder a suspect. CSU attached a picture of the ticket.* Sunny swung her phone so that KD could get a quick glance.

"Let's head to the hospital and then that movie theatre after we leave the new crime scene," KD decided. "We need to follow every lead."

At the nurse's station, Sunny flashed her shield. "There was an Elaine Hogan admitted late last night."

The nurse directed the detectives to a man in a dark suit down the hall standing in front of Elaine Hogan's hospital room. The man turned out to be Lester Crain, the local precinct detective who initially caught the case. Manhattan South Homicide was called to determine if there were similarities: gang, West Side.

"It came down from the chief of detectives that I was to wait for you two to arrive. The MO here resembles your assault," he glanced at Sunny, "and the Christine Lowry murder." Detective Crain filled the detectives in on the crime scene, location, and assault specifics before entering Elaine's hospital room.

The woman's swollen face looked ready to burst, her skin taut, severely bruised, purple and black. Long brown hair lay over her ample breasts under the sheet. Sunny had no idea what the woman really looked like. She didn't even look human, the beating so complete.

Lester Crain introduced the detectives to Doctor Shirley Johnson. "The doctor here says Elaine has bleeding in the brain. That hose there," he pointed to a spot near Elaine's puffy ear, "it's there to relieve cranial pressure."

"What are her chances for a full recovery, Doc?" KD asked, still studying the drainage tube.

The youthful doctor sighed heavily. "She was lucky to make it through the night. She has about a ten percent chance."

Sunny rested her clasped hands atop her head and took a deep breath. The brutality. And again, this could have been her fate were it not for Camille.

"What're the rape kit results?" Sunny asked, dropping her arms heavily to her side, seething.

"No need for a rape test," Detective Crain contributed as he prepared to leave. "Elaine was born Jeremy Hogan." He turned to the doctor. "What did you call it? General aff...huh...aff—"

"*Gender-affirming surgery*," the doctor bit off the words in frustration, eyes locked on Detective Crain as she impatiently swung her stethoscope around her neck. "She's a transgender woman." The doctor sighed. "*Elaine*," Dr. Johnson emphasized, still glaring at Detective Crain but speaking to Sunny and KD, "has had top surgery, but not bottom surgery." The stern doctor finally took her reprimanding eyes off Detective Crain. "Give me your business cards so I can call you when...and if Elaine recovers."

Chapter Eighteen

Before visiting Saint Anthony Hospital, Sunny and KD had read Detective Crain's DD-5s in the NYPD Case Management System, the digital database holding the evidence and events surrounding Elaine's brutal and senseless beating. The DD-5s filled in the details of their earlier phone conversations with first-on-the-scene uniform police.

Outside the hospital, KD started the car. "Let's get over to the crime scene for a look at what the DD-5s described. The location isn't far. It's on the opposite side of Twelve Avenue—the West Side Highway—from where we found Christine's body. Close enough to warrant our attention."

"Has to be the same gang," Sunny said. Camille's text message identified a three-block radius of strong perp scent trails near, but not at, this crime scene, matching scents at her and Christine Lowry's crime scenes.

Fifteen minutes later, KD pulled to the mouth of the alley. A blue and white NYPD radio patrol car plus yellow crime scene tape blocked the alley.

The DD-5s described the Hell's Kitchen crime scene accurately. The deep alley ended with a loading dock. Garbage was strewn and blowing everywhere. The surrounding area was a mixture of nightclubs and wholesale businesses. Not far away, Sunny could hear the heavy, impatient traffic on the West Side Highway, the same traffic that helped her orient her blurry mind on its opposite side during her assault along the Hudson River Greenway.

She strode to the rear of the alley while KD canvassed the front. She searched for security cameras but found none, just as the DD-5 read. The wind funneled into the dead-end alley, spawning small tornadoes that churned the garbage in circles, blowing her hair into her eyes. There was a dumpster to her left. Sunny carefully lifted the lid, not sure what would jump out. An indiscernible stench immediately assaulted her nostrils.

"Pssst!"

Sunny dropped the lid with a bang and jumped back. There was a sound from the dumpster… At least, she thought she heard something. She slowly lifted the edge of the lid to peek back inside.

"Pssst! Down here!"

She dropped the lid again and immediately unsnapped her holster as she cautiously searched around back of the stinking dumpster.

"I'm sure those pieces of shit thought Elaine was a biological woman," KD shouted above the swirling wind from the front of the alley. "Once they found out otherwise, they beat her mercilessly," he growled. "She was one of our citizens, McGraw," he went on. "I want their asses in the worse way!"

Sunny was only half listening, distracted by the sound around the dumpster. She slowly knelt, hand on the butt of her gun, to look under the huge putrid garbage container.

"I'm sorry about Elaine," the huge gray rat said. "Last night, before I flew to Wounded Knee, I started my Manhattan grid flight on the West Side." The rat's long whiskers fluttered as he spoke. "The beating she took must have happened shortly after I flew over this area. This alley didn't have scents at the time. I picked up the scents a few blocks north of here. I came back to the area to try to reduce the radius."

"Camille?" Sunny said, unbelieving, her mouth agape. But she was growing more at ease with his shifting now.

"Yeah. It's me," Camille responded from under the dumpster. "This watch has one of their scents on it." He moved to the side and pointed at an expensive-looking silver watch with his right front paw. "The watch slid into the rain drain under the Dumpster and partially down the pipe."

"Who are you talking to, McGraw?" KD asked as he headed toward the dumpster.

She looked up to see KD approaching. "Just talking to myself, partner." She quickly rolled the dumpster with a grunt and lifted the rain grate.

"Okay. Just don't answer yourself, or I'll put in for a new partner."

KD suddenly leaped in the air as a humongous gray rat scurried from under the dumpster. After landing, he attempted to kick the filthy rodent to New Jersey.

"No!" Sunny suddenly stooped and grabbed KD's leg. The skittering rat bolted up the alley, tail high, legs a blur of long strides.

A few moments went by while Sunny watched Camille dart to safety. She still had hold of KD's leg.

"Are you going to give me my leg back, McGraw?" She quickly released her grip and smiled sheepishly, looking up.

"McGraw, you are one strange puppy. If you weren't an excellent detective, I would trade you in for the new model." KD looked up the alley at the quickly disappearing rat. "There must be one rat for every New Yorker, and you want to save the filthy creatures." He shook his head woefully.

Sunny knelt back down to look under the dumpster. She retrieved the watch by looping it around her ink pen to preserve any DNA. She stood and presented the new evidence that could possibly break the case open.

At the end of the pen, she dangled the sparkling pricey watch at face level for examination. "Found it hidden a little ways down that rain drain." She pointed her boot at the opened grate as she brushed at her sleeve to help sell the...fib. Sunny didn't like the feeling of not being truthful, but she had no choice. No way was she going to say a talking rat found the watch.

"I could see how CSU could miss it...but how did you know to look?" His perplexed expression lingered.

She skillfully switched the subject. "It's not weather-beaten," Sunny observed. "Hasn't been here for long. Has to belong to one of those bastards." The bright sun highlighted the shine of the watch.

KD's expression smoothed. He extended his fist for a bump. "Good catch, McGraw!" Their fists met. "I think I'm going to keep you around," he said with a broad smile. "Get it over to Forensics for prints and DNA. And tell them no more information leaks. I'll update the Loo."

Chapter Nineteen

It was just past noon when Sunny jumped the movie ticket line, garnering angry stares at the West Fifty-Fourth Street theater. She asked the older man behind the ticket window to call the manager to the front.

The tantalizing smell of buttered popcorn hung heavy in the air as the two detectives stood in the lobby of the ten-screen theater. Sunny couldn't remember the last time she'd been to an actual brick-and-mortar movie theater. With DVDs, streaming, and little patience, she watched her movies from her apartment sofa in her pajamas.

"What was the last movie you saw in an actual movie theater?" she asked KD. He had his eyes on the popcorn machine, watching the tasty kernels explode behind the glass.

"Angela wanted to see *Spencer*, that one about Princess Diana." He pursed his lips and rolled his eyes. "The things we do for love," he said about his fiancé. "But then again, she sat through *Ford vs Ferrari* for me." He walked toward the popcorn machine until a voice caught their attention.

"Detectives, I'm Rosa Cardona, the theater manager." She was a tiny woman, less than five feet tall, with a Spanish accent. Sunny put her in her mid-fifties. "How may I help New York's finest?" She extended her small hand.

Sunny and KD glanced at each other. This was not going to be like moving a mountain. At the mention of law enforcement, most people clammed up, not wanting to get involved.

Rosa Cardona smiled, waiting. "My brother is a police officer in the Bronx, out of the Forty-Ninth Precinct." New York City was divided into seventy-seven precincts, with each precinct divided into sectors that were roughly neighborhoods. "His name is Carlos Cruz. Do you know him?"

They didn't. Nearly forty thousand on the NYPD force, and people thought you knew them all. It was a sweet, innocent question, but even KD, who seemed to know everyone in NYC, had to shrug.

"Well then, how may I help you?" she said above a raucous in the lobby as security escorted a loud couple out of the theatre. "Startin' to make out in the back of the theater," Rosa Cardona explained, shaking her head, thumbing at the horny couple. "Getta motel already, will ya!" she shouted at them.

From KD's phone, he showed the theater manager the picture of the movie stub found at Christine Lowry's crime scene. Rosa Cardona glanced at the screenshot of the ticket. "Monday evening, screen seven. That evening, we were showing the new *Fast and Furious* movie on screen seven." She looked back curiously at KD. "What's this about, Detectives?" She stepped closer, whispering, "Is this about those women here on the West Side? I'm hearing in the news, one assaulted, one dead, one clinging to life?"

114

Sunny didn't let on that she was the assault victim. "People, especially women, are in such fear in the city. Catch them soon, please."

"Sorry, but we're not at liberty to talk about an ongoing investigation. We're doing everything to apprehend those responsible," KD said. He pointed to the security cameras above the ticket registers. "We need to get access to those camera recordings in order to correlate this ticket timestamp to the face of the purchaser." He held out his phone again.

Sunny and KD left the movie theater with assurances that the NYPD would get access to the camera feed once corporate approved. They also left with a medium tub of hot buttered popcorn and a bag of Twizzlers, which Sunny couldn't resist.

Chapter Twenty

The fourteen-story building immediately on the Manhattan side of the Brooklyn Bridge was NYPD headquarters, One Police Plaza, 1PP. The NYPD police commissioner's office occupied the top floor. KD and Sunny rode the elevator to the eighth floor, which housed the Real Time Crime Center. Sunny had always wanted a reason to visit 1PP and the RTCC, and KD sought to expose her to as much of the NYPD organization as possible. Good to her word, Rosa Cardona had gotten the NYPD approval to access the movie theater video surveillance system.

The elevator door opened, and they stepped out on the eighth floor. A high wall of color video monitors displayed live scenes around New York City, some of the video feeds from Aviation Unit helicopters. Detectives and civilian analysts worked at approximately twenty workstations. They spoke live to the NYPD staff throughout the five boroughs.

"I see you're admiring the center." Sunny looked down from the wall monitors to see a tall, blonde-haired, forty-something man approaching, his hand extended. "You must be Sunny. I'm Kurt Lewis," he said. "KD, long time." The two men greeted. KD told her that Kurt was born and raised in Manhattan and was a former detective out of Harlem's Twenty-Eighth Precinct.

"The place is state-of-the-art technology," Kurt began. "Our analysts here have access to all the public cameras around the city, license plate readers, gunshot detection equipment, and databases filled with criminal information. Follow me, please."

They walked to Kurt's cubicle. On his desk were three monitors and a soccer ball. "You still play?" Sunny asked, pointing at the red and white soccer ball.

"Yeah. A pickup game here and there on the weekends," Kurt said with a wide smile, his relish of the game shining through. "I used to play in college."

"Sunny played basketball in college," KD put in. "A forward."

"And you were a football wide receiver, right KD?" Kurt said as he dragged in one more chair from an empty cubicle. They all took seats.

"Yep. Wide receiver. But *tackle* football is not one of those games you keep playing in perpetuity." KD laughed as he extracted his phone. "Here's the theater's access information."

Kurt moved the mouse, and his display came alive. "Excellent. Let me pull up my remote access application. This must be some hot case. We just can't arbitrarily use facial recognition on New Yorkers. The command came down from the chief of D's." He pointed at the ceiling, indicating the thirteenth-floor office of the chief of detectives. "I received the proper and legal orders to work with you guys. Can't have some suspicious detective tracking his or her significant other, if you know what I mean." He chuckled. "And we're not a surveillance state like China and others where all citizens are constantly monitored live with facial recognition software."

Kurt typed, glancing back and forth from the monitor and KD's phone. "We're in. Looks like a live feed judging by the timestamp." He pointed to white letter information on the bottom right corner of the display. "Let's back up to Monday." On the display, the moviegoers walked in reverse. The screen went dark a few times as the theater closed for the night, then light again on Monday. Kurt slowed the reverse speed, faces becoming clearer. "Oops. Went past the ticket timestamp." Slow-motion forward ensued. He finally slowed to step mode as each ticket was purchased. "There!" He pointed to a young African-American male.

"Can you get a better shot of his face?" Sunny asked.

A few more clicks of the mouse stepped the image forward. "Here we go." Kurt stopped the video. The young man was looking up as he stuffed his wallet back into his pants pocket. "Let me capture his face." With the mouse, Kurt drew a square around the man's face to import into facial recognition software to scan NYPD databases for matches. "He may not be in our databases, but let's give it a try."

On the monitor, there was a blur of faces racing past at electronic speed as the software compared the unidentified probe image of the movie-goer to the NYPD photo repositories. They desperately needed a lead. The software chugged along, faces flashing, Black, white, male, female.

Suddenly, the screen froze. The man in the screen matched the man in the movie photo.

"Yes!" the detectives exclaimed in near unison, pumping a fist in the air.

"Chris Mitchell," Sunny read the name beneath the photo in BADS. The Booking, Arraignments, and Disposition System contained arrest records and criminal activity of those processed by the NYPD. Court records completed the database.

"Chris Mitchell is a parolee, busted for gang activity," Kurt read from the display. "I can start a search for the suspect against citywide archived camera footage we've collected and saved. Obviously, there'll be some manner of delay because it's saved footage. I don't know how long the search will take. The collection is vast. I can send the results to your phones." The detectives were in agreement.

"Give us his address in the meantime," KD pressed. The address was in Chelsea—Sunny's neighborhood—and not far from the Hudson River Greenway.

"I have a meeting I must get to," Kurt informed. "I'll let the software keep running, sending you hits from the collected images."

After thanking Kurt, the detectives left for the Chelsea address.

Chapter Twenty-One

In the parking garage below 1PP, their phones chimed simultaneously with a new message. KD clicked the car doors unlocked as Sunny read the new message.

"Nix Chelsea," she abruptly announced. "Chris Mitchell was in the Upper East Side not long ago, according to the timestamps in these pictures. The facial recognition software sent us several still shots of him."

KD stood with the car door open, viewing his phone. "In this pic, he's headed into Duane Reade on Sixty-First. He's wearing a green New York Jets cap. Maybe he's still up that way," KD speculated, stroking his goatee. "It's a shot, but let's try this. On your laptop, pull up the live feed on the NYPD camera on that corner."

He hurried around to the passenger side as Sunny set the laptop on the car roof and started the NYPD remote camera application. In moments, they spied the green Jets cap and Chris Mitchell buying a dog.

"We must be living right," KD exclaimed. "Hop in!"

From 1PP, KD caught Third Avenue rushing north. The flashing emergency lights, screaming sirens, lots of cursing, and occasionally driving in the bus lane allowed them to escape much traffic. They were trying to nab Chris Mitchell before he could escape into the big city. Sunny kept the live feed going that showed Chris Mitchell step up to a hotdog cart for a tube steak. The suspect stood at the curb watching the world go by as he alternately downed the dog and a can of soda.

At Sixty-First and Third Avenue, KD silenced the siren to make a stealth approach. They didn't want to alert the suspect. Sunny kept an eye peeled for the green New York Jets cap while KD navigated the congested street. The car hung a left and headed west on Sixty-First. Duane Reade and the hot dog vendor were a block away at Sixty-First and Lexington Avenue.

"Shit!" KD suddenly leaned toward the windshield, his eyes fixed on something ahead.

"What?" Sunny strained to see over the car in front of them. Her view was blocked.

Suddenly, Sunny knew what. Gunfire erupted. Was Chris Mitchell shooting? She instinctively placed her hand atop her Glock.

"Road rage," KD shouted, pissed off. He threw the car into park, and they both hopped out, guns drawn.

"That sucka hopped outta that black Land Rover," KD cried above the traffic sounds, "and shot out the headlights on that white Chevy Equinox SUV. He's aiming for the tires now!"

The detectives charged at the incensed gunman. Both guns were aimed at the angry man's center mass.

"Drop the gun!" KD yelled. The woman in the SUV was still screaming her head off. The gunman eased his gun to the street and held his hands high, surrendering, his eyes ablaze.

With her Glock aimed at the Range Rover driver,

Sunny caught sight of a green cap bobbing in the distance. It was Chris Mitchell. And he was on the run.

"KD! Over there!" Not interrupting her deadly aim, she threw her chin in the direction of Chris Mitchell as she held the Glock steady with both hands.

"Shit! Shit!" KD muttered. "I'll take care of this friggin' jackass and the fender bender. You go after Mitchell."

Sunny jumped to the sidewalk, gun tight against her leg. The green cap was crossing Lexington.

"Chris Mitchell," she shouted. "Police! Stop!" Sunny shouted again and again amidst the car horns, squealing brakes and tires, and loud delivery truck engines. She could barely hear herself. She raised her nine, and Mitchell bolted east across Lexington and down Sixty-First.

Sunny didn't have the traffic light on busy Lexington Avenue, but she darted into the street anyway in hot pursuit. To her right, a large FedEx truck came to a sudden front-end nose-dipping stop, brakes squealing. The bug-eyed driver peered down through the huge windshield at the crazy woman with a gun pointed at the sky. She held her left hand, palm out, pumping it, stopping the other lanes of traffic, cars slamming on their brakes, tires screaming, cabbies hurling expletives out their windows. She angrily slapped a cab's hood as a warning. The cabbie slid low in his seat, his eyes pinned to her gun.

She survived the vehicle obstacle course, but now, where was Chris Mitchell's green cap?

Her heart racing, she spun in a complete circle on the sidewalk. Down Sixty-First were apartment buildings, a vape shop, and restaurants. With her 9mm at her side, she crept along the sidewalk. She heard sirens in the distance. She suspected KD had radioed Central for officer assistance.

The green cap was nowhere in sight. Maybe he'd ditched the cap, Sunny decided, her head on a swivel, crouched, as she cautiously crab-walked sideways.

On the opposite side of the street, a female postal carrier was pushing one of those three-wheel mail carts. She urgently pointed to a spot just ahead of Sunny. Rain or shine, bullets flying, the Postal Service delivered.

A dentist's office sign marked the spot where Sunny's new postal friend pointed. A stairwell down led to the office. Sunny first spied the top of a green cap. She lowered her weapon to eye level.

"Come out with your hands up!" she commanded.

The man Sunny saw on Kurt Lewis' display monitor at the Real Time Crime Center emerged with his hands held high.

Chapter Twenty-two

Sunny knew, at some point, liars couldn't keep track of the webs they weaved. A story could shift ever so slightly. The brain tired after repeated questioning. The interrogator waited for that one slip of the lip. Sunny kept up the pressure in MSH Interrogation Room 2. A radio patrol car had brought Chris Mitchell to MSH since the detectives had to hang back to add their eyewitness account for the frickin' road rage scene.

"So again, Chris, why did you run from me down Sixty-First Street?" Sunny put to the squirming man.

Interrogation Room 2 smelled of pine disinfectant. The evening cleaning crew was now in Room 3. Sunny studied Chris Mitchell, who shook his head in aggravation. Chris Mitchell sat while KD and Sunny roamed the interrogation room, one of them always behind Chris to keep him off balance, unsettled. The detectives called it their impatient strategy. Sunny always pictured that lone hyena in the nature shows surrounded by a pride of snarling, nipping lions.

Chris possessed a thin face with large eyes, and at the moment, his eyes flared. "Like I told the cop on the ride here, I heard gunshots. I'm in *New York City*, and the next thing I know some"—he looked warily at Sunny—"some crazy woman with a gun was running toward me."

Shots certainly were fired. Some nut in a gorgeous triple black Range Rover decided to *kill* a Chevy Equinox SUV over a minor fender bender. It was only property. Fortunately, no one was hurt. Though, there was a terrified mother with a child in a rear car seat.

"And stop calling me Chris. You have my wallet, my ID, and my Mennen Deodorant Stick from Duane Reade." He smirked. The stick deodorant was in his pocket, along with a Duane Reade receipt. For the moment, the ID was held as fake.

KD's phone chimed with a message, then Sunny's a moment later. Sunny upped the pressure.

"Where were you Monday night?" she demanded. Christine Lowry, the Army veteran, was murdered Monday. Elaine Hogan was savagely beaten Wednesday night. Sunny was taking it a step at a time, looking for lies and inconsistencies along the way.

"*What?*" KD blurted, eyes bugged, interrupting the interrogation as he read something on his phone. His roaming had brought him near the interrogation room door. He looked up at Sunny and ran his hand across his throat, indicating to stop the interrogation. He beckoned for her to step outside.

Once the door closed, KD spoke. "Kurt at RTCC must still be at his meeting because the facial recognition software is still running." He pointed at Sunny's phone. "You just got the same message. RTCC facial recognition software shows Chris Mitchell," KD raised his eyebrows, "exited the subway not long ago at Twenty-third Street and Eighth Avenue." Thirty-eight blocks from the fender bender.

A long distance. "We need to get a live feed from the street camera. It appears he's headed to his apartment in Chelsea."

Sunny slowly turned her head to the interrogation room door as if seeing through it. They placed a uniformed officer to stand guard at Interrogation Room 2's door while they struck out for Chelsea.

Chapter
Twenty-three

Sunny pulled back her jacket, exposing her Glock. "Get your hands out of your pockets," she said in an authoritative voice to the PPH gang members.

All five gang members threw their hands into the air in mock surrender and stood spread-eagle against the Perry Public Housing Complex red brick wall where Chris Mitchell lived.

"Yo, Five-O, ya gonna stop and frisk us?" one gang member provocatively drawled over his shoulder. He wiggled his ass for emphasis. The slang term Five-O originated from the '70s cop show, *Hawaii 5-O*, the fiftieth state.

"Get outta the way!" KD shoved Mr. Backwards Cap from the complex doorway.

Sunny imagined the PPH gang assaulting her in the park Monday night. She closed her jacket and followed KD through the door. The gang members started laughing and fist-bumping, congratulating each other for their antics.

The elevator door slid closed. Gang graffiti decorated the interior.

"I remember discussing Stop and Frisk at the police academy," Sunny said.

"You're lucky you didn't have to implement it." KD shook his head ruefully.

The controversial NYPD policy allowed New York City citizens to be stopped, questioned, and searched. The only basis the police needed was "reasonable suspicion."

"It didn't sound fun at all," Sunny remarked while peering at the elevator floor indicator. They had just passed the fifth floor.

"It devolved into racial profiling of black and brown communities. Citizens were stopped multiple times in a day, spread-eagle." KD sighed loudly. "We didn't concentrate on contraband around the city's colleges on Friday nights or crimes on Wall Street that would cause our next global financial meltdown. Noooo," he drew the word out. "We went after the weak. It damaged community trust. The policy got struck down, but we're still trying to recover. A federal judge finally declared the policy as a violation of the Fourth Amendment's prohibition against unreasonable search and seizure. Today, we must reasonably suspect a person is armed before a stop and frisk."

The elevator door slid open on the ninth floor. KD sniffed the air. "Smells like pork chops." It was the dinner hour. Several music categories—Hip Hop, R&B, Salsa, jazz—emanated from behind doors.

At apartment 903, Sunny placed her ear against the door. She shook her head to KD. She heard nothing from inside. But then she heard what sounded like the metallic clang of a cooking pot placed on a stove burner. She knocked hard.

"Police! Open up, Chris Mitchell," she shouted. They both withdrew their guns, aiming the weapons at the floor for the moment. Several latches slid before the door opened. They both charged inside.

"What did I do?" Chris Mitchell pleaded as he was handcuffed and sat at a small kitchenette table.

"Anybody else here?" Sunny asked, scanning the tiny apartment. A double bed was in the living room, where most people had a sofa.

"My grandmother is in that bedroom," Chris used his slender chin to point, "taking a nap. This," he indicated the living room bed, "is where she sleeps at night. What's this all about?" He strained at the uncomfortable handcuffs and looked with the same large moon eyes as the *other* Chris Mitchell back in Interrogation Room 2.

"I'm going to take a quiet look around," KD said as he carefully opened the bedroom door where Grandma slept, his gun pointed down.

The cramped apartment turned out to only have two small bedrooms and four beds, including the one in the living room. The kitchen could only accommodate one person at a time.

"Who else lives here?" Sunny asked as she holstered her weapon.

Chris sighed heavily. "My mom, pops, and little sister live here too."

"Where are they?" KD said, looking around for a seat. He first eyed the living room bed, then took the other dinette chair across from Chris.

"At the grocery store," Chris said grudgingly. He squirmed in the chair. "They'll be back soon. The pot of water on the stove is for some rice they're bringing home to have with dinner."

Sunny looked closer at Chris's forearm. "Nice PPH tattoo," she needled. "Still running with them, I see." She had memorized many of the city's gangs and their symbols. Now, she added this one. The detectives glanced at each other. They were equally confused. Who was back at the precinct in Interrogation Room 2?

Chris peeked at his tattooed forearm the best he could in the handcuffs. "Cost money to remove it. Money I don't have," he snarled. "And I'm not in a gang anymore."

KD apparently saw an opening for their main reason for being here. "If you save your *movie* money, you can remove your gang affiliation symbol."

"Why're you sweatin' me, man?"

Extracting his phone and locating the movie ticket picture, KD slid the device across the tiny table. Chris glanced at it and shrugged.

"It's *your* movie ticket," KD clarified. "*Fast and Furious* three hundred and one." Sunny couldn't catch her snicker in time. It burst out. Chris Mitchell frowned. KD prodded the young man. "Are you picking out the next car across the street you're going to steal?" Getting a suspect angry sometimes made them spill involuntary truths.

Across the street from the Perry Public Housing Complex was a ten-story kindergarten through twelfth grade, lavishly remodeled, state-of-the-art school. The information was all in Chris Mitchell's criminal record. The school cost up to fifty thousand dollars a year per student. Parents drove up in Mercedes, Land Rovers, Escalades, and Hummers. For those at PPHC, kids with little, the shiny new cars were fish in a barrel. Follow the cars, steal them, sell them to chop shops. Unfortunately for Chris, he was caught heisting a Lexus.

"I have a job," Chris spat defensively. "I don't need to steal anything." The young man leaned his head to the side as if in pain. "I got my GED while I was locked up," he volunteered in a voice loaded with pride. "I want to go further, but money is tight. I'm looking for a second job, but my criminal record is a problem. While in prison, I learned that it cost fifty thousand dollars a year to lock me up." He shook his head woefully. "Same as the cost of a good college. Things seem backward." He signed deeply, clearly the thought troubling him. "Anyway," he snapped out of his dejection, "my little sister wants to attend that school across the street, and I want to help my parents get outta this shithole public housing. And like I said, I don't do that gang stuff anymore."

"That's well and good," KD pressed on, pointing at his phone. "But we found your ticket stub at a murder scene near the Hudson River."

Chris sat up bolt straight, his arms pinned behind him. He scowled at KD. "That's what this is about? A murder?" he said, his head now shaking vigorously from side to side. "I go to the river sometimes to escape the madness around here. It's peaceful."

Sunny was still trying to picture Chris and his PPH gang assaulting her. Like back at the precinct in Interrogation Room 2, she was listening closely to his voice, trying to place him at her assault scene, but her head was so groggy that night from the head blow. She couldn't identify any voice inflection or unique words.

"You and your boys were *wilin'* in the park Monday night, weren't you?" Sunny remarked. She purposely left out details to see if Chris would slip and incriminate himself with information only the assailants and murderers would know.

Chris suddenly twisted in his seat to face Sunny standing at his side. His face was a mask of insult.

"I don't run with them, I told you! That gang is threatening to do...things...to me...to my little sister...if I don't join them again. She's only eleven," he emphasized. "She's smart. Straight A's. When I was eleven, I was already smoking and selling weed." He hung his head, shaking it. "That prison scared me straight," he said softly, sniffling.

"You're coming down to the precinct with us," KD said, unlocking the handcuffs. Sunny turned off the fire under the rice water.

Chapter Twenty-four

An hour's drive from Rapid City Regional Airport, Amber Smoke's rideshare was now south of the Badlands of South Dakota—an area of rock erosion creating spectacular pinnacles and spires. An eagle—Amber swore it was the same eagle near the airport and at the Cherokee Nation— danced on the warm air currents above, dipping, soaring, screeching. Soon, a road sign proclaimed they were entering the Pine Ridge Indian Reservation.

In forty-five minutes, Amber was scheduled to meet with Sioux leaders to discuss the political action committee idea. But first, she wanted to visit the mass grave just southeast of there to pay her respects.

She bent forward toward the driver. "May I bum a cigarette if you have one?"

The driver leaned and, without taking his eyes off the road for long, rummaged through his glove compartment. Over the seat, he handed Amber a pack of Marlboro. She shook out one and thanked the man. He extended a cigarette lighter.

"Thanks. I don't smoke," she declined. The driver peeked incredulously into the rearview mirror.

Another half-hour drive and the car parked next to the Wounded Knee Memorial sign. In studying the attempted genocide of Native people, Amber had read of this massacre in history books. Now, she was actually here.

The location's name was derived from a Native American who sustained a knee injury during a fight at what was now Wounded Knee Creek. Lieutenant Colonel George Armstrong Custer's old Seventh Cavalry took its bloody revenge there following the cavalry's defeat at Little Big Horn in 1876 at the hands of Crazy Horse.

She paid the driver and thanked him again for the cigarette. The eagle screeched above. Amber shaded her eyes from the sun to see the majestic bird. Her mind wanted to go to irrational places as she felt the bird was following her. But she had work to do.

Fifty yards ahead on a slightly inclining, twisted dirt path stood a decorative metal arch. She weaved her way under and through it.

It was a late, very warm morning, but tourists were already surrounding the chain-link fence—the perimeter of the mass grave, which was about the size of a large backyard swimming pool. Inside the fence, a six-foot monument topped with an acorn-like apex stood proudly commemorating the dead.

Some tourists around the fence snapped pictures. Others were quietly meditative. One man had Slavic features and a lazy eye, and Amber thought he was on her flight. He must have an interest in Native culture. A tall, middle-aged man in jeans was the tour guide. A red bandana held back his hair.

"Joe, how many are in this grave?" a woman with a heavy Scandinavian accent asked the man with the bandana.

"From two to three hundred," Joe responded as he walked around the perimeter in Amber's direction.

Joe shot out his hand to shake Amber's as he walked past. "The timing is right, so you must be Amber," he said in a respectful whisper. "I was expecting you. I'm to escort you to the meeting and then get you back to the airport," he informed her, continuing his walk to answer more tourist questions.

Amber leaned against the chest-high, chain-link fence, her knees feeling weak with reverence. Grieving hands had tied red, yellow, white, and other fluttering prayer ribbons through the fence links. Her eyes scanned the breadth of the grave. Somewhere under all this dirt lay Native men, women, and children arbitrarily tossed into a giant hole in the ground, clearing the way for civilization.

The Marlboro cigarette would have settled her nerves, but that wasn't the reason she bummed one. She withdrew the cigarette from her purse and began jamming it into the fence link next to multicolored prayer ribbons and more cigarettes. The tobacco smoke would send prayers and greetings to the Creator.

After the tourist left, Joe led Amber to the Administration Center adjacent to the mass grave. An hour later, she emerged and hopped into Joe's car, telling him about the successful meeting.

As Joe had promised, they immediately headed to the airport. A half-hour on the road and the barren landscape still went on for miles. It was as though they grew rocks there—what the Sioux were left with after civilization rolled through.

"If you need to stretch your legs, let me know," Joe said, piloting his old gold Pontiac that seemed to have finally hit its stride.

"I'm good, thanks."

Joe pointed to the right. Amber followed his direction and immediately recognized what was up ahead.

Joe proudly smiled as he looked through the windshield at the Crazy Horse Monument sculpted into the mountainside.

"We want the world to know that we, *too*, have great heroes!" he declared of the Sioux war hero who famously defeated Custer at the Battle of Little Big Horn.

Following the sightseeing, Joe accelerated the Pontiac. He promised she'd make her flight after one more small detour. Ten minutes later, they caught sight of Mount Rushmore. Joe slowed the car.

"*Paha Sapa*," he spoke solemnly. "The Black Hills. They were *never* for sale." He gazed thoughtfully at the US presidents carved into the Sioux axis mundi, their spiritual center. He explained some of what Amber already knew. When gold was discovered in the hills, prospectors descended on the Sioux homeland guaranteed in the Fort Laramie Treaty.

"We use US treaties to line our bird cages," Joe chuckled. "In 1980," he continued, "the Supreme Court ruled that the United States illegally *dispossessed* us of the Black Hills and more. The US was demanded to pay us, but we didn't want their stinking money. There's over a billion unclaimed dollars."

Amber knew the Black Hills story but not the dollar amount of a settlement. She was still gazing at *axis mundi*. It was the oft-repeated story of Natives forced from their homes, forced from their lands.

Joe shook his head at Washington, Jefferson, Roosevelt, and Lincoln. "And then they carved their leaders' faces into our holy place."

The old Pontiac up ahead smoked slightly, especially on hills. In his fast airport rental Mustang, Sergey discretely tailed Amanda Smoke and Joe, the tour guide. Back at the Wounded Knee gravesite, he looked for every opportunity to kill the woman. Sergey hadn't risked bringing a gun on the plane. He stalked her to secretly inject her with a syringe of poison or stab her in the back of the head with an ice pick, but there were too many eyes around him and no escape route.

The Pontiac slowed at something carved in a mountainside. The carving didn't look complete. The name *Crazy Horse* was on a sign. Sergey was still trying to understand his new adopted homeland. He dug out his trusty tablet to quickly search Crazy Horse while the Pontiac paused, its brake lights shining. Oh, Crazy Horse was the one who defeated that General Custer guy. Sergey continued to read Crazy Horse's words: *We wanted to hunt as opposed to a sedentary life on a reservation, where we were forced to live against our will. We only sought to live in peace and be left alone.*

The rusting Pontiac accelerated back onto the route. Sergey slid the Mustang gearshift from park to drive, hanging back as far as he could, peeking over hills. The route was lightly traveled with a few cars driving in either direction. But forcing the Pontiac off the road and flipping it wouldn't guarantee her death, and with the Joe fellow in the way, there would be collateral damage.

Sergey was dragged back to the present when the pair pulled to the shoulder again to view four faces carved into a mountainside. *What's with all the mountain carvings in this country?* But this one he now remembered. That Lincoln president he could always pick out of a crowd. Those others, not so much. He reflected on American history again. It resembled a lot of history from his Eurasian birth land. The Vikings, Mongols, Goths, and Huns, all invaded Western Europe, plundering and slaughtering any in their path.

They finally made it to the airport. His target sat at an airport restaurant table, eating a muffin and drinking tea. Sergey stood just outside the empty restaurant pretending to be on his cell phone call while he watched the woman's back. She seemed so innocent. Sergey always wanted to know as much about his targets as possible beyond physical features. This woman was pretty with a family, but such sentimental things could never get in the way of work. His Russian organized crime boss had told him some corporation wanted the entire family killed out of revenge. He dug deeper and found out the corporation was named Excorp Industries. Its CEO was Larry Exford. The corporation sought to purchase some Sunadaga territory but was rebuffed. Something to do with rare earth elements for secret advanced warfare technologies. Whatever. It was going to be Sergey's biggest payday, far beyond any past hit jobs in the United States or back in Europe.

An elderly white-haired waitress—probably without the money to retire—approached the table to see if the woman needed anything else. Amber Smoke placed her hand over the cup, declining. The old waitress smiled and went through a saloon door to the kitchen. Amber's phone rang. She said hello several times before standing to walk to the back window, apparently for a better signal. Sergey saw an opportunity to get paid.

He reached into the inner ankle side of his left sock. There, he withdrew the plastic packet. He checked to see if the Indian woman was still on her call, looking out the window at the airport runways. She talked animatedly to someone, her free hand gesturing. The saloon door was still.

He jammed his phone into his pocket, strode nonchalantly to the table, and, with a furtive twist of the wrist, dumped the packet's contents into the teacup. He got out of there and watched from across the airport hall. The woman continued her conversation as the saloon door swung open, and the old waitress exited.

The waitress looked around while drying her hands on her apron, not seeing her customer who was near the window. Walking to clear the table, the old woman frowned at no tip. She stacked the few dishes on a tray and headed for the kitchen. She shouldered the saloon door open and then stopped on the other side. Sergey saw her take a bite from the leftover muffin. Next, her head lifted, appearing to drink the tea.

No, no, no! Sergey screamed in his head. *Shit!* The strychnine would have the collateral damage foaming at the mouth.

Chapter Twenty-five

The man who insisted his name was Lester Atkins, not Chris Mitchell, sat in Interrogation Room 2. NYPD databases finally confirmed his claim. Nothing was faked. Lester's spitting image waited in Room 3 as the detectives entered. KD described Sunny's and Elaine's assaults and Christine's murder. The true Chris Mitchell's mouth dropped open.

"So, you say you're down by the river a lot at night?" Sunny probed to see if Chris's story shifted.

He squeezed his large eyes shut as if in pain. "Like I told you back in the projects," he said, referring to Perry Public Housing, "I'm afraid of that gang. They own the neighborhood. You're either one of them or a victim of them. I try to arrive when they're gone. Call my boss." He jotted down the number. KD handed the number to the officer outside the door to call right away.

Sunny was now believing more and more that Chris had nothing to do with the crimes. "Do you think your ex-gang had anything to do with this?"

He was shaking his head, then something clicked. "I

was down near the water Monday night. I remember hearing some voices somewhere behind me. Men." He gazed up at the ceiling in thought. "Rowdy, drunk-sounding men, come to think of it." He was nodding. "They used the words "rad" and "awesome" a lot. Nobody in our gang talked like that."

KD beckoned Sunny into the hall outside the interrogation room. Immediately, a civilian aide told them that a couple awaited them in the squad room.

As requested, Reggie and Jackie Mitchell had arrived at the MSH precinct. They were told about what appeared to be identical twins in the interrogation rooms. Chris' employer did vouch that the young man was in Queens painting the interior of a home in Forest Hills, the residents due back soon from their Florida vacation.

Using their phones, the Mitchells showed pictures of Chris at home late Monday night for his sister's birthday party after dinner. Chris donned a shiny cone hat in one of the pictures. The family later played bingo, with Grandma winning twice.

In the precinct Interrogation Room 1, Jackie Mitchell reached into her purse to extract an envelope. Her large eyes pleaded for the detectives to read its contents. She uneasily slid the envelope across the tabletop to KD and Sunny.

"See if this helps," she said in a shaky whisper, then turned to her husband, a thin-faced, mustached man. The couple held hands. Sunny was witnessing a loving scene that one day she too wanted to experience, but right now, there were crimes to solve. KD beckoned for Sunny to open the envelope.

Inside the envelope was a yellowing newspaper clipping. The detectives leaned close for a few moments to read the article. Sunny was shaking her head in confusion until realization struck. "Holy shit!" she let escape, then apologized.

"Yeah," KD muttered, sliding the envelope back

across the table. "Your son Chris is in Room Three," he said to the Mitchells. "But would you mind first talking to the young man in Room Two?" The Mitchells agreed.

The detectives and the Mitchells stood outside Interrogation Room 2. Sunny swung the door open, and Mrs. Mitchell gasped, slapping her hand to her mouth. Mr. Mitchell stared with his brow deeply furrowed.

Lester Atkins looked up at the couple in the doorway, his large eyes darting suspiciously between the two, clearly not knowing what to make of the scene. During the detective's interrogation, Lester Atkins turned out to be an architect whose fiancé lived not far from the Duane Reade on Sixty-First Street. Lester and his fiancée were at a Yankees game on Monday night and a Broadway show on Wednesday night. There were receipts for both events. Sunny made the introductions to the Mitchells.

"What's going on? When can I leave?" Lester Atkins pressed, clearly not wanting to stay a second longer.

Jackie Mitchell was reaching into her purse for the envelope again, even before Sunny had to ask her. Sunny took the envelope and handed it to the apprehensive Lester Atkins, who, after a few skeptical beats, finally took the envelope from Sunny's outstretched arm. The Mitchells took a seat, not taking their eyes off Lester, while the young man read.

Lester Atkins' expression suddenly morphed from impatience to distress. The yellowing news article shook nervously in his hand. He slowly raised his teary eyes to the Mitchells.

"This explains a lot," Lester announced, waving the article. Both Reggie and Jackie Mitchell were nodding their heads, agreeing vigorously.

In the initial interrogation of Lester, he related his family background in an effort to get the detectives to believe that he was no murderer, no gangsta. Several years ago, both his parents had died in a horrific apartment building fire in the Bronx caused by a faulty E-Bike lithium-ion battery charger. Eight residents died. He was their only child. The older Lester got, the more he questioned his family. He didn't possess their physical traits. The yellowing article spelled out the hospital abduction of one of the Mitchell's twin sons.

KD nudged Sunny for them to give the family a moment alone. The detectives spoke in hushed tones in the hall.

"We didn't catch *anyone* responsible for the assaults and murder," Sunny remarked, disappointed.

KD was nodding his head. "I've been doing this for ten years. It happens. CSU finds leads, and we have to pursue them to the end." He shook his bald brown head in frustration at the reality. "Sometimes investigations just inch long. But remember what Chris said." KD pointed to Room 3. "Remember when you asked him if he thought his ex-gang had anything to do with the crime? Remember his description of the language?"

"That's right. I remember." Sunny wasn't feeling as bummed out now. "Chris said that he never heard the PPH gang members using words like 'rad' and 'awesome.'"

The investigation had reunited a family and reasonably eliminated PPH so the detectives could focus on other leads.

Somebody on the other side of door number two was really wailing. The detectives had yet to introduce Lester to his identical twin behind door number three. Sunny wondered if Camille's powers could somehow determine if Chris and Lester were definitely twins beyond their outward appearance. The thought of Camille's powers brought her mind to the T-Rex bone necklace of KD's open Murray Hill case. The necklace wasn't much to go on, but like KD said, *Sometimes investigations just inch long.* She was learning as a rookie detective.

Twenty minutes later, a huge family hug took place

in the hall outside the interrogation rooms. Lester mentioned his upcoming wedding, and the glee reached a new level, squealing, hopping. Sunny reminisced about her family's together time...before her father was shot dead.

After the detectives saw the jubilant family out of the precinct, they returned to their desks to process fives from the interrogation. The day wasn't over until the paperwork was done.

Chapter Twenty-six

With her apartment TV muted, Sunny called her mother in Oklahoma City. It was Sunny's turn. Jennifer had called several days ago. Margarette McGraw invariably inquired about Sunny's love life, or lack thereof. But this time, Sunny was ready. Lunch with ADA Greg Ross at Sally's Deli in the Meatpacking District had led to another date request. Sunny hadn't decided on a good time for the next date.

"A lawyer, huh?" Margarette McGraw harrumphed on the other end of the phone, joy riding on her tone. "Well, don't keep him waiting too long. I like it. A lawyer in the family."

"Mom, pump the brakes. You're getting way ahead of yourself," Sunny cautioned.

The telephone call always veered into talk about Sunny's father. At least he hadn't taken his own life as far too many law enforcement personnel did these days. The Job's unique pressures forced some to the brink.

"Do you still believe that there's more to your

father's death?" Margaret McGraw asked in a shaky voice.

OKC Police Officer Louis McGraw was shot through his opened patrol car window at close range in the temple as he sat in the idling police cruiser while his partner ran into the convenience store to take a leak. Sunny's mother received his pension, which enabled her to keep their home and feed twelve-year-old Sunny and her older sister. Uncle Joe stepped in wherever he could. Sunny was never satisfied that her father's killer was probably still out there. For the same reason, Margarette McGraw was a virtual recluse, sticking close to home, the burglar alarm armed every night.

Sunny never wanted to lie to her mother, but she also wasn't going to stress her out. Yes, she was still suspicious of the circumstances surrounding her father's death. Sunny took the conversation in a different direction. Margaret McGraw couldn't resist a hearty conversation about Pepe.

"He's looking up at me right now with his bug-eyed self. His tail is wagging a mile a minute." Pepe was the chihuahua Margaret's daughters had bought her. The sisters knew that Pepe would bark if anyone approached the house—a second burglar alarm.

After saying goodnight to her mother, Sunny unmuted the TV set, let Tuffy out onto the fire escape, and powered up her laptop on the kitchenette island. She started her fourth viewing of the security camera video from business establishments in the vicinity of Elaine's savage beating. Sunny was home…but still on the Job as usual. If only she could collect the OT for all the extra hours she spent off the clock.

On TV, microphones were shoved into the faces of Mayor Roland Myers and NYPD brass for comments on the wolfpack terrorizing the city. Ever since African-American hair from the crime scene was inadvertently leaked, several of the more lurid-oriented, shock-driven stations started asking when the NYPD would start concentrating on Black gangs. But law enforcement was careful not to jump to conclusions.

A new e-mail hit Sunny's inbox. Following the subpoena, Elaine's cell phone provider granted access to her phone records. Sunny immediately dialed Elaine's last called number, Gina. They talked for a minute. She planned to meet Gina at an LGBTQ club called Club Posh. She then dialed KD at his home in Brooklyn. It was late, and she was still a ball of energy. She convinced KD to stay at home with his family.

Sunny had enough of the sensational news. She turned off the TV. Her cell phone chimed with a new text message. It was Camille. He asked her to drop by tonight. She texted back, *OK. Right after I finish some investigations. Any leftovers?*

On the Upper West Side, the refreshing night air brought out the club crowd even on a weekday in Manhattan. Sunny read *Club Posh* on the flashing neon sign in the club's window. She heard live music. She entered behind a hand-holding couple in their fifties.

Small couples' tables filled the club. A bar was situated to the right. Sunny weaved between tables to make her way to the bar.

"What will it be?" A huge African-American bartender who reminded Sunny of the prisoner in the *Green Mile,* wiped the bar counter and then draped the towel over his huge shoulder. With kind eyes, he waited.

"Not tonight," Sunny responded. She flashed her detective shield. "I'm supposed to meet Gina Duncan."

The bartender pointed to the stage in the back of the club. "That's her performing now."

Sunny spun on the barstool to face the stage. She was looking over the heads of club patrons seated in red cushioned chairs that matched the stage curtain. Heads bobbed and swayed to Cindy Lauper's "True Colors." In an

NYPD sensitivity training seminar, the detectives were taught to listen. Since Elaine was a transgender woman, and the bartender had used the pronoun *her* to describe the Cindy Lauper look-alike on stage, she now knew to use female pronouns.

Gina Duncan belted out a not-so-bad version of "True Colors." Her big blonde hair bounced to the beat. Her black sequin dress sparkled under the bright stage lights. The band—a drummer, a keyboardist, and a guitarist—filled the club with vibrant notes. Three minutes later, the crowd stood and applauded. Sunny went backstage to the dressing room and introduced herself.

"Detective, sorry to give you the bum's rush on the phone, but I was getting ready for my show. What's this investigation all about?" Gina Duncan asked as she sat before a wall mirror, primping her blonde wig.

Curly wigs, straight-haired wigs, more blonde wigs, and redhead wigs were situated around the dressing room. Flashy stage outfits hung on a rack. The dressing room transported Sunny back to her *Toddlers and Tiaras* days. The same heavy perfume smell. The same bright lights above the mirror. Makeup was scattered everywhere. It was a bit much as a child and still a bit much. But this was Gina's preference.

"Elaine Diaz's last call was to you," Sunny said.

Gina was applying lip gloss as she gazed at Sunny through the mirror. "The call was to switch schedules with her last night, Wednesday, and tonight also. I'm doing the early shows for several days, and Elaine is performing her Shakira act in the late shows. You should stay to see her perform "Hips Don't Lie" tonight. She's doing half the routine in Spanish." Gina placed the cap back on the lip gloss. Her bubbly expression failed. She turned on the stool to face Sunny, recognition in her eyes.

"Something bad has happened to Elaine? I can just feel it," she said in a shaky voice.

Sunny nodded. "I'm afraid so. She's in the hospital, beaten up pretty bad."

"Oh my God!" Wide-eyed in shock, Gina threw her hand over her mouth. Sunny rubbed Gina's back as the woman hyperventilated. "Where is she?" Gina managed to say while sobbing. "I have to see her." Gina rose quickly off the stool, wobbling in her heels. Sunny stood.

"It's past visiting hours," Sunny said in a calming voice. She didn't want to go into Elaine's extensive injuries. "Do you know where Elaine was going after work last night?"

With the tissue, Gina dabbed at her running mascara. "She said after work she was going to hail a taxi to her Hell's Kitchen apartment. Elaine didn't like the subways at night because of all the harassment." Gina shook her head in despair. "I shouldn't have switched schedules with her." Gina's crying started anew.

"It's not your fault," Sunny soothed.

"Why can't they just leave us alone?" Gina wailed. "Let us live our lives." She shook her head in despair, the wig rocking. "We're not bothering anybody." She slammed her fist on the makeup counter. "They bully us, scapegoat us, criminalize us."

Sunny continued to rub the woman's back comforting her.

On the drive south from Club Posh to the Meatpacking District and on to MH Construction, Sunny called KD. She heard silverware clinking in the background. KD's halting words suggested the family was at the dinner table. She hurriedly informed him about her interview with Gina Duncan. Once she got off the phone, she contacted the Taxi and Limousine Commission. Elaine's Wednesday night driver was off tonight. They would try to reach him at home, but tonight, they would give her access to the onboard taxi camera footage. A few minutes later, Sunny parked in front of MH Construction under a bright streetlight. She tossed the police ID plate on the dashboard and made her way to the second floor of the shop.

It didn't take long for Marshall to serve, not leftover Indian tacos, but rather corn soup.

"My compliments to the chef!" Sunny shouted to Marshall, who was in the shop's tiny kitchen. The savory dish was another Haudenosaunee delicacy of corn, pork loin cubes, carrots, celery, beans, and rutabaga.

"We're going to make you an honorary Native American if you keep eating our cuisine like that," Marshall quipped.

That got a huge laugh from both Camille and Sunny, who were seated across from each other eating corn soup at the same two-seat window table from the night before. Out the window, streetlights reflected off the cobblestone streets below. Club and restaurant patrons strolled the Meatpacking District sidewalks.

"When I'm done in here," Marshall went on, pots banging in the sink, "I'll show you how to use that special saddle."

Sunny looked at Camille for meaning. He hid an impish smile behind his large soup spoon. "What does he mean 'Show me how to use it?'"

"You'll see. Let's finish our soup first," Camille reassured her. He leaned forward, resting his forearms on the table. Weightlifting, heavy punching bag workout, and construction work were evident in his huge biceps and broad shoulders with well-developed deltoids.

"I'm sorry about Elaine," Camille said with melancholy in his voice. "I wish I would have started a little later. Maybe I could have caught that gang out in the open."

"No! Don't beat yourself up." She grabbed his warm hand across the table. "It's my job to solve this case." She squeezed his hand. "You rat, you! You found that watch." That got a big chuckle out of him.

149

"And almost got squashed underfoot by your partner," he said, relief on his face. Now it was Sunny's turn to laugh.

"There should be DNA on that watch, which will hopefully break my case open, and it's all because of you." Sunny released his hand and leaned back in her chair. "Your other text message indicated that you found another scent hotspot on the Upper West Side."

"Yeah, there's about a four-block radius of strong scent trails up there. Same scents as at your assault scene. Same as at Christine's murder scene." He reached for a writing pad on the windowsill and quickly sketched a rough street grid. He tore the sheet away and handed it to Sunny.

"Any idea how we can narrow that down?" she asked, viewing the sketch. She tried to recall all the restaurants and clubs in the target area. Sunny was giving Camille free rein. He had found the watch. Maybe he had some more creative ideas.

He considered her question for a moment. Then his eyes went bright. "I can transform into a bloodhound or German shepherd, and we can scour that area at street level when you're ready."

She, with Camille on a leash, wouldn't look out of place. But how would she explain her new canine friend and findings to KD and the Loo?

"Searching with a dog is an excellent idea, Camille." She would make up some far-flung canine explanation. *Dog sitting my neighbor's dog?* This case needed resolution fast. "But let's see how much mileage we get from the watch first." Now, she wanted to know about his trip to South Dakota. "How did Wounded Knee go?"

"I flew almost nonstop. A stiff tailwind once I was over Pennsylvania helped a lot. I'm so proud of my sister Amber." Sunny could feel the love between the siblings. She and Jennifer had that same bond. "One day you must meet Amber."

150

"I'd love that."

"So, you say you grew up in Oklahoma?" Camille slurped a spoonful of corn soup and chewed. "Tell me about it."

Sunny related her youth, her reluctant beauty pageants, the painful teen years after her father was killed, and how her uncle Joe taught her farming, crop duster airplane piloting, horse riding, and barn cleaning. Camille pinched his nose.

"That piloting and horse riding will serve you well tonight," Camille replied, wiping his smiling mouth with a napkin.

"Piloting a plane and horse riding will serve me well? What's going on?" Sunny asked, observing a mischievous gleam in his eyes. He remained mum. "Okay...then tell me about your life and how you gained those superhuman powers you have." He started to talk—

"You two ready to test the saddle?" Marshall said as he came out of the kitchen, drying his hands with a yellow and white checkered towel.

"What's he talking about?" she asked, confused.

"Let's do it, Marshall," Camille agreed, grinning, raising his six-foot-one frame from his chair. "I'll tell you about me and my powers in a few moments. I'll meet you guys out back." Sunny's expression was part worried, part puzzled. "Come on! It'll be fun," Camille gushed.

Chapter Twenty-seven

The tall wooden stockade fence behind MH Construction concealed the back of the shop from prying eyes. A motion sensor floodlight above the shop's garage door burst to life like some Broadway theater stage, illuminating the ground in front of the garage door. The shadowy figures of backhoe tractors, excavators, cement mixers, mobile electric generators, several lengths of aluminum ladders, a dump truck, and other construction equipment Sunny didn't recognize filled the yard behind her.

"We can't thank you enough for helping to vindicate Camille," Marshall said as he punched in the garage door security code on the pad next to the huge door. Immediately, the chain-driven metal door clattered, lifting on its rollers with a racket.

"I'll investigate Camille's case during any lulls I have in my current NYPD assault and murder cases." She watched the door groan, slowly opening. She still wasn't certain why they were out back of the construction company.

The floodlight washed illumination under the creaking, now two-foot-opening garage door.

Sunny suddenly caught her breath.

On any other day, the fight or flight instinct would have dominated her mind, sent her headlong to eliminate the threat, or, conversely, fleeing, avoiding death to fight another day.

Marshall stood, hands on hips, coolly watching the door rise to face level. Sunny could tell he had experienced this many times. But not her. She finally took a deep, relaxing breath, blowing out the air with puffed-out cheeks.

She couldn't take her eyes off the tremendously large, razor-sharp talons of whatever remained hidden behind the still-rising door. She decided to take her cues from Marshall. She finally blinked, but the dreamlike quality remained.

The grudging garage door went quiet as it reached its fully open state. The enormous falcon lowered his massive head to clear the top of the garage door threshold. Sunny was aware that she hadn't said one word.

The falcons she had seen in her life were only the size of chickens. *This!* This towering raptor.... She instinctively took several steps back as the bird of prey stepped out under the spotlight. A great hooked black beak for tearing flesh dominated the bird's head. The falcon had slate gray wing feathers with brown and white bars on the underbelly and a white throat.

The bird's intense, miss-nothing eyes gazed down at the small humans before him. Marshall broke the silence.

"You're not as big as you usually are," he said, looking up at the falcon.

The raptor turned its enormous head to Marshall. It's gigantic, hooked beak opened. "I'm not flying with *you* on my back." The bird's eyes smiled. "The load is much less. I scaled down to size for Sunny."

Marshall cracked up in laughter. With a *smack*, he slapped his protruding belly. "Too many Indian tacos and too much corn soup."

Camille took a few more steps forward, his talons scratching the ground. He crouched and lowered his neck so Marshall could fit the saddle and bridle. Marshall adjusted the stirrups.

"Now you see why horse riding and airplane piloting would come in handy," Camille reminded Sunny. "Hop on. I'll tell you my story while we we're up there," he said, throwing his head to the dark night sky.

So this is what he meant the other day by "we", he and Marshall, fly upstate. She was so absorbed in solving cases she missed the gist of Camille's description. Sunny wondered when she was going to wake up.

But against her inhibitions, and with a toothy grin, she ran and vaulted onto Camille's back. She stroked his soft, downy neck feathers that were aerodynamically swept backwards for speed greater than an airplane. With fluid, practiced motions, she grabbed the bridle reins.

"What are you waiting for?" she shouted with glee, pulling back on the reins to aim Camille's head skyward.

"Hold on tight!" Camille joined in the frivolity.

Feet in the stirrups, Sunny gripped the reins and tightened her legs around Camille's muscular neck and sides.

Camille spread out his wings as Marshall moved out of the way. With his enormous falcon wings outstretched, he began to slowly flap up and down, warming the muscles. With each wing beat, Sunny felt Camille's powerful bunching muscles under her legs.

Marshall shielded his eyes as dirt and dust churned with Camille's faster and faster wing beats. *Swoosh, swoosh, swoosh!* The wide smile never left Marshall's face, even with a mouthful of dust.

"Here we go!" Camille's wing strokes grew more powerful, swifter.

"C'mon already!" Sunny yelled above the tremendous swooshing wing beats.

From a crouch, Camille kicked away from the ground, springing into the air. Sunny's heart skipped a beat as he lifted off, airborne. This wasn't her uncle's horse or crop-dusting airplane. This is incredible, unbelievable!

Still shielding his eyes below them, Marshall waved to the couple as they lifted into the dark heavens. Sunny returned his wave. He grew smaller and smaller as Camille gained altitude. Camille craned his neck back toward Sunny to speak.

"We're not far from the Hudson River. We'll stay low and hidden in the shadows until we pass the George Washington Bridge."

Sunny hardly heard a word, distracted as the exhilarating, breathtaking ride mesmerized her, sending happy chills up her spine.

With greater wing sweeps and powerful strokes, Camille discreetly flew them through the dark night over warehouses and wholesale businesses in the Meatpacking District. Once they were over the waters of the Hudson, he seemed to shift gears, relaxing. Sunny gazed above at glittery stars in the heavens, the same heaven she saw upside down as the gorilla scrambled up the birch tree with her draped over his massive furry shoulders. She stroked Camille's soft neck feathers as a gesture, thanking him for saving her life and including her in his life, trusting her to keep his secrets.

With his expansive falcon wingtips skimming the cool, dark waters of the Hudson, Camille and Sunny quietly, leisurely, passed under the George Washington Bridge, leaving New York City's bright lights and ceaseless hubbub behind. Effortlessly, Camille's powerful, steady wing beats carried them north. He craned his neck to her.

"Riding is old hat to you. I almost gave up on Marshall when he first started flying. Slipping and sliding all over my back, throwing me off balance and wobbling all over the sky. I was ready to drop him off at JFK airport to buy himself a plane ticket to Sunadaga territory."

The wind whipped her hair behind her. "All that farm work *finally* paid off," she said with a laugh.

Sunny's cell phone rang. She held the reins with one hand as she fished her phone from her pocket. *Damn. Don't drop it in the Hudson.* It was KD. Why was he calling her this late? This must be important.

"What's up, partner?" she answered with more amusement in her voice than she intended.

There was a pause. "Where are you? Sounds like you have your head stuck out a car window like one of those slobbering dogs."

Close. Sunny pulled back on the reins as she did with Thunder on her uncle's farm. Camille slowed, cruising now.

"Crime lab just call me," KD said. "They're still working the DNA but they found a nearly invisible laser cut serial number etched into the back of the watch."

"Fantastic!"

"They said the watch was sold in a jewelry store in Poughkeepsie."

Sunny was still learning New York, especially upstate New York. She finally felt confident about traveling the five New York City boroughs: Manhattan, Brooklyn, Queens, Staten Island, and the Bronx, and most of Long Island. But upstate? She deferred to KD, who was born and raised in New York.

"I went to a friend's wedding in Poughkeepsie a few years back," KD added.

"So we need to go to Poughkeepsie?" She thought she heard a toilet flush. "Where are *you*?"

"I'm hiding in the men's room at a Broadway theater. I promised Angela that I wouldn't allow the Job to ruin the stage performance and dinner tonight. Didn't think that Forensics would come back so fast with something. And since the brass is up our asses, we should get a head start."

"What do you need me to do?" Sunny asked.

Camille started having a little fun. He rocked smoothly from one side to the other, sending them zigzagging above the sparkling waters. Sunny smiled at the antics, then jerked the reins twice, signaling for him to knock it off.

"I'm forwarding you the e-mail with the watch serial number in the attachment. Get us a subpoena to take to the jewelry store with us. I'll be home pretty late."

"I can handle it. Give me about an hour."

"Cool. I'll pick you up at your place in the morning, and we'll head upstate."

Chapter Twenty-eight

With a moonless, cloudless, star-studded sky above and cool Hudson River waters rushing below, Sunny jabbed her cell phone back in her pocket after talking to KD. She took the bridle in both hands. Camille flew at a steady pace. Like a horse jockey, Sunny timed her body roll to each strong wing beat, moving as one.

"The watch you found could pay big dividends, Camille," Sunny said with the crisp wind in her face, windblown hair flowing backward.

"Glad I could help."

Aloft on great falcon wings for nearly twenty miles north of New York City, they glided toward the three-mile-long Governor Mario Cuomo Bridge spanning the Hudson River connecting Rockland and Westchester Counties. Tonight, soft LED lighting illuminated the lengthy span in red, white, and blue.

"I'm going to turn here to get you back so you can continue the investigation. That'll give me a chance to tell you my story."

Sunny knew bits and pieces of Camille's life. Now, she would finally get the whole story. "This I want to hear."

Camille dipped his long, outstretched wing to the left, banking in a wide arch. With effortless, rhythmic wing beats, they headed home.

"I should have listened to my mother and gotten my butt in the house," Camille started. "I was twelve, up in the tree in our backyard playing with Jake, my pet chameleon. A storm was brewing and the tree was swaying, but I needed to see Jake shift to one more pattern, so I continued to play. The way Jake transformed always amazed me. Five minutes later, I put Jake on my shoulder so I could climb down, but it was too late. A bolt of lightning hit my shoulder where Jake was."

"Oh my God!" Sunny interjected. "Were you okay?"

"Hell no! Knocked me right out of the tree, ten feet below. I was in a coma for a week. The doctors didn't think I was going to make it. My parents were planning my funeral."

"So that's how you got that big burn scar on your shoulder?"

"Yep. The doctors pulled a few pieces of what was left of Jake out of my shoulder. Jake took the direct hot lightning bolt hit. Most of Jake was boiled and mixed into me. Once I can come out of hiding, I want geneticists and scientists to examine me. Tell me how this happened. But in the meantime, I did some research on gene editing—transforming genes and manipulating the genetic makeup of living things. I read that shocking the cells with electricity—like lightning in my case—kickstart their transformation. I acquired extra powers, morphing, transforming, shifting."

"Like into a humongous falcon," Sunny snickered from behind Camille's head.

"Or a gorilla...or rat. I can go on and on. Anyway, once I went to prison, I really focused on my new powers. One night, a little mouse escaped the prison, leaving behind a pile of prison clothes in my cell."

"And that tiny mouse was you?"

"Yours truly." He dipped one wing, then the other, playfully veering from side to side. "I'm sure my cellmate was baffled when he woke up. And the warden must have been beside himself." He threw his beak forward. "Look up ahead." The New York City skyline glistened in all its glory in the distance. "I'll tell you about transforming into war mode later."

"*War mode?*" Absorbed in her cases, she vaguely recalled him expressing the term in relation to using his hair as string for the bow in his footlocker.

"Yeah. I can only go war mode when I'm *actually* threatened."

Sunny wished she could ride all night, but she needed to get to her apartment to continue working the cases. She wondered if Elaine had gained consciousness. But then again, her doctor hadn't called as promised if the savagely beaten woman improved in the least.

Camille glided back under the George Washington Bridge. To the left, the Hudson River Greenway commenced, running the length of Manhattan Island. Camille banked left, reversing his outbound path, staying low, out of sight, in the shadows. A block away from MH Construction, he kept his massive wings extended on a perfect glide slope. Rooftops passed beneath. Sunny held the reins tightly, preparing to land.

Camille's mighty falcon wings started a slow backstroke, gently applying the brakes as they dropped out of the pitch-dark night sky. He spread his tail feathers wide, then aimed them down further braking. Sunny felt forward inertia as he passed over the company's stockade fence, shedding more momentum.

As they stalled in midair, he beat his wings faster, causing the grass below to waver, bend, and flatten from the tremendous air downwash under his wings.

Back winging even faster now as the ground drew closer, Camille's great, sharp, curved talons touched down first. He landed gently and folded his wings.

Marshall exited the back door with a broad grin, wanting to know how the flight went.

The next day, the warm morning promised a hot summer day as Ariwiio Smoke stepped out on the porch of his house on Sunadaga territory near the Canadian border. A large part of Canada was once home to the Haudenosaunee Confederacy, Ariwiio's people freely moving throughout their ancestral home.

"Meow."

To Ariwiio's right, in his late wife's white Adirondack chair, the cat was back. The one who several days ago he thought he saw turn into a goose, but he wrote it off to poor late evening light and his aging eyesight.

The yellow-eyed cat lying comfortably in Angel's chair appeared to ignore Ariwiio. The cat gazed lazily at the Adirondack Mountain foothills in the distance. Ariwiio took a seat in his Adirondack chair, a small table separating him from the lounging cat. The cat opened his mouth in a silent meow of acknowledgment. In the quiet warmth, the two took in a few moments of nature together.

As president of the Sunadaga Nation, Ariwiio couldn't rest for long. Five minutes later, he groaned as he rose from the chair, his sore knees complaining. He was headed to his office in the Administration Building. Behind him, he heard the cat leap to the wooden porch with the double beat of front then rear paws. The cat followed him down the porch steps to his Ford Taurus parked in the gravel driveway. Ariwiio opened the car door, and the friendly cat leapt onto the car seat.

"Well, aren't you presumptuous?" The cheeky cat did another silent meow, no concern in his yellow eyes.

The Taurus crunched driveway gravel until Ariwiio got to the end and turned onto the rural county road. The cat curled in the passenger seat for another nap. As Sunadaga president, Ariwiio knew most of the families in the territory, but he didn't know whose cat this was. He wondered who was missing a cat.

The car weaved down the quiet two-lane road through the woods of ancient pines, woods Ariwiio's ancestors called home for thousands of years...until the colonials, including George Washington, forced the Haudenosaunee from their ancestral home.

Ariwiio blew his horn as he passed their cultural center on the left. Big Jojo and agile Anteweeno of the boy's lacrosse team mowed the grass before it was too hot out, getting the center ready for the visitors. The center educated and brought in much-needed income to the nation. The boys wiped sweat from their brows as they waved at the president.

A quarter mile farther, Ariwiio slowed to a stop to allow a mother goose to escort her young, about ten goslings, across the road to a nearby pond. The gaggle reminded him of his own family. He took the moment to think of his son Camille. Right here, Ariwiio decided to call his lawyer to direct him to make a deal with the prison for his son's remains. Ariwiio was tired, weary. He needed closure.

With the car still idling at a stop, the stray cat stood in the car seat. The cat hunched its back in a tremendous stretch while yawning widely, its tongue jutting out. Ariwiio reached over and rubbed the cat's head. "I guess I need to give you a name." With his son still on his mind, the cat lived in two worlds. Ariwiio named the cat Tee, a takeoff of Camille's Native name, Teeyeehogrow.

Moments later, he pulled into the Sunadaga Administration building parking lot. The cat hopped out the car and followed Ariiwio inside.

"Ready to scratch some naked chest?" Doris Trail, Ariiwio's secretary, shouted from her office.

Doris only recently retired as Ariwiio's full-time secretary. She was staying on part-time until Ariwiio hired a new secretary. Doris was renowned for her Native jewelry designs, something she wanted to spend more time doing in retirement.

Ariiwio entered his small office. The Sunadaga flag, the yellow sun with radiating rays, hung behind him on its pole next to his credenza. The cat hopped onto the credenza and laid his head against a picture of Ariiwio's late wife. Doris entered carrying a folder of Sunadaga Nation enrollment applications. She plopped a folder on his desk. Ariiwio groaned.

In the past, Ariiwio's people and all Indigenous people were subjected to one indignity after another—scratching the chest being but one. To determine the level of "Indianness," government agents concocted a subjective system of dragging a fingernail across the chest of a Native person. If the scratch reddened, the specimen possessed a larger degree of European blood and was thus deemed more intelligent. No mark. Unfit. True Indian.

"As usual, the ones on the bottom are wannabes," Doris explained. Many wanted to be Native these days, bitten by the casino bug.

Doris turned on her heels to leave but then spotted the cat lounging on the office credenza. "Who's cat?"

"Search me." Ariwiio swiveled in his chair to face the credenza. "Comes and goes as he pleases. I was going to ask you if you knew. You know everybody in the Haudenosaunee Confederacy."

The cat stood, stretched, then padded to the opposite side of the credenza to rest against Camille's photo now. The cat's eyelids hung lazily at half-mast.

Ariiwio was shaking his head. "This cat..." He didn't want to sound spooky. "This cat seems familiar...seems to know me."

"I'm outta here." Doris headed for the door, laughing. "You're creeping me out, Ariiwio."

His cell phone rang. He swiveled back to his desk. The phone display read Marshall.

"Well, well, if it isn't a voice from the past," Ariiwio answered. "Hey, Marshall." The cat bounded from the credenza onto Ariiwio's desk, caterwauling loudly, his tail straight up.

Camille and Marshall grew up together on the territory. Sleepovers, fishing, hunting, and lacrosse, the boys were inseparable. As men, they were still close—that was until Camille went to prison.

"When are you visiting the territory again?" Ariiwio asked. "Home." He stressed the word.

"I'm making some time, but I do have someone who wants to visit and help Camille's cause."

Ariiwio listened as Marshall described NYPD Homicide Detective Sunny McGraw, who found Camille's life and circumstances intriguing. She wanted to know how the court arrived at a conviction. She dabbled in writing novels and would donate much of the proceeds to Camille's legal fund.

"Give the detective my number," Ariiwio sighed, stroking the cat to quiet him. He didn't see how Detective McGraw could help, but she couldn't hurt either.

"That is one loud cat you got there," Marshall observed.

"You want one?" Ariwiio offered. "You can have this one."

"Naw. I have one here with a cop—" He stopped in midsentence. "A copy of...a copy of," he stammered, "a copy of a star on his back."

Ariiwio frowned in confusion. "Okay," he dragged out. "But the offer stands."

"What's with that noisy cat?" came loudly from Doris's office.

"Is that Doris? Doris *Trail*? Tell her I said hello," Marshall said, sounding glad to change the subject.

Many emphasized Doris's surname, Trail. And she was always eager to elaborate. The ancient runner of the trails once relayed communications throughout the Haudenosaunee nations. Those from other continents were astonished at how quickly word spread from one Haudenosaunee nation in America to another. The Haudenosaunee used a labyrinth of trails connecting their nations throughout the northeast. In a relay system, long before the Pony Express, hundreds of miles along the Ambassador Road were covered by runners in a single day, contributing to the strength of the Haudenosaunee Confederacy with a tight communication system. These and other Native highways extended throughout the Americas, diffusing culture and trade far and wide. Later, Native highways were used to build the United States.

Following the call with Marshall, Ariiwio gathered his pen, pad, and notes for the council meeting to be held at their alternative location—the longhouse. He also grabbed blueprints of the new boy's and girl's lacrosse field. A new field probably wouldn't help the boy's losing record, but he had a plan to address their flagging spirits. Ariwiio was once their coach until Camille took over. Ariwiio decided to use the same sweat lodge strategy his coach used to get his old team back to a winning record.

Unsurprisingly, when Ariwiio left his office, he realized the cat had disappeared...again.

***

Sergey's Russian organized crime boss threatened to bust him back down to a bit player, shaking down shop owners for protection money and drug dealers for shorting the mob's cut in a transaction. The thirsty waitress at the South Dakota airport ruined his well-laid assassination plot. Airport security personnel raced into the restaurant as Sergey boarded his flight. He would try to be more careful with the remainder of the Smoke family.

He watched the Taurus leave the Sunadaga Administration building. Sergei anxiously fondled the small T-Rex bone that hung from his thin leather necklace, the second one he'd made. He peered from behind a huge maple tree at the edge of the property. Where was the man driving? *This is one active family.* Sergey darted into the woods to retrieve his Jeep.

He gunned the engine, searching for the Taurus. He rounded a bend on the two-lane road and spotted the car about an eighth mile ahead. The Jeep stopped accelerating, and Sergey finally sat back in the seat. He checked the glove compartment for his gun. Last night, he'd done more research on the family. The old man's wife was dead, and his son was missing...from prison. In the news article interview, Ariwiio Smoke believed his son was dead. The old man was suing the prison system for his son's body. Damn! This family had been visited by much grief. But Sergey knew what the Russian mob would do to him if he didn't finish a job, so he kept reminding himself that this was only work.

The Taurus's left turn signal lit up, and the car turned. Sergey couldn't see where the car went until he drove casually by. The structure looked...tunnel-like...a long, dome structure with one door in front. The parking lot was half full. Sergey didn't return.

Chapter Twenty-nine

On warm Friday morning, a horn blew out front of Sunny's Chelsea apartment. It didn't sound like an NYPD department-issued unmarked. The car out front possessed a higher-pitched horn. While she could hear many horns— New Yorkers laid on their horns as an audible middle finger, this odd horn was right below her window. She was expecting KD about this time so they could travel to the jewelry store in Poughkeepsie.

The horn blew again. Somebody out front was persistent. Sunny went to the front window of her fourth-floor apartment. A red convertible Corvette sat double parked, its emergency flashers on.

"Nah, he didn't!" she drawled, faux-Bronx, her neck moving side to side.

Sunny dumped the remainder of her coffee down the kitchen sink. After double-checking Tuffy's food and water, she raced down the apartment building's center staircase and onto the stoop. The Corvette Stingray was low-slung and curvy, with rumbling chrome side pipes that ran under each door. KD's wide smile said he knew she would be surprised. His arm hung out the car in a dashing fashion, too cool.

"May I drive?" Sunny knew the answer but had to bust his chops just for sport.

He shook his bald head vigorously, playing along. "Not now! Not ever!" He flashed his pearly whites. "This is my baby." He slapped the steering wheel with both hands. "Not even my fiancé touches this steering wheel."

Sunny allowed a car to pass. She opened the passenger door and hopped in.

KD drove the same route west as Sunny used to jog to the Hudson River Greenway, where she was assaulted, and Christine Lowry was killed. Early in the morning, people were already walking atop the Highline elevated park as the rumbling Vette passed underneath.

"No way was I driving a piece of shit unmarked to Poughkeepsie," KD said as he turned north onto the West Side Highway. "I got music. I got my coooool car."

He turned on the stereo. Lady Gaga's silky voice seemed to surround Sunny. Speakers were in the door, behind her head, and she believed under the seat judging by the vibrations to her butt. She had the feeling of being at a live concert. Sunny joined in with Lady Gaga singing "Take my hand."

"Please. No!" KD interrupted. The Vette roared in first gear. He stabbed the sports car into second, throwing them back into the white bucket seats.

"What? I have Lady Gaga on my iPhone," Sunny remarked.

"So. You wanna make my ears bleed?" He laughed, then joined in with her singing the tune.

In the morning rush hour, people in adjacent cars stared at the two songbirds in the little red convertible. A few bobbed their heads to the music. Others seemed annoyed.

It wasn't until the drive approached the proximity of Elaine's crime scene that they grew serious. KD turned down the music.

"I called the hospital yesterday evening," he said. "Elaine hasn't made any progress. It's not looking hopeful."

Sunny felt a tightness in her stomach. Elaine had taken such a vicious beating. Somewhere under all the bloated skin and bruises was a human being clinging to life.

"As I told you already, I didn't get much from Club Posh or the cab's interior video, but I have a feeling this wristwatch lead will help this case," Sunny said assuredly.

KD glanced at her, then back to the road. "You sound confident."

Yes. She was confident. A big rat told her. "We're going to nail these bastards."

Once she returned from Poughkeepsie, Camille had promised to investigate with her the *second* four-square-block scent trail hotspot in the Upper West Side, scents related to Elaine's assault and battery. He certainly couldn't walk around as himself. She wondered what shifting he had in mind. A bloodhound? But she'd never seen anyone walking a floppy-eared bloodhound in NYC. Maybe a poodle.

Five minutes later, at a stoplight, KD dug in his pocket and extracted a twenty-dollar bill. He handed the bill to Sunny.

"Call her over and give it to her, please." Sunny complied.

A homeless woman with dirty red stringy hair, pushing a shopping cart filled with soda cans and blankets, shuffled to the car. The light had turned green, and horns were already sounding behind them. KD raised his arm high, giving the agitated crowd the bird. The thankful woman smiled toothlessly with a "God bless you."

"You hand out a lot of cash," Sunny observed, remembering the cash handout in Alphabet City.

The traffic was thinner as they drove farther north along the West Side Highway of Manhattan. KD shifted to third gear, the Vette growling. "There's far too much economic disparity in the US," KD explained his charitable handouts. "Let's get out of New York City so I can show you what I mean."

The George Washington Bridge came into view. The bridge connected New York City to New Jersey. In the light of day, Sunny was trying to figure out which section of the bridge she and Camille quietly flew under last night. A pleasant smile crossed her face.

Chapter Thirty

The sign ahead announced the Henry Hudson Bridge out of Manhattan and into the Bronx. A few miles later, KD merged the Corvette onto the Saw Mill Parkway. Soon, they were in the city of Hawthorne on the Taconic State Parkway. The Vette ate up the miles. KD enjoyed the experience, his left arm still dashingly hanging out of the car. Sunny adjusted her Saint Laurents against the sun's glare.

The scenery here wasn't the congested Manhattan skyscraper and apartment on top of the apartment landscape. Trees. So many trees. Everywhere. That was what first caught Sunny's attention. Neighborhoods. Expensive. Well-manicured lawns.

KD shifted into fifth gear and the engine rumble changed to a purr. They both wore dark shades. A few white fluffy cumulus clouds floated in the blue sky.

"I want one of these." Sunny patted the car door, indicating she wanted a Corvette also. "How long have you had it?"

"It was my father's. His hobby. I take him for drives when he feels up to it. A stress buster, he called it."

Sunny could never forget how she tragically lost her father to a gunshot in the left ear while sitting in his patrol car or how KD's father was left paralyzed by a stroke.

"He would take me on Sunday rides in this car," KD continued. "Just the two of us." His voice went wistful. "The beach...ice cream. We had a blast." He laughed loudly. "They're going to have to bury me in this bad boy." His hand affectionately stroked the top of the steering wheel.

He reached for his cell phone. "Let me show you this while the Taconic State Parkway is straight. It's a roller coaster just north of us. And I love it!"

Deftly, with his thumb, he entered his password to unlock the phone. He passed the device to Sunny. She raised her shades atop her head.

"You asked about the money I give to the needy. My father taught high school history. He knows American history backward and forward and was obsessed with *general* poverty in the wealthiest nation in world history. My old man broke down for his students what he believed the major causes of poverty in the US, the Three E's: attempted extermination of Native Americans, enslavement of African Americans, and exploitation of the poor from Europe and other places." KD pointed at the cell phone. "My father grew up surrounded by African American poverty. He concentrated on one aspect of African-American poverty because the indisputable commerce numbers are in every history book. He found a way to translate the vague statistics from the highfalutin language of academia so that his young students and the person in the street could understand. This template can work for any pocket of poverty." He instructed Sunny on how to access the pictures on his phone.

Sunny puzzled at the numbers and graphs on the screen until KD filled her in on the meaning.

"Cotton—*White Gold* they called it—at its yearly

height constituted sixty percent of US exports—goods and services—the US sells to other countries. That created a lot of good-paying US jobs. Cotton kicked off the first industrial revolution. It was a large part of the foundation of the US economy." KD glanced at the sideview mirror. "Pop researched and figured today's equivalent of cotton at its height would equate to Americans purchasing nearly *two years'* worth of brand-new cars and trucks—approximately one and a half trillion dollars. Mind you, slavery went on for two hundred and fifty years. Two hundred and fifty years of "free stuff" as they say, going to other American families. And we haven't even included the internal US market of cotton, tobacco, sugar, and rice." He paused looking over at Sunny. "Do you think this wealth should be returned to African Americans?"

It was something she had pondered in the past. If someone took something of great wealth that she was in line to inherit, she would pursue it to the hilt. "If the wealth were mine, I would want it returned." She shook her head. "This is such a complicated subject. I never owned any slaves. What am I supposed to do?"

KD signaled to get in the left lane to pass a white Mercedes. He drifted back into the right lane of the Taconic State Parkway. Without taking his eyes off the winding road, he nodded his head toward the phone. "I'm not trying to be facetious, but it doesn't say *Sunny's* exports on that screen. It says: *US* exports. The US—North and South—was advantaged. Slavery was enshrined in the US Constitution." He raised his shades and momentarily glanced at Sunny, then back to the parkway. "Cotton *Union* flags flew over people wearing cotton in the north, also using it in their homes and businesses. Cotton *Confederate* flags flew over people wearing cotton in the south, using it in their homes and businesses."

She was nodding understanding. "So, you're saying that the wealth gap should be addressed at the national level?"

"That's what I believe. Sue the company, not the individual stockholder," KD said while checking his sideview mirror again.

She looked at the last graph on the screen. It showed one line hovering high above another. It was entitled: "White vs Black Wealth Gap, 10 to 1."

"This certainly can't be me. I don't own a Corvette." She stabbed her finger at the graph and laughed.

KD glanced at the phone, then back to the road. He laughed along with her. "That's funny." He lifted his hand from the stick shift and raised a let-me-have-your-attention index finger. "Remember, I said Pop wanted to address *general* poverty? I believe he was truly trying to be fair. There are varying depths and reasons for poverty in our nation, and these variations must be considered. Listen to this. If a burglar steals one hundred thousand dollars from one neighbor and then fifty thousand dollars from the next neighbor, when the burglar is caught, each neighbor isn't owed seventy-five thousand dollars apiece." He jacked up his eyebrows waiting for a response.

"You make a lot of factual and logical sense," Sunny reasoned. She knew that women today sought economic justice also. They earned between sixty and eighty cents on the dollar of men. Giving them both a dollar raise wouldn't fix the wage gap. And her family certainly could have used some *general* poverty help, especially when she was a little girl. Growing up in the trailer park, she understood the sting and shame of poverty. She was too young to fully grasp the cruel taunts of the wealthier kids at her elementary school, but she knew she was different.

The Vette crested the hill, and Sunny had that lifting-out-of-her-seat rollercoaster sensation. A BMW pulled up to KD's side, challenging him to race. KD flashed the peace sign and his signature smile. The Bimmer accelerated away.

"He'll end up crashed on this winding, twisting road," KD said, shaking his head. The Vette maintained a steady speed, the side pipes droning. He draped his hand over the stick shift, relaxing. "So, that's where I get my interest in poverty from. It just shouldn't be like this in such a wealthy nation...considering our past."

The Taconic State Parkway inclined, the area quite hilly. KD shifted to fourth, and Sunny felt herself glued to the seat as the engine's torque increased. Her shades fell over her eyes, but she lifted them again.

Sunny handed KD his phone back. She hadn't known this side of her partner. Her respect grew even more. The life lessons their late fathers taught still propelled them in their adult lives. Louis McGraw wanted to make the world safer, starting on the streets of Oklahoma City. He lost his life pursuing his convictions, but not before instilling in his youngest daughter the same ambitions.

"I'm going to make certain I keep some cash on me," Sunny said as she lowered her shades. They turned and smiled at each other.

Portions of the Taconic State Parkway were cut through solid granite so close Sunny felt she could almost reach out and touch the rocks. KD slowed as they rounded a deep curve. A blue and yellow New York State trooper cruiser was pulled to the side, its rooftop beacon flashing red.

KD downshifted and switched to the left lane as per New York law when passing an emergency vehicle. As they passed, they saw the Bimmer driver slumped embarrassingly in the car seat. KD couldn't resist honking the horn to rub it in.

A little over an hour north of Manhattan, they exited on a loop to Interstate 84 West back over the Taconic. The expressway skirted southern Dutchess County. KD momentarily floored the car, pining Sunny to her seat as they merged into the fast-moving traffic, tractor-trailers and all.

Two miles later, KD's phone rang. It was Elaine's surgeon, Dr. Shirley Johnson. He put it on speakerphone.

"Please give us some good news, Doc," KD pleaded.

"Afraid I can't. I told you I would keep you up-to-date on Elaine's condition. We had to rush her into surgery and drill a few more holes in her skull to relieve more pressure. Sorry."

KD thanked the doctor just as they approached Route 9, the original main north-south drag from the New York state capital of Albany to Manhattan.

"Elaine's parents disowned her," KD finally commented as he headed north on Route 9.

Sunny sighed heavily. "That's awful. She's alone...at death's door." Sunny massaged her forehead in agony. Elaine was rejected by her family and beaten to within an inch of her life by a cruel society. Poor woman. Sunny wanted KD to step on it to get to Miller Jewelers right away. The scum who bought the watch had assaulted her, stole Christine's life, and nearly killed Elaine. Her foot pressed into the passenger side carpet to move the car faster.

Stoplight after stoplight, the detectives made their way along the business district of Route 9. KD knew the Poughkeepsie area after attending a friend's wedding several years ago. This felt more like Oklahoma City to Sunny, with plenty of grocery stores, salons, fast food chains, and working-class neighborhoods with swing sets and above-ground pools in the backyards.

She thought about suggesting a quick lunch at one of the many restaurants but decided to forge ahead to solve this case now before someone else was assaulted or killed. Another slow twenty minutes of stop and go, and the detectives caught sight of the Galleria Mall on the left. Miller Jewelers was an eighth-mile north of the mall. It was going to feel good to stretch her legs.

A tiny bell tinkled above the jewelry store door as the detectives entered. A man behind the counter peered around a father and daughter admiring a new bracelet on her arm. She wore spiked heels and very formfitting tan pants.

"I'll be right with you," the clerk said.

The woman, in her mid-twenties, gushed at the beauty of the bracelet on her arm. She flipped her blonde highlighted hair to her back as she raised her arm to eye level, rotating her wrist and admiring the bracelet. "This is gorgeous!"

Sunny supposed the diamond-studded bracelet was a birthday gift or perhaps a college graduation present. Sunny had received nothing of the sort when she was growing up. She remembered her sister's hand-me-downs and Goodwill. But once her father landed the policeman job, the family would shop across the street and half a block down at the department store with the layaway plan and the new smell.

As the father turned to view his daughter's outstretched arm, Sunny did a re-calc. The man in the dapper dark suit could be her grandfather.

"Ralph, I want it," the young woman said, then kissed him on the cheek.

"We'll take it," the man simply said to the clerk. The much older man placed an age-spotted hand on the young woman's butt.

Is there an arrest here? Sunny groaned. She glanced to see if KD took in any of this. He was busy comparing watches.

A few minutes later, the bell above the door tinkled as the odd couple left Miller Jewelers. The detectives approached the counter.

"Wedding? Engagement?" the clerk asked with a big smile, the smell of onions wafting from him. He was a short, slight man with tiny ears. He wore a black bowtie, a Peewee Herman look.

Sunny quickly looped her arm through KD's arm. She leaned her head against his shoulder, looked up at him, then at the clerk. "What's your most expensive wedding ring?"

KD's eyes smiled, but he sighed exasperatedly as he quickly unlooped their arms. "We're NYPD detectives, Mister—" he announced, pulling back his jacket to reveal his belt-attached shield. Sunny did the same. Here, too, they didn't announce they were *homicide* detectives.

"I'm Eugene Miller, owner, operator here. How may I help you, Detectives?" The slight man with the onion breath started out quite solicitous.

From a large envelope, KD pulled out enlarged photos of the watch found in the sewer pipe under the Dumpster. Sunny's mind flashed to Camille transformed into a rat, pointing out the hidden watch.

"There's a serial number right here," KD pointed out. "Who did you sell this to?"

"Umm. That's one of my top-of-the-line Rolexes," Eugene Miller shared proudly. He stroked his chin thoughtfully. "But I'm afraid I can't help you, Detectives."

They headed Eugene Miller off at the pass. KD produced the subpoena, flipped it open, and held it high. The jeweler got the message. He studied the subpoena and then took the photos from KD.

"It was sold here alright," Eugene Miller confirmed. "Let me see..." He turned on his heels to type the serial number into a computer, several times glancing at the photo to get the serial numbers correct.

"Oh!" the jeweler exclaimed, his back to the detectives, scratching his tiny ear.

"What do you have?" Sunny asked impatiently.

The man returned to the display counter. "Mr. Chambers of Chambers Realty here in the Hudson Valley. He used to sell real estate in New York City. You may have heard of him. I sold the watch to him. May I ask what this is about?"

"No," KD answered flatly, simply. "We'll need a copy of the sales receipt, address, and all."

The slight man printed the sales transaction and gave directions to an address in Millbrook. KD was familiar with the location about half an hour away.

"We thank you, Mr. Miller," Sunny said as she folded and pocketed the sales printout and took a quick step back. She needed fresh air to wash away the onion smell. She was at least glad he wasn't spitting also.

The bell above the door jingled as the detectives left for Millbrook.

Chapter Thirty-one

The Sunadaga Council meetings alternated between the Administration Building and a replica of an original Haudenosaunee longhouse that Ariwiio and others constructed decades ago on Sunadaga territory. The elm bark siding replica kept them in touch with the spirit and tradition of their forebears, who lived on this same soil for thousands of years. They were the Haudenosaunee—the People of the Longhouse.

Ariwiio entered the front door of the longhouse, distracted by the call he was going to have with his attorney to propose the release of his son's remains in exchange for dropping the lawsuit. He wasn't sure what Detective McGraw could do at this late point.

Councilmembers talked idly to each other as he passed. Sunlight beamed in through the back door, sixty feet away. The structure was windowless. Above, a latticework of small elm branches lashed together with elm strips served as rafters. Still higher, the sun spilled in through several smoke holes fifteen feet overhead. The longhouse was twenty feet wide. Two-tiered bunks lined each side wall running the length of the structure, the bottom for sleeping, the top for storage.

Ariwiio strode to the rear under the bowed roof. He greeted ten council members on his way to the spot where he usually stood when the meeting was going to be short. How was he going to get through this meeting with his anxiety rising? But closure for his son's death was in reach. He should have delayed the council meeting to call the family attorney first, but he was here now.

He was going to make this a quick meeting. Fortunately, there wasn't much on the council agenda besides the new lacrosse field. He would get out of there and get the private time he needed.

But Richard Big Tree soon upset Ariwiio's plans. Richard was from the more radical wing of the council. In 1492, he would have advocated building a wall around America to keep out the illegals. Richard stood and walked to the center of the longhouse before the entire council. In his mid-fifties, he reached for his *gustoweh*—pronounced *go-SHOH-weh,* a feathered headdress worn in the Haudenosaunee nations. He swept the turkey and hawk feathers from his eyes and hiked his jeans. Directly under a smoke hole in the roof, he commenced straightening fire stones with his black New Balance sneaker. A huge black kettle hung above the circle of stones.

Richard stood in the perfect spot to start a Smoke Dance, Ariiwio observed. But there was no smoke today.

It was said that the Smoke Dance originated from the need to force smoke through the roof hole. The longest recorded Haudenosaunee longhouse measured four hundred feet in length with over forty smoke holes to release the cooking smoke that also cured meat and corn. Through matrilineal order, Haudenosaunee women owned the longhouses. An elder mother, with her daughters,

181

granddaughters, and so on, kept extending the longhouse as marriages occurred. All lived under one roof.

Ariwiio brought the meeting officially to order. He was certain what Richard wanted to discuss—the grapevine informing him—but he asked anyway.

"Richard, let's open with your agenda item."

The man stopped manipulating the fire stones and took a seat on the platform. Above his head hung a gorgeous blue and white handmade black ash basket and a few dried ears of corn.

"We must build a casino," Richard expressed flatly, and exactly what Ariwiio had heard was on the man's mind.. "We need the jobs."

"Richard, our rural location, far from any city center, is unlikely to attract customers. It's too risky." A few nations of the Haudenosaunee Confederacy operated casinos, but these were near large cities.

"Ariwiio, you hold us back," Richard parried. "You and your family are too soft, too cautious," he blurted.

An elder councilwoman, April Shenandoah, seated across from Richard, reflexively clasped her hands in her lap. She and Richard Big Tree had a heated exchange at the last council meeting in the Administration Building. Richard favored selling parcels of Sunadaga territory to outside developers. April and others, including Ariwiio, would have none of it.

Wringing her snarled hands, April glared out the longhouse backdoor, ignoring Richard. Divisions within the council ran deep, but all maintained the proper decorum the longhouse demanded.

The council took a quick vote to put down the casino idea. Richard Big Tree wasn't finished. In the Sunadaga elected system, Richard vowed to run against Ariwiio in the next presidential election. The council moved to other subjects.

Ariwiio wished Camille were here to discuss the new lacrosse field. At every opportunity, he had called on Camille and Amber to attend the council meetings as subject matter experts and to expose them to politics, conflict, and leadership. Ariwiio shared the latest lacrosse field blueprints, and a few routine budget matters with the council and later adjourned the meeting. Next week's council meeting was in the Administration Building. What fireworks awaited?

It was noon when Ariwiio arrived at the cemetery on the edge of the territory. Under the warm sun, he stood before his wife's grave. Her mysterious one-car accident still haunted him. He needed to offload some of the torment of losing two family members in such close order, a one-two punch in the gut.

He surveyed the Smoke family burial plots, his, Amber's, Camille's. A parent shouldn't have to bury a child, he pondered sadly, gazing at Camille's plot. That was just not Nature's order. On his wife's grave, he laid yellow roses snipped from Angel's flower garden, a piece of home.

"Angel," Ariwiio began, "I'm going to call our attorney to drop the prison lawsuit in exchange for Camille's remains." He wiped damp eyes with the back of his hand. The prison claimed Camille just *disappeared*. "I'll be the next to join you and Camille."

Route 44 out of Poughkeepsie wasn't the congested West Side Highway, nor the FDR on the east side of Manhattan, and that suited Sunny just fine. The drivers here were actually courteous. Route 44 narrowed from four lanes to two, and drivers politely allowed the dovetailing of cars. If this were New York City, she could just see the fender benders and road rage of those getting cut off.

Sunny spotted a McDonald's in a village called Pleasant Valley. The hunger was too great. KD pulled into the drive-thru and killed the thumping engine in order to hear the server in the speaker.

Back on the road, burgers in hand, Sunny received a text message from ADA Greg for dinner tonight. She told him where she was and that dinner was a maybe.

GPS guided them through the village of Millbrook, shops, cafés, and restaurants. Ten minutes later, as they wound around a wooded country road, a lone white house appeared in the distance. KD drove closer. The house was a mansion resembling *the* White House.

In the center of the vast green lawn, a fountain squirted a jet of water twenty feet high. Four two-story Greek columns supported the portico's roof.

"I think we should have driven the Rolls-Royce instead," KD quipped as he pulled under the portico's roof. The Corvette's side pipes echoed with a rumble until he shut the engine off.

On Sunny's side of the car, a massive front door opened, polished copper hand and kick plates glistening. A woman with a deep scowl on her regal face appeared. With not one hair out of place in her blonde hair, she looked to be in her late-fifties. Pearls the size of marbles adorned her neck. Sunny quickly flashed her shield as she exited the car.

"NYPD Detectives Sunny McGraw and Kevin Douglass, ma'am," Sunny announced. The woman reached for her pearls.

"Mrs. Shelley Chambers," the woman replied in a haughty voice, her head raised high. "What's this all about?" she demanded, clipping each word.

KD walked around the back of his car to join Sunny. He disregarded the woman's question. "Is Mr. Chambers here, Mrs. Chambers?" The husband's name was on the watch receipt. For a moment, the woman stood stunned, mouth agape like one used to getting her way. Then, she led the detectives inside.

The place was cavernous—antiques, expensive rugs, and exquisite oil paintings on the wall.

"Wait in the morning room." She pointed to a room to the right. "Rosa! Rosa!" Mrs. Chambers called into the house. A maid appeared. She was Latino, wearing a gray uniform and a white apron.

"Yes, Mrs. Chambers," Rosa replied.

"Get Mr. Chambers. I believe he's in the greenhouse."

"No, ma'am. He in the vineyard. I see him drive tractor there," Rosa said in a thick, Spanish-accented, broken English.

"Have the gardener stop trimming the hedges and go get Mr. Chambers," the woman ordered. She turned back to the detectives. "Sorry to put you in the morning room so late in the day. Rosa hasn't cleaned the parlor yet. I'll go get us tea while we wait for Mr. Chambers." The woman walked away, calling Rosa to help her in the kitchen.

Sunny was the first to enter the morning room and immediately jumped back at the snarling canine teeth that met her. An enormous bearskin rug lay at the entrance to the room. KD snickered at her startled reaction.

"A *morning* room?" KD whispered, turning in a circle to take it all in.

"Really! This is almost as big as my entire apartment." Sunny looked around. "I feel like one of the *Beverly Hillbillies* my father would watch in re-runs." KD got the sixties comedy reference and laughed.

KD walked through the spacious room, sun flowing in from floor-to-ceiling windows. He opened an oversized book labeled *Westdale*, which lay on its dedicated table. Sunny observed the pictures as he flipped the pages. It was a history of the property. The original mansion was built before the Civil War. One diagram showed the vast property layout: lakes, orchards, horse stables, slave quarters, fox hound kennel, a mill.

"Slave quarters?" KD mock shuttered.

Mrs. Chambers returned, Rosa in tow carrying a tea tray. Rosa placed the tray on a table next to the bearskin rug and asked how they liked their tea.

"And I can't get you to tell me what brings you here all the way from Manhattan?" Mrs. Chambers prodded.

KD slurped his tea dramatically, and the woman raised her chin higher. "I'm sorry, Mrs. Chambers, but the answer is still no."

Mrs. Chambers didn't get her way again, and Sunny was certain this wasn't her last attempt at ferreting out their reason for speaking to Mr. Chambers exclusively. Sunny changed the subject.

"This is quite a place you have here." She was certain the lady would elaborate.

The elegantly dressed Mrs. Chambers sipped her tea and placed the cup down gently. "My husband's family built it." Sunny was sure KD would like to add that surely those enslaved had a big hand in building it. Mrs. Chambers pointed at the property book that KD left open. "This area of upstate New York was once wilderness until his family tamed it." She turned to tell Rosa to hurry Mr. Chambers on.

KD rolled his eyes while Mrs. Chambers wasn't looking. Sunny had seen KD squirm uncomfortably in the past at certain subjects. She did the same on drunken Irish subjects. KD probably knew the exact Indigenous nations forced out in the taming to make way for Château Chambers.

Rosa reentered the morning room with a large smile on her face. She clasped her hands before her. Footsteps were behind her on the marble floor. A large man in a floppy beige safari hat with piercing gray eyes entered the morning room. Mrs. Chambers quickly rose and went to his side.

"Howard, to no avail, I tried to get these detectives to tell me what this was all about," she huffily announced. Mrs. Chambers held onto her husband's forearm, leaning into him.

"It's okay, darling," he said, removing his gardening gloves. He handed the gloves to Rosa. "Detectives, how may I help you?" He pointed to the tea tray, and Rosa prepared his cup.

"Mr. Chambers, just a few questions," KD began. "Where were you Monday night?"

He looked at his wife for an answer. "I was here. Shelley here can vouch for me." He scowled as he spoke the words.

"Absolutely," Shelley Chambers agreed, still standing next to her man. "We were bottling wine from our vineyard."

"Can anyone *outside* of this household verify that you were here?" KD asked. Sunny noticed KD headed off, using the help as corroboration.

The Chambers gazed at each other for a few beats before Mrs. Chambers suddenly remembered something. "Howard, the UPS man. You signed for the delivery at the door. It's all on our security camera."

"And what about Wednesday night?" Sunny asked. The night Elaine was beaten and left for dead.

The Chambers said they had been at Westdale all week, processing grapes, bottling wine, and labeling.

Sunny removed a photo of the watch from an envelope. Without words, she handed the photo to Howard Chambers. She wanted to study his reaction. Something wasn't adding up. She was trying to picture this man, who wore fancy gardening attire, in New York City, assaulting, raping, killing...but then again, a psychopath could be the PTA president, the softball coach. The detectives had to check all the boxes. Mrs. Chambers spoke first.

"Look, Howard, someone has a watch just like Howard Jr.'s," she observed to her husband, pointing at the picture with impeccable nails.

Howard Chambers nodded in agreement, studying the photo. "So what is this?" he finally asked.

"We're investigating an assault and a homicide in Manhattan," KD explained. The Howards stiffened. "This was found at one of the crime scenes."

"Okay. Rolex makes plenty of these watches, so—" Howard Chambers started, but KD cut him off.

"Not with a serial number leading to you," KD countered. "Where is Howard Jr.? We need to ask him some questions."

"Well, I'm afraid that's impossible," Mrs. Chambers said, her voice cracking. She started nervously fingering her pearl necklace again, looking up at her husband.

"When can we speak to him, ma'am?" Sunny pressed onward.

The woman's other hand flew to her mouth. "He's dead. Died in a cliff climbing accident several years ago." She buried her face in her husband's shoulder.

Mr. Chambers elaborated that the expensive Rolex was a gift to Howard Jr. for placing number one in wrestling in the lower Hudson Valley region.

"Follow me," Howard Chambers directed. "Something's not right. My son's watch is in its case in the parlor. The watch you have can't be my son's. We keep it in the parlor on the mantle with his many trophies."

They all made their way down a wide hall with luxurious paintings of fox hunts, steeplechases, and landscapes. To their left spread an immense dining room with a table for twenty, chandeliers, china closets, cut flowers in vases. Sunny inwardly whistled at the opulence. There would be no drinking *Kool-Aid* from a mayonnaise jar here like she did as a little girl. The Chambers finally turned into a room four times the size of the morning room.

"I apologize. Rosa hasn't cleaned the parlor today," Mrs. Chambers apparently felt obligated to say. The marble floor was mirror-shiny.

Mr. Chambers lifted a watch case from the huge fireplace mantle. Wrestling trophies and pictures surrounded the case, a veritable shrine to Howard Jr.

"There seems to be a huge mistake, Detectives," Howard Chambers said, holding the royal blue Rolex watch case with reverence. "Here's Howard Jr.'s watch." He handed the case to Sunny, who was the closest to him.

Sunny attempted to open the case but chose the wrong side. She spun the case and tried again. It snapped open. The case was empty. *Is this some kind of joke on law enforcement these people are playing?* she thought. She turned the case for all to see.

Mrs. Chambers gasped, and her mouth fell open. She clutched the pearls. Mr. Chambers cursed under his breath. KD glowered at the Chambers.

Then, out of nowhere, Mrs. Chambers screamed, "Rosa!"

When Rosa didn't immediately appear, the woman shouted Rosa over and over. The stress in a lady's voice rose until she was nearly hoarse.

Rosa suddenly appeared, breathless, at the parlor's threshold. She was wiping her wet hands on her apron, a bewildered, terrified expression on her face.

Mrs. Chambers was red-faced as she glared at Rosa. "You said you have family in New York City, right?" Rosa nodded her head, fear in her eyes. "You stole my son's watch and gave it to them, didn't you?"

Rosa's eyes fell on the empty case in Sunny's hand. "No, ma'am. I only clean around watch case. No touch, ma'am. I never—"

"You're fired!" Mrs. Chambers shouted. "Get out now!" She pointed at the door. After Rosa left in tears, head hanging, Mrs. Chambers straightened her dress and cleared her throat. "I will have none of that."

Sunny was shocked at the suddenness of termination. Following the woman's outburst that sent poor Rosa packing, Sunny stepped to the mantle to replace the empty watch case. Her mind was working the Rosa theft angle, but the puzzle pieces weren't fitting. She placed the case among the many trophies and pictures of Howard Junior. But on closer inspection, she realized that there were two different young men in the mantle pictures. And all the trophies were for wrestling...but a few were engraved with *Luke Chambers*. Sunny discreetly inquired.

"Luke is our youngest son," Howard Chambers said proudly. "He's a student at West Side University in Manhattan."

Even in the short time Sunny had partnered with KD, the two had developed nonverbals to relay messages between them. *Don't tip off the Chambers.* It was time to visit West Side University.

As the Chambers led the detectives out of the parlor, suddenly crashing and cracking sounds echoed in the expansive hall. When they reached the dining room, a raging, red-faced Rosa had the priceless china closets open, flinging fine china with both hands against the wall, trashing the place. Sunny couldn't understand the Spanish words, but she picked up the angry emotions. The Chambers held onto each other, flinching with each expensive crash.

On the outskirts of rustic Millbrook, KD pulled off the road at the sign for a help-yourself vegetable stand. Next to small wicker baskets of cucumbers, tomatoes, and ears of corn was a large glass jar of dollar bills and coins.

KD selected a basket of tomatoes. "My mother loves vine-ripened tomatoes." He dropped a few dollars into the jar.

Spending plenty of time on her uncle's farm, Sunny could tell that the owner of the Millbrook vegetable stand was no slouch. She dropped several dollars into the jar for a basket of sweet corn.

"Thank you." The voice came from a tall, lanky, seventy-ish man wearing a huge straw hat and dirt on his jean's knees. The only thing missing was a corn pipe. He carried vegetable replenishments for the stand. He introduced himself as Craig Wagner.

"You wouldn't happen to have some green tomatoes out there, would you, Mr. Wagner?" KD inquired, pointing at the garden. "My mother fries them."

"A woman after my own heart." The friendly man placed his hand over his heart. "Give me two minutes," Craig Wagner said as he fast stepped back toward the garden and disappeared behind tall cornstalks. Moments later returned with an armful of green tomatoes. "On me. Tell your mom to enjoy."

With the Corvette filled with fresh Millbrook vegetables, they were merging onto the Taconic State Parkway when Lieutenant Sanchez called. KD clicked to the speakerphone.

"I was about to call you with an update, Loo," KD said, checking his side view mirror to merge into traffic. "We're leaving Mill—"

"Later," Lieutenant Sanchez interrupted. "You two worked with those identical twins, right?"

"Right," KD responded. "Chris and Lester."

Sunny heard trouble in the lieutenant's voice. The twins had been cleared and released. They were one big happy family now.

"Lester, the architect...is dead," came over the speakerphone.

"Dead?" Sunny croaked.

"Lester Atkins was shot dead in front of the Perry Public Housing Complex. The precinct detectives believe it was gang related."

Wait a second, Sunny thought, shaking her head in confusion. "Lester wasn't a gang banger." She saw the error in her thought process before Lieutenant Sanchez said it. She angrily slapped her leg.

"Gang Unit believes there's some kind of mistaken identity at play here," Lieutenant Sanchez went on.

Sunny sighed heavily, squeezing her eyes shut in sorrow. "Can you text me Chris's number, please? I want to offer my condolences to him and then to his family." She recalled the young man's pride in lifting himself against tremendous odds and acquiring his GED in prison. He had big dreams for himself and his family. Sunny's family had escaped the trailer park. Chris sought to escape the projects.

"No need to send you the phone number," the Loo replied.

Sunny leaned toward KD's phone to be better heard above the car pipes and the wind through the convertible. "Why won't you send me the phone number, Loo?"

Lieutenant Sanchez cleared his throat. "He ate a gun while sitting on a park bench overlooking the Hudson River."

Following the traumatic phone call, the Vette's purring exhaust was the only sound for many miles. Sunny broke the silence.

"This stinks!" she said in aggravation. "It just stinks!" She was shaking her head. "I want to be part of that investigation."

"Count me in, too." KD was driving with both hands on top of the Corvette's steering wheel, tension evident in his tight grip.

They had reunited a family…if only temporarily.

Chapter Thirty-two

A lemon scent filled the air in Ariwiio Smoke's kitchen as he swept wood shavings from the black and white checkerboard tile floor. The warm running water from the faucet whipped up a froth of bubbles, and the sweet lemon fragrance rose from the sink. Amber submerged their lunch drinking glasses, silverware, and dishes into the water and then started putting away previously washed dishes from the rack.

"Where did this Tupperware come from?" Amber asked. "I didn't bring it from my house." She rotated the blue plastic Tupperware bowl, analyzing it.

Ariwiio stopped sweeping. He pointed the broom handle in the direction of the front door. "I'm finding them between the screen and front door." He grunted as he bent to sweep wood shavings from under the kitchen table.

The curly wood shavings were from carvings Ariwiio did for the dispirited boy's lacrosse team. Ever since the team lost Camille—Coach T—their record fell in the toilet. Ariwiio was using the same strategy his lacrosse coach used many years ago to motivate his boyhood team. But he should have done the carving in his garage workshop. Angel never would have approved of the mess he made in the house.

"Since we lost your mother and brother, somebody evidently knows that I've been distracted, just meeting myself coming and going," Ariwiio said of the Tupperware meals. "No time for much else as Sunadaga president, coach, etcetera. I'll have to thank somebody when I figure out who it is."

"Sounds like you have a secret admirer, Pop," Amber ribbed her dad as she placed saucers in the cupboard.

"Huh?" Ariwiio removed the dustpan from a hook near the backdoor.

"Pop, put the broom down for a moment and please look at me."

Amber sounded and looked like her mother with long, gleaming black hair and soft but firm eyes. Ariwiio took his seat. Amber sat across from him at the kitchen table. *It was just a simple meal left at his door*, he mused. He didn't see what all the fuss was about. Amber leaned forward.

"Mom would never want you to be alone," she whispered.

Ariwiio dismissively pursed his lips. He thought it was too soon to think about anyone except Angel. But he nodded his head in resignation.

"Good. You're out of practice." Amber squeezed his old hands. "We're going to work on it," she said with determination, rising to finish the dishes.

Ariwiio went back to sweeping. "Guess who called today."

"Who?"

"Marshall called as I was leaving the Administration Building. He says there is a New York City detective named Sunny McGraw who's interested in Camille's story. She wants to research his life and how he was convicted and then write a book. She says the proceeds can go toward our lawsuit." Ariwiio was back on the fence again, stressing himself. He could keep the lawsuit alive and find out what they really did to his son.

"When is she going to start?"

"Should be here tonight for introductions. Says she's flying in. I'm meeting the lacrosse team at the sweat lodge tonight. She'll contact me when she's close."

"Detective, huh? She can't bring him back to us but she sounds like just the person who can help get justice and clear Camille's name." Amber placed the last lunch plate in the strainer and wiped her hands dry. "I better get home." She kissed her father on the forehead.

"Look at all that traffic," Sunny said from the Corvette's passenger seat headed to NYC. Evening rush hour commuters fleeing New York City on the opposite northbound side of the Taconic State Parkway sped home bumper-to-bumper just south of Fishkill in Dutchess County.

"What do you think about our boy Luke?" KD said, shifting into a cruising fifth gear.

"I think we truly have a solid lead."

The location of West Side University was within Camille's scent zone in the Upper West Side, which bolstered the likelihood that Luke Chambers was the key to breaking open this case of assault and murder. It was personal for Sunny. She couldn't wait for the face-to-face encounter with someone who'd tried to snuff out her life. They didn't have PC yet, but Sunny could feel that probable cause to arrest was right around the corner.

Ten minutes later, KD's cell phone rang again. It was Elaine's doctor once more. KD placed the call on speakerphone. "Detective McGraw is here with me. Tell us something good, doc."

"I wish I could, Detective," Dr. Johnson said, her voice depressed. "I have bad news." She paused. "Elaine died."

Dammit! Sunny tensed and gnashed her teeth. The case had just increased to three murders, including Christine's baby. And her resolve doubled.

"Detectives, I'm sorry. We did all we could. Her brain just couldn't recover from that much trauma. I gotta go. They're calling me over the PA system. Her body will be in the hospital morgue."

With her family disowning her, Sunny what what would happen to Elaine. New York City operated a cemetery in the Bronx called Hart Island, where unclaimed and unidentified bodies were buried one on top of the other. Inmates from Rikers Island prison dug the graves. Elaine would probably end up there in an unmarked grave. Sunny loosened her jaw before she got a migraine.

Halfway to Manhattan now, even traffic on their southbound side of the Taconic was increasing. KD didn't want to get stuck in NYC traffic with low fuel, so he stopped forty-five minutes north in Yorktown Heights for gas. Sunny took the opportunity to stretch and give Greg a call to cancel dinner tonight.

"If I didn't know any better, I'd think that you were avoiding me," Greg said, humor in his voice. Sunny adored this side of him. She also sensed a little hurt in his tone. But she had to cancel in order to fly to Sunadaga territory with Camille tonight.

Greg had already gotten the news that Elaine didn't make it. "You folks get any new leads upstate?" he asked.

"We believe so. We'll be able to tell you more in the morning. We're still on the Job."

"No pressure, but you guys need to solve this soon. It's all over the news."

Yeah. No pressure, Sunny thought.

The Honda Civic at the pump ahead of KD's Corvette displayed a rainbow flag bumper sticker. Sunny couldn't help but think about Elaine. How could one American hate so strongly that he took the life of another American who was just minding their own business, doing nothing illegal? What gave them the right to be bully, judge, jury, and executioner? If the tables were turned, they would surely cry bloody murder!

With the car full of gas, KD flipped down the silver gas cap. Sunny thought of buying a Coke but soon thought better. If they hit heavy traffic, she didn't want a full bladder. Life in the city.

The scenery started looking familiar as KD drove the reverse commute back into Manhattan. It was slow going in New York City rush hour, but they finally made it to the Upper West Side and then on to the West Side University campus.

Chapter Thirty-three

Late Friday afternoon while looking for the Student Administration building at West Side University, the detectives studied the campus layout on a large sign next to the parking lot. Students, backpacks laden with textbooks, walked past, many with their heads down, manipulating electronic devices. In Sunny's lifetime, she had witnessed this new head-down posture in people, sometimes to disastrous ends—walking into light poles, falling into fountains, missing the curb, getting hit by cars.

The Admin Building turned out to be on the opposite side of the campus. Determined, the detectives sucked it in and started their trek. The case had to come to an end before another woman lost her life.

"Do you remember your college days?" Sunny asked, gulping air at the fast clip walk.

"You're talking like I'm ninety years old. I'm only a few years older than you, I'll have you know." Ten to be exact. He increased his walking speed. "Sure, I remember.

Went to college in Indiana. That's where I met Karen." There was a catch in his voice.

Four-year-old Layla's mother, Karen, a social worker, was driving home on the LIE. Karen was on the phone with KD when she suddenly screamed, and the call abruptly dropped. The wrong-way drunk driver on the Long Island Expressway was also killed. KD took an extended leave from work. His mother helped him raise Layla. Then Angela came into his life. They met at a library, both bringing their young daughters to check out storybooks.

"KD, again, I'm sorry for your loss," Sunny said as the two suddenly walked single file to allow two skateboarding young men room to pass.

"Thanks," KD replied.

They were walking shoulder to shoulder. While looking straight ahead, KD reached out and tapped Sunny on the forearm to get her attention. "We can't be this lucky. I think that's our boy coming toward us."

The young man was quite fit, athletic, and slightly bowlegged. How KD was so adept at remembering faces was beyond Sunny.

"Are you sure that's him?"

"Yep. From the picture on the Chambers' mantle," KD said. "Maybe it was from a wrestling injury, but I noticed how his left brow is lower than his right. Plus he looks like his father."

Before she could answer, KD stepped right in front of Luke Chambers, who scowled, looking down eyeball to eyeball at the detective. Sunny watched her fearless partner in admiration.

"Luke Chambers? NYPD Detectives Jackson and McGraw," KD announced, flashing his shield. Luke said nothing. "We'd like to ask you a few questions." They inquired about his whereabouts on the assault and murder nights.

Luke Chambers didn't immediately respond but kept his challenging eyes squarely on KD. In Sunny's experience, innocent people rattled off a response right away. "Am I under arrest?" Luke asked calmly, with a slight slur. A group of three girls strode past. Luke twisted to get an eye full. He grinned broadly, licking his lips lasciviously. He faced the detectives again.

The detectives didn't have probable cause to arrest Luke just yet. If it turned out to be his DNA on the watch, then they would have PC to drag his pompous ass into the interrogation room.

Sunny listened closely to Luke's voice inflections, trying to compare it to those she heard in the dark the night of her assault. He must've been quiet that night. She didn't recognize it. "You're only a person of interest," she said. *For now.*

Luke finally broke the intense eye contact with KD to turn to Sunny. "Well good, Croc-*quette* and Tubbs," he goaded, referencing the Black and white detectives, Tubbs and Crockett, on the TV show *Miami Vice*. He sounded and acted as though he had little respect for women.

KD cocked his head to get Luke's attention. Luke turned back to KD, who had stepped back an inch.

"We found your watch," KD said, his voice filled with innuendo.

"I didn't lose one," the brash young man retorted.

If the situation could get any tenser, it did when Luke suddenly reached into his gym bag. Sunny pulled back her jacket to grab her Glock. Luke retrieved his wallet. Between his index and middle finger, he presented KD with a business card.

KD looked closer at Luke's extended hand. "Where did you get those bruises?"

Luke didn't even glance at his hand. "Wrestling," he said matter-of-factly. He impatiently thrust the business card closer. "My lawyer, if there are any more questions." Luke stepped around KD, brushing shoulders while walking away.

KD executed a precision military about-face. He called out to the young man. "Does this mean I'm off your Christmas list?" Then he started stretching, yawning. "Let's call it a day. I'll call the Loo. We'll do DD-5s in the morning."

Chapter Thirty-four

With saddlebags filled, Camille flew the same path tonight out of the Meatpacking District as the night before. In the darkness, he and Sunny cruised under the GWB. Camille's falcon wing beat steady as Sunny adjusted herself in the stirrups in preparation for the burst of speed falcons were capable of, especially one with Camille's powers.

Tonight's meeting on the Sunadaga territory with Camille's father, Ariwiio, would be an introduction. Her book required an in-depth understanding of Camille and Sunadaga life, culture, traditions, and what led up to Camille's incarceration. The book research would give her entrée to exonerate Camille. Subsequent flights upstate were probably required.

Camille's powerful wing strokes a few feet above the Hudson River soon brought them to the Mario Cuomo Bridge and its three-mile span between Rockland and Westchester Counties.

"After this bridge, we'll gain altitude and speed," Camille said over his shoulder.

Sunny repositioned herself like a jockey in the Kentucky Derby. As on her uncle's horse, Thunder, she raised her butt slightly from the saddle and leaned forward, reins held tightly, ready for speed.

"Let's do it!" she shouted into the wind. She was all in.

At the Bear Mountain Bridge in Peekskill, thirty minutes north of Manhattan, Camille was nearly up to full speed. With great wing strokes, they had gained height, soaring over the bridge. The cool, clear, starry night enveloped the travelers up the Hudson River Valley.

Sunny leaned close to Camille's ear to talk above the whistling wind. "What does it feel like when you shift?"

"First, I have to concentrate on what in the animal kingdom I want to transform into. Second, I must decide how large. And lastly, I must decide what extra powers or abilities I want. I can even add external animal powers, like the speed of a cheetah, to my human form if I wanted to. Then, I could run the length of Manhattan in no time. But I don't want the attention for obvious reasons."

"You can shift into anything? A bear? A bee?"

"A human with wings, a horse with wings," he laughed. "Yes. *Anything* in the animal kingdom. For a split second, I blank out as the transformation occurs. I can best describe it as an internal earthquake in me when the shifting happens, and especially when I transform to what I call *war mode*, muscles like steel, skin like armor, claws grow longer, stronger fangs, all my senses supercharged."

Her imagination ran wild. *So that's war mode.* She recalled him using the term during their conversation of using his hair as string for his bow in the footlocker.

The Franklin D. Roosevelt Bridge streaked underneath them. Soft blue lights outlined the span over the Hudson River at Poughkeepsie. Sunny remembered driving past the bridge in the daytime after leaving Miller Jewelers on their way to Millbrook. She liked the night aerial view from above much better. In no time, they zipped over the Kingston/Rhinebeck and soon the Rip Van Winkle Bridge. Camille seemed to be just warming up.

"Marshall said my father would be at the sweat lodge tonight. We'll have to fly hard to get you there in time."

"What's a sweat lodge?"

Just past the New York capital city of Albany, Camille loosely followed the Lake Champlain Canal, which connected the Hudson River to Lake Champlain. The only sounds amidst the quiet, glistening waters below were the steady swoosh of Camille's tireless, powerful wing beats.

"A sweat lodge is a place of healing and cleansing," he said, "of purification of the spirit, the body, and the emotions. The sweat lodge responds to whatever one needs."

It sounded like some spiritual experience to her. "What does a sweat lodge look like?"

He described the shape as similar to an igloo but made of willow tree saplings a thumb's diameter, bent in the shape of a dome. In ancestral times, the sweat lodge was covered with tree bark and animal hides to keep in the healing heat.

"Today, we may go to the hardware store for canvas tarps and other modern amenities to construct a sweat lodge," he explained.

Camille roughly pointed out the Proclamation Line a few miles ahead. It was essentially the spine of the Appalachian Mountains running along the east coast from Alabama, through New York, and on into Canada. He craned his neck to speak.

"To keep the peace, nonindigenous people once remained east of the mountain range, but that didn't hold." The next barrier was the Mississippi River, but that, too, was reneged on. "If Marshall needs to get to Sunadaga territory in the *daytime* in a hurry, we take a short drive out of

Manhattan into Jersey, and then we fly roughly up this Proclamation Line ridge, low, just above the treetops. You and I can do the same if we need to one day in the daytime."

Sunny couldn't tell a soul what she was experiencing up here. Who would ever believe her anyway? It still felt like a dream.

An orange glow in the dark woods beneath them indicated they had arrived in Sunadaga territory. Wings outstretched, gliding in a slow circle, Camille described the orange glow as a bonfire heating stones. His father's house was a short walk through the woods to the sweat lodge. Camille recounted that since he couldn't hear drums beating, they were still early. He came to a smooth landing in his father's backyard. Sunny dismounted and removed her phone and a large canvas shoulder bag from the saddlebags.

"Shit!" Sunny huffed as she checked her phone.

"What is it?" a small, unfamiliar voice responded in the darkness.

"Where are you?" She spun in the darkness using her phone display as a flashlight, just as she had done in the tree the night she was assaulted.

She heard a high-pitched bark somewhere near her feet. She aimed the phone down.

"Put me in your bag and then text my father that you arrived."

Camille had transformed into the cutest teacup Yorkie. Sunny had been so excited to fly on the back of a falcon that she hadn't thought what Camille would do as she investigated his life, leading to imprisonment. It relaxed her to know that he would be by her side one way or the other. She stuffed the Yorkie into her shoulder bag and followed the dog's directions into the quiet night, only broken by crickets, and on to the sweat lodge.

"Just received a message from Forensics. No usable DNA on the watch." She exhaled in exasperation. "And the fingerprints are smudged, useless." They had the watch's serial number, but anyone could lose or have a watch stolen. She wanted desperately to nail the smug son of a bitch, Luke Chambers. She was sure he was involved, but they needed hard evidence. Three dead, one assaulted, Rosa lost her livelihood, Croc-*quette* and Tubbs.

"There's a fallen tree we need to step over in about twenty feet," the Yorkie said from the shoulder bag. Sunny aimed the phone light to the ground, swinging the light from side to side. "When we get back to the city, I'll snoop around for more evidence since that watch didn't pan out," Camille promised.

Her phone chirped. She received Ariwiio's response to hike to the orange glow in the woods, which she was already doing according to the direction of the Yorkie in her bag.

Drums started beating in the direction of the glow. Camille explained that the boys lacrosse team was in a funk after they lost Camille as their coach. Their dismal season record reflected their low spirits.

Sunny swung the phone light as she stepped along the well-worn dirt path through the woods. The orange glow was getting closer.

"Whew! You smell that?" Camille said from the shoulder bag.

"Smell what? I don't smell anything."

"Oh yeah. It takes you humans a lot longer. Give it a moment. A dog's sense of smell is thousands of times stronger than a human."

Sunny consciously sniffed the air, and then it hit her. "Phew! A skunk. Where?"

"Shine the light to your left," Camille advised. There in the darkness, a skunk foraged for food.

"Hey buddy, you mind moving it along?" Camille chided the skunk.

Sunny's human ears only heard disgruntled squeaks and growls from the black-and-white critter.

"You say what? We're interrupting your meal of juicy grubs?" Camille repeated.

"You can understand that skunk?" Sunny said in surprise. Then she remembered how the animals on her uncle's farm, chickens, ducks, horses, and cows would all mingle, vocalizing, seeming to understand each other on some level.

"Yep. I told you I have more powers. I can commune with animals, *even* as a human. The animals thought that COVID-19 was going to be the human equivalent of an asteroid striking the Yucatán Peninsula, killing all the dinosaurs. They would have a habitable planet again, all to themselves."

They stopped as the skunk crossed the dirt path, giving the animal a wide berth. The pungent smell lingered for a moment before Sunny resumed her hike. *Animals would be better without us,* she contemplated. He can communicate with animals. She shook her head.

"Now I smell that dinosaur bone necklace again. You brought it with you?" Camille asked, nose twitching high, sampling the air.

"No. It's back in NYPD evidence storage."

"Okay. I caught a whiff of what smelled like that necklace." He shook his head in befuddlement, his big Yorkie ears flapping.

Past the trees in a clearing, yellow, red, and orange bonfire flames leaped into the dark night sky. Melodious chanting, drumbeats, and rattles filled the night air. Sunny, with Camille in her shoulder bag, stepped into the clearing and was met by a white-haired, smiling older man. He extended his hand.

"Sunny, so glad you could make it. Marshall says you're a detective who's writing a documentary about Camille's life and can maybe help us clear his name. We can use all the help we can get."

Sunny released Ariwiio's hand. "That's right. I'm intrigued, and I want to help." Repay Camille for saving her life. For assisting with the ongoing investigation...she could go on and on. She didn't believe he was capable of murdering anyone.

"And who is this little fella?" Ariwiio reached and rubbed his son's head. The Yorkie ate it up, licking Ariwiio's hand excitedly.

"Oh. This is...Brooklyn." She didn't know where that name came from, but it worked. Then she recalled a police K9 by the name.

"It's going to be a tad warm inside the sweat lodge for him, but we'll be quick. Also, the boys have school in the morning, so I'm not keeping them out too late."

Ariwiio quickly explained the raging bonfire. Firekeepers added logs to heat the bowling ball-size stones to cherry red, sending brilliant sparks upward into the pitch night. The fire popped and crackled. Inside the sweat lodge water would be ladled onto the stones, creating steam. Drumbeats, chanting, and the sound of rattles emanated from inside the lodge.

"Hot rock here!" the firekeeper shouted. With a pitchfork, the firekeeper lifted a glowing hot stone from the bonfire and walked to the sweat lodge. The entrance flap flew open, and a pair of hands took hold of the pitchfork handle and disappeared inside. A few seconds later, the sweat lodge flap opened again, and the empty pitchfork was handed back.

Sunny's phone rang. It was a uniform patrol officer from Manhattan named Holly Thorne. She was at Saint Anthony Hospital. Jennifer McGraw was there being treated for assault and battery.

"Your sister told me you are a homicide detective and to call you," Officer Thorne said.

"Thank you, Officer. How is she?" She caught her breath. Her heart raced. She took a few steps away from the sweat lodge. The Yorkie clawed his way high in the canvas shoulder bag and growled.

"She has a cut on her head where she fell forward after the pummeling. I've seen worse," the officer said calmly. "She should be released soon. A nurse is attending her right now. I'll hand your sister the phone."

Sunny's mind careened with horrible thoughts. Who attacked her sister? Did Luke Chambers have anything to do with it? Or...Timothy Wong, the escapee?

"Sunny?" Jennifer's shaky voice came through the phone.

"How are you, Sis?" Sunny held her breath.

"Just a little shaken up. I almost made it home. Attacked me from behind. Didn't rob me of anything," she rattled on breathlessly. "Do you think this has anything to do with your job?"

Sunny took a moment to breathe. Her sister seemed scared but safe now. "I don't know. I'm just glad you're safe."

"The hospital is releasing me in a few minutes. I'll call you when I get home. The nice officer here says she'll drop me off." Jennifer handed the phone back to the officer, and Sunny thanked her.

"Is everything okay?" Ariwiio asked over her shoulder as she clicked off the call.

"Y-yes," Sunny stammered."Shall we?" Ariwiio got to his hands and knees and crawled inside the sweat lodge. Sunny followed, her attention divided.

Chapter
Thirty-five

In the dark woods, the Russian lowered the silenced rifle's night vision telescopic sight as the old man crawled into the sweat lodge. Earlier tonight, his muffled rifle shot had missed the man when he bent to step over for something in the path between his house and the sweat lodge. Sergey thought to take a second shot, a headshot. The old man was a slow-moving target. But then some kids showed up, all boys. He ejected the high-powered rifle's magazine. Some woman carrying a dog in her bag crawled into the sweat lodge behind the old man.

Eww! Where was that damn skunk? He squinted into the darkness for the repulsive creature.

The red glow of lava hot stones and a few candles provided sufficient light inside the sweat lodge. Ariwiio watched the wonderment on Sunny's face as she found a spot to sit in the straw on the ground around the periphery and folded her legs. In the center of the sweat lodge, a pit of incandescent stones glowed. The boys' lacrosse team was already inside, a couple bare-chested, the rest in tank tops, faces glistening with sweat. Ariwiio introduced her and spoke of her documentary about Camille's life. The boys, in turn, said their names, some warm words about their former coach, and returned to their mesmerizing chants and hypnotic drumming.

For Sunny's benefit and a refresher to the boys, Ariwiio expanded on the use of the water drum and its place in Indigenous culture. Not much larger than a coffee can, the base of the water drum had a plug to release or add water to keep the buckskin top moist and supple. It was another gift— as lacrosse—from the Creator to give the people entertainment and joy. The drum's beat was never played faster than the human heartbeat, heard as a baby hears his or her mother's heartbeat in the womb. Its top a circle, it had no beginning, it had no end. Ariwiio handed the detective a horn rattle. She merrily joined in. Ariwiio could tell that the phone call still bothered the detective. She seemed a little distracted. Law enforcement work was stressful. It was night. She should be off duty, but he surmised her mind multitasked wherever she was. But she also seemed eager to learn, to tell the world of his son's life, and to help clear Camille's name. He moved the event along.

"I know you're wondering why I asked the lacrosse team to meet me here," Ariwiio said, scanning the youthful faces. The boys nodded. "When I played lacrosse long, long ago, our team...well, our team stunk one season. I know you miss Coach T." And I miss my son. "He wouldn't want you to lose your spirit—your medicine. So, I want to do this pep rally like my coach once did for our team."

He reached behind himself to retrieve his bag. His *gustoweh* feathers fluttered with each head movement. The wood shavings all over the house were worth it to him. He gestured to subdue the horn rattles, to beat the drum softer, and lower the chants. He dribbled a ladle of water over the hot, hissing rocks. Steam rose in a red fog. Ariwiio continued the rally.

"I'm sure each of you has had dreams of great skills on the lacrosse field. You can only realize your greatness when you accept who you are." He looked over the team. Sunny did the same, clearly soaking up information for the book. The Yorkie started panting, but it looked like a happy pant, his eyes sparkling.

"You have an animal spirit of greatness!" Ariwiio emphasized. The young faces took him back to when he was a boy. "We are here to discover your spirit."

The single mesmerizing water drum maintained a steady beat. The lodge was filled with a red fog.

The smallest team member, Jana, an attackman on offense, looked across the hot pit at brawny Antewenno, a midfielder on defense. In unison, they turned their eyes to Ariwiio, a look of wonder on their faces. The water drum beat rhythmically, and the rattles rasped in time, all mingling with the earnest, hypnotic chants and bobbing heads.

"Close your eyes," Ariwiio implored. "Listen to your inner self to know your animal spirit." He picked up the ladle of water and spread it over the red-hot rocks. They hissed and sputtered, a new plume of steam rising and filling the sweat lodge, the air opaque and moist with water vapor. The chanting and beating continued for another minute. Sweat poured in rivulets off the young men, their foreheads and chests glistening. They were finally inwardly focused. Ariwiio saw the detective peek at her phone. He was a busy man, and she was a busy woman.

Ariwiio reached behind himself for the suede pouch he'd brought. In the glowing red light, he searched inside.

"Antewenno?" Ariwiio called, and all the young men dreamily opened their eyes from their trance. "Antewenno, tell me your dream, your animal spirit!"

The husky goalkeeper closed his eyes again and shook his horn rattle intensely to bring forth his dream. "The bear!" the young man exclaimed confidently.

Ariwiio bowed his head, accepting the dream while he searched his pouch in the glow of the hot rocks. Among the nearly twenty amulets he had carved for the pep rally, he located a bear relief carved into an oval of wood with two suede straps attached. Ariwiio motioned for Antewenno to hold out his right arm. On the young man's large bicep, Ariwiio tied the bear amulet armband.

"Tremendous strength," Ariwiio declared of the bear, straightening the powerful amulet on Antewenno's bicep.

Next, Tracy, an aggressive defenseman, told Ariwiio his dream was the mountain lion. Ariwiio found the amulet in his pouch. Ariwiio believed that Camille would have chosen the mountain lion for himself.

"Fierce! Untamed!" Ariwiio uttered. In the red glow of the sweat lodge, Tracy accepted his amulet. He smiled broadly, admiring the armband, straightening it to his liking.

The falcon, swift and agile, donned another boy's bicep, while the raven, cunning and crafty, wrapped around still another. Ariwiio added another ladle of water to the incandescent rocks, steam soaring.

Detective Sunny McGraw turned the page of her writing pad. She jotted something onto it. The woman seemed truly interested. She started back, shaking her horn rattle to the water drum beat.

Ariwiio turned to the hefty goalkeeper. "JoJo, what was your dream?"

"The tortoise!" There was no doubt in his voice.

It took Ariwiio a moment to find the animal in his pouch. "Immovable! Indestructible!" He tied the amulet to JoJo's beefy bicep.

Then Ariwiio turned to Jana, the smallest player on the team. The lad shamefully dropped his eyes. Though the young man was slight of frame and not very tall, he could score and step up when they needed him. He cleared his throat.

"The chipmunk," Jana announced softly, and the team smiled, still shaking their horn rattles and chanting, heads bobbing in unison.

Ariwiio smiled at the apt choice and searched his pouch. A young man from Ariwiio's boyhood team had once chosen a chipmunk, so he was ready. It took him a few moments in the dim light, but he found it.

"Even the *tiniest* creatures have worth to the Creator," Ariwiio began. "They prove it over and over." The diminutive young man received his amulet. Ariwiio now turned to Sunny.

"Sunny?" Ariwiio called. She seemed startled. "Marshall has told me much about you, the dangerous work you do, your tenacity. I want you to have this as you pursue justice in your homicide cases…and justice for Camille and all people." Ariwiio reached into his bag and pulled out a badger carving. "Indomitable spirit! Fearless!"

"I'm honored," Sunny responded, allowing Ariwiio to tie the amulet over her arm. The Yorkie barked his approval, and they all laughed.

In the red light, the amulet recipients admired their honors. Ariwiio quenched the hot stones with scoops of water as the lacrosse team left for home. He rubbed the Yorkie's head. Outside the sweat lodge, the busy detective took another phone call. She appeared relieved this time.

The two—three including the frisky Yorkie—sat around the dwindling bonfire outside the sweat lodge. The tiny Yorkie hopped in Ariwiio's lap, his tongue lolling happily, his tail wagging briskly. Ariwiio filled Sunny in on more of Camille's life—the parts Marshall hadn't told her. His son had lived a normal Native boy's life of school sports, pets, adoration of his mother, racism, and appreciation of his culture. The murder conviction nearly broke Camille. His mother's mysterious death while Camille was in prison, unable to attend her funeral, tore out his son's heart.

Ariwiio turned on his flashlight as the bonfire slowly died. They sat on a log outside the sweat lodge. The Yorkie acted as though he didn't want to go home. Every time Ariwiio handed the tiny dog to Sunny, he jumped back into Ariwiio's lap. They walked the dark trail to Ariwiio's house, where Sunny promised to return soon. She thanked Ariwiio for the wonderful, informative, and enlightening evening.

Saturday morning was like any other day at Manhattan South Homicide for Sunny and KD. They worked the West Side cases until they hit a wall. Following Sunny's sister's assault last night, an additional cautionary bulletin was sent to all involved in the Timothy Wong and West Side cases. Sunny was told by local precinct detectives that it could have been a random assault or Jennifer could have been targeted. No one knew for sure at the moment.

This morning, they were completing their DD-5s of Miller Jewelers and the Chambers interviews. With no identifiable DNA on the watch, only a serial number, the investigation had hit another snag. The detectives were certain Luke Chambers had something to do with the assault and murders. After completing the DD-5s, they would investigate Luke's friends.

"Look at this?" KD laughed, slapping his desk. He slid his laptop around so Sunny could read the news page on the display. "Last night some junkie said he saw a winged man flying around shooting arrows." KD shook his shiny head in amazement.

The article related that not one—but two arrows were shot from high up and a distance sniper-like through the fifth-floor window of a drug stash apartment. Authorities reported that the arrows fragmented upon impact delivering a payload of cleaning solvent which contaminated the drugs.... Sunny slid KD's laptop back to him as her mind puzzled out the event.

Camille? Sunny wondered. After they landed last night behind MH Construction, he told Sunny that he was going out to further search the new scent zone. He evidently did more. She idly fingered the sweat lodge badger amulet under her shirt sleeve. *Arrows? Payload?* She pictured the black footlocker, the bow strung with his hair.

"I bet you other New Yorkers saw that man with wings and just kept on walking. Just another day in the city." KD cracked up causing the other precinct detectives to look their way.

"Detectives Douglass and McGraw, there's a gentleman here to see you," the office civilian aide announced as he approached.

Sunny twisted in her chair to see the high-held head of Howard Chambers. He wasn't wearing the cultured expression of a wine connoisseur this time. He glowered at the detectives.

"May I speak with you two...in private?" he said from across the precinct room.

Interview Room 2 was not in use. The room was constructed of battleship gray cinderblock walls. Before completely entering the room, Sunny asked the aide to bring her bottled water. She stood in the doorway.

"Mr. Chambers, coffee, tea, water?" she asked.

"Water," he simply demanded. The man impatiently took a seat at the table. He immediately interlaced his fingers, always a sign of contention in Sunny's opinion.

She closed the interrogation room door. KD kicked things off with small talk.

"Incredible place you have upstate," KD began.

Mr. Chambers pursed his lips, clearly in no mood for beating around the bush. "My son, Luke, called me. Says you two are harassing him. Have him as a person of interest."

"That's true, Mr. Chambers," KD nonchalantly confirmed while walking to the door to retrieve three bottles of water from the aide.

"We have two murders." Sunny didn't include Christine's baby since that news hadn't been released to the public yet. "And an assault," she said from across the table. "We have to check all the boxes, sir."

Seething, Howard Chambers snatched his bottle of water from the table, unscrewed the cap, and took a long, angry swig, air bubbles gurgling in the bottle. He slammed the battle to the table, a small amount of water splashing. "Murder? Chambers aren't capable of such an atrocity," he announced haughtily.

"Mr. Chambers," KD said, standing in front of the one-way window. No one was on the other side of the window this time. "Law enforcement follow the evidence wherever it leads us."

"Have you pursued that Mexican angle?"

Nice try! Sunny's knee-jerk reaction was to throw water in the man's face to wake him up, but she kept her head. "We don't share investigation strategies, sir."

Howard Chambers suddenly stood. "Well, you pursue your rash investigation." It sounded like a threat as the man glared up and down at the detectives. "We have what it takes to defend ourselves!" He walked to the door. "We're offering a twenty-five thousand dollar reward for whoever committed these murders. Those people need money. Someone will come forward."

Those people stuck in Sunny's craw. She wasn't born with a silver spoon in her mouth. She was those people. But this prick didn't see it that way. She was steaming mad. Fortunately, KD spoke before she exploded.

"Mr. Chambers, can you please hold off on a reward? All kinds of crazies will come out of the woodwork."

"I'm not only *not* going to hold off the reward, I'm calling Roland."

KD stood his ground, eyeing the man intensely. "Don't threaten us with calling the mayor. You can leave now...sir." Her partner clipped each word.

The man looked down his nose at them before slamming the door shut.

Ten minutes later at her desk, Sunny perused West Side University student athlete photos on her laptop, searching for Luke Chambers' friends. Luke Chambers was captain of the wrestling team, pictured in the center of three rows of hulking wrestlers. Suddenly, Sunny realized she had forgotten she had placed her text notifications on silent before entering the sweat lodge last night. She had two messages, one about giving blood at the Red Cross, which she did regularly following her dad's example, and the last message was from Camille...early this morning. When did he sleep?

The message directed Sunny to log into an NYPD pole-mounted surveillance camera on the Upper West Side. Camille caught a man's recent scent in the open this time. Sunny used the camera location and timestamp to view the saved footage. A large man in a red and white sweat suit was running from a...rat. Camille? The streetlight provided excellent illumination of the man's terrified face, a face she had just seen in the West Side University wrestling team photo.

"Detective Jackson, we need your signature here." The civilian aide waylaid KD for paperwork as he returned to his desk with a cup of coffee. Sunny quickly shut down the camera page. She couldn't tell KD that a rat positively ID'd one of their suspects. What was up with her and rats, he would say. How could she focus their attention on this one man running from a rat? They needed to get this case solved.

Chapter Thirty-six

KD peered over Sunny's shoulder at the West Side University wrestling team photo on her laptop. Three rows of twenty-one men total, dressed in WSU wrestling uniforms, filled the screen. Captain Luke Chambers was kneeling center on the first row.

Three African Americans peered back at her from the laptop screen. African-American hair was found in the hoodie of Sunny's turquoise sweat suit, suggesting close contact. Aaron Thomas, in row two, was the one running from the rat. Camille captured Aaron's scent at Sunny's, Christine's, and Elaine's crime scenes. Their eventual investigation would get around to Aaron, but they needed to save lives now. It would sound illogical to KD not to start with the African American named Jesse Moore in row one, next to Luke. The men looked like pals, arms draped over each other's shoulders. A third African American named Carl Payne stood in row three.

As Sunny expected, KD, the consummate detective, saw the camaraderie between Jesse and Luke and invariably pointed to Jesse Moore. "Let's start with questioning him." He walked back to his desk opposite her.

"Woman's intuition," Sunny blurted. It was bullshit but worth a try to hurry the investigation along. "Let's go with this Aaron Thomas guy first." She jabbed her index finger into the screen.

KD clicked his tongue in resignation. "Your spidey senses want to go with door number two first?" he jested.

More like rat senses. "Work with me on this, KD." She searched for any priors and found a public drunkenness arrest for Aaron Thomas.

KD shook his bald head and pursed his lips in befuddlement. "Whatever! Let's get moving. Get his cell number from the record, and let's see where its pinging."

At Lunch hour, the streets and sidewalks of Manhattan were filled with foot traffic and shoppers. During twenty minutes of driving, every turn of their fleet car proceeded excruciatingly slow as pedestrians crowded the crosswalks, cell phones to heads.

"He's on the move again," Sunny said from the passenger side, viewing Aaron Thomas' cell phone ping on the laptop.

"Once I complete this turn, we should spot him." Jaywalkers slowed their progress. When the crosswalk cleared, KD was finally able to turn onto West Eighty-eighth.

"That's him!" Sunny pointed excitedly. "That's him there!" She slammed the laptop shut and had her hand on the door handle in no time.

"We can cut them off over there." KD pointed to a section of the sidewalk. He sped ahead and double-parked. They both leaped from the car.

Dark shades hid Aaron Thomas's eyes. He was certainly a wrestler—huge, veiny, WWF arms. Six feet tall, about two-thirty, all muscle, he sucked on a red 7-11 Big Gulp, the straw lodged rakishly in his cheek.

Sunny flashed her tin with KD. "Aaron Thomas, we're NYPD Detectives McGraw and Jackson. We need to ask you a few questions." It was all she could do not to groin kick the guy.

Sunny demanded he tell them where he was the nights in question. She was seeing her reflection in his shades. It was irritating and distracting.

Aaron took a dramatic slurp of Big Gulp, finally removing the straw from his cheek. He smacked his lips with a taunting this-is-so-delicious sound. Sunny's fists were balled. All she could see was this sonofabitch choking the life out of her in the park.

"I was barhopping on those nights," Aaron said cockily. He sucked his teeth.

"Do you have witnesses?" KD chimed in.

"Yeah, but I was too blasted to remember," Aaron replied lamely. The straw returned to his cheek, and the annoying slurping resumed. Sunny saw herself slapping the cup of red stuff from his huge mitt.

"Would you mind removing the shades, Aaron?" Sunny asked politely but not feeling it. It was only lunchtime, and he seemed inebriated or something already. Drugs?

Aaron didn't readily comply, but then slowly removed the shades to reveal bloodshot eyes.

"Are you on *something*?" KD asked.

"Just tired. Partying can be exhausting," Aaron said with a wry smile while arrogantly bouncing his shoulders. "If I'm not under arrest, I have things to do and places to go." The big man slid the shades back on, jacked up his eyebrows, and strode off with his Big Gulp.

From a discrete distance, the detectives followed Aaron Thomas, the car creeping. The wrestler finished his drink and tossed it in a corner garbage can. Once Aaron was out of sight, KD rolled the department car next to the smelly garbage can. Sunny didn't bolt out the car this time. She looked at KD. "Rock, paper, scissors?"

"I don't think so. I'm driving *and* the senior detective," he quickly said, pulling rank on the rookie. He pointed to the glovebox for a pair of latex gloves for her to collect the abandonment sample.

Sunny held her breath as she fished through the waist-high garbage can. She pulled out the Big Gulp cup, but no straw. Another dive. *Damn. What's that sticky stuff?* She found the straw wedged in the garbage can's side.

"You need to ride in the trunk with your stinky self," KD ribbed as she made her way back into the car. "Let's get that cup to our FBI task force contact. The fibbies are good for at least *one* thing. They can analyze DNA in hours, not days like the NYPD. The fed has resources far beyond what any state." The chief of detectives was still pulling one detective from each homicide precinct throughout the five boroughs, but the FBI contact was already established.

The other two African-American wrestlers, who the detectives interviewed were more cooperative and had verifiable alibis.

On the drive back to the precinct, Lieutenant Sanchez called. He gave them the Upper West Side address of a woman found dead in an alley. If they didn't solve this string of murders soon, he was going to pull them off the case when the complete task force was finally constituted. Sunny switched on the car's emergency lights and sounded the siren. KD executed a tire-screeching U-turn.

Chapter Thirty-seven

Four blocks north of West Side University, news vans were already at the newest crime scene with their broadcast masts extended to transmit the latest homicide news. Sunny and KD weaved through the crowd of onlookers. Sunny recognized a woman reporter from the night of her own assault heading toward her, microphone ready.

"Detective McGraw, did the West Side Wolfpack strike again, the one who tried to kill you?

Sunny pushed the mic from her face. "No comment." She lifted the yellow crime scene tape to enter the alley. The Loo's warning to remove her and KD from the case propelled her forward. They had already turned their files over to the developing task force and their FBI contact.

"KD, you piece of work!" A tall, stout woman detective walked over to greet them.

"Phyllis! Long time," KD said, extending a hearty handshake. He introduced Sunny. "Phyllis Mayfield here was once a part of Manhattan South but then moved on up

223

north to Manhattan North Homicide." MNH handled cases above Fifty-Ninth Street.

"My boss called your boss," Phyllis began, "because this homicide may fit the pattern and location of your cases. Crime Scene is already here collecting evidence. The ME's van is here, too, but I wouldn't let them remove the body until you folks got here." Phyllis led the detectives deeper into the alley.

The victim was a small white woman, barely five feet tall, maybe thirty years old. Sunny looked closer for strangulation marks.

"So far, it's fitting the pattern, KD," Sunny observed. Strangulation bruising encircled the dead woman's thin neck. And the location was right.

Out of courtesy, KD slid only the side of the sheet to reveal the DOA's bare, skinny hip. The woman had no underwear on. He slid the sheet back and scanned the alley.

"On second thought, I don't know now that she fits the pattern," Sunny said, vacillating while bending closer to examine the dead woman's hands. "She didn't spend any time on her hands." The woman's nails were unevenly clipped. "And she's so skinny." The perpetrators had thus far selected fit, well-maintained women as targets.

"Good points, McGraw," her partner agreed. "You're thinking not their type?"

"Yeah. Something's a little off."

"Okay. We'll pursue this as one of our cases if or until we find out otherwise." KD threw his chin up the alley. "Let's canvass some of the businesses and apartments around here. See if anyone saw or heard anything."

The ME arrived in the alley with the body bag to remove the dead woman. The count may now be up to four: three women and Lowry's baby.

***

Two hours later, back in the squad room completing DD-5s for the third dead woman, all KD and Sunny could do until the ME provided her analysis was wait. They were also standing by for FBI DNA results of Aaron Thomas's Big Gulp. Wait, wait, wait. At a standstill. Maybe a perfect time for Sunny to take a quick trip upstate.

Lieutenant Sanchez informed his detectives about the first task force meeting at 1PP tomorrow. He reassured them not to take it personally. On the case, he had the best detectives MSH offered. But that didn't keep Andrew Rizzo from ragging on them.

"You two are killing our numbers," the chubby man said, pointing to the board's statistics.

KD ignored him, but Sunny was in no mood. She could care less that his father was an NYPD captain. "Rizzo, if you don't shut your pie hole, I'm going to take that statistic board and ram it up—"

"McGraw, let's take a break," KD interrupted. "I want to take my kid to the park."

It was a good idea. She needed a breather. But if any results came in tonight, she was back on the Job in a heartbeat. Unfortunately, their day wasn't about to end.

Lieutenant Sanchez hung out his office door. "You two over to Chinatown. Now!" He pointed one, two at KD and Sunny. "Your boy just resurfaced. He's giving the local precinct a hard time. You two know him. Go re-cuff him, then get back on your West Side cases."

Chapter Thirty-eight

Fifteen minutes after rushing down the stairs—no elevator, too slow—from Manhattan South Homicide on East Twenty-first Street, KD executed a tire squealing right turn onto Canal Street, siren blaring, grille and headlights flashing. Canal was the main drag through Chinatown in lower Manhattan.

A month ago, Sunny and her sister were there one bright Saturday afternoon for lunch. Chinatown was known for its delicious foods and affordable restaurants. Sunny had ordered fried dumplings and hand-pulled noodles. Jennifer had opted for honey-glazed pork over white rice. They'd eaten in a park watching a tai chi class of young and old, graceful as ballerinas.

But today was serious business. KD veered into opposing traffic as they sped west on Canal Street. The destination was familiar...and distressing to Sunny.

After a quick left turn off Canal Street, they encountered news vans setting up to broadcast. Several blocks down were NYPD barricades in the street. Past the barricade were blue and white police cars, several fire trucks, and a two ambulances. Blue lights. Red lights. White lights. All flashed strobe-like for several blocks. Two flat black Emergency Service Unit armored vans were parked near an apartment building. Everyone was looking up.

KD rolled their black unmarked Ford slowly forward. They flashed their detective shields to gain entrance behind the barricade. Next to the apartment building, firefighters inflated a rescue air cushion—a giant air mattress to break the fall of a jumper. Sunny stuck her head out the car window for a better look.

Timothy Wong wobbled precariously at the edge of the roof of the five-story apartment building. Memories of the helpless dead infant in Sheryl Chen's apartment 304 flooded Sunny's mind, along with plenty of anger. This was not the way she wanted to find the escaped convict. She had imagined the coward drawing a gun—too late for her faster hand. She wasn't proud of the thought...but there it was. Crimes against children set her off.

"So you're the two detectives who know this guy?" the ESU lead, dressed in a Kevlar vest and black helmet, said as he pointed at Timothy Wong at the roof's edge.

Responding wearily, KD replied, "Unfortunately, that would be us. Let us take a crack at talking him down."

The lead ESU radioed to his officers throughout the apartment to allow the homicide detectives access to the roof. Sunny and KD ascended the stairwell. ESU officers, in all black, carrying assault rifles, were stationed on each floor. And although the residents had been evacuated, the smell of savory hot cooking oils permeated the halls.

So as not to startle anyone, at the roof access door, KD eased open the metal door. Twenty feet away, Sheryl Chen's petite body spun around to see the detectives step out onto the hot, flat, white, rubbery roof. Her white dress flapped in the wind. Her eyes were red and wet with tears.

She quickly turned back to Timothy Wong, his shirt fluttering as he perched dangerously on the two-foot high ledge. His eyes registered shock at seeing the detectives.

"You two don't come any closer or I'll jump!" he yelled at the detectives. "You're the reason I went to prison."

No. You're the reason you went to prison, you murderous, delusional son of a bitch, Sunny wanted to say, but she held her tongue this time. She didn't want to upset the man any further. They wanted to capture him, put his ass back in prison, and throw away the key.

KD placed his palms forward, indicating Timothy should calm down. Timothy Wong stuck out his arms, swaying to maintain his balance following a particularly strong wind gust.

Sunny wanted to know if Timothy Wong had orchestrated the attack on her sister. Oh, how she dreamed of snatching his ass off that ledge. But this wasn't the time to think about revenge.

"I need you to forgive me, Sheryl," Timothy whined.

No damn way, Sunny thought, seething. The last time she saw Sheryl Chen, the grieving woman was being helped out of the courtroom at Timothy's trial, hysterical at the loss of her baby. No way would Sunny forgive this bastard. Timothy claimed he "accidentally" shook Sheryl's five-month-old daughter, who wouldn't stop crying. Doctors discovered brain bleeding, evidence of shaken-baby syndrome.

"I'll come down if you forgive me, Sheryl." Timothy twisted to see behind himself to the apartment building across the street. A group of guys with beer cans in their hands taunted him.

"Jump! Jump! Jump!" they cried in unison, laughing, chugging down beer, clinking their bottles.

Teetering, the desperate man turned back to Sheryl. Sunny pictured the firefighters below adjusting the inflatable mattress to break the man's fall. After bouncing unpredictably off five stories of fire escapes, she didn't believe he'd be alive once he hit the cement sidewalk.

"Please forgive me, Sheryl, and I'll go back to prison," he wailed. "I can't live in there without your forgiveness."

Then, Sheryl Chen did something extraordinary. She held out, accepting arms. With small steps, she walked stiffly toward Timothy. Witnessing the powerful emotion, Sunny stood agape. Love. She brushed windblown hair from her eyes.

"I'll be damned," KD muttered unbelievingly.

Of course, Sunny loved her mother. She loved her father. She loved her sister. But love outside of her family had eluded her. Here, on a hot roof, she saw love.

Timothy continued his pleading. "Please!" He started raising his arms, and then the beginnings of a smile blossomed on his face.

Sheryl moved closer. "Don't jump," she croaked.

The rooftop tension subsided with each slow, small step Sheryl took forward.

Timothy Wong would be returned to a secure prison—no more leaves granted for any reason. No bloody mangled mess on New York City's sidewalk.

Sheryl inched closer. "Don't jump," she begged, reaching out for Timothy.

A huge smile crossed the dangling man's face, then he gasped, eyes wide, as Sheryl dropped her hands to his waist…and pushed.

"No!" the detectives shouted simultaneously in high and low-pitched voices. They stood frozen.

Sheryl Chen stood stockstill, her back to the detectives, not stepping forward to view her handiwork on the impenetrable sidewalk. *Was she going to jump?* Sunny wondered.

The beer drinkers were cheering and high-fiving. KD was taking slow, cautious steps toward Sheryl. His tense posture said he was ready to sprint if need be to catch the woman before she took a flying leap.

The thin woman finally made a move. Her dress flapped in the wind. Without looking back, she nonchalantly placed her hands behind her back. KD started reciting her Miranda rights.

With a sweep of his hand, he gathered the wood shavings into a pile on the table. His father had taught him the craft of wood carving. Camille rotated the carving at eye level, pleased with his production. Now, he needed to give it to Sunny.

Downstairs at MH Construction, he could hear Marshall using the zinging air impact wrench to remove a flat tire from the company trailer. Below, outside the window, New York bustled, its restaurants and bars filling. At sunset, Camille planned to go for a jog to relieve his cabin fever. His phone rang. It was just who he was thinking about.

"I'm back at the precinct poring over recorded interviews, DD-5s, and security camera footage," Sunny began.

"When do you take a break? It's Saturday," Camille snickered.

"Actually, that's what I'm calling you about. I need a little breather. We're still waiting on DNA results. We should have it soon. Can we quickly go to the territory—up the Proclamation Line along the mountains? I want to do some preliminary investigating before I request your records from the court and police."

"Sure," he said excitedly, watching couples strolling hand in hand on the sidewalk below. Anything to get his conviction vacated. He wanted desperately to come out of the shadows and lead a normal life. But mostly, he wanted to visit his mother's grave as a human, not as a tawny fawn or a hovering ruby throated hummingbird—her favorite.

"Fantastic! That checks off one thing I want to get done this evening. I have to get back for a dinner date tonight, the second thing...then back to work," she chuckled self-consciously.

"Oh." Camille attempted to hide his disappointment.

"Are you okay?"

"Yeah," he fibbed. But then he realized that she had a life before he met her. Who was he to intrude? The guy she was with at Sally's had a cool car, dressed in nice suits, had a good job, and was not a fugitive. *Who would be interested in a freak like me anyway?* There were crimes to be solved and people to save. That was where his time should be spent. With his powers, he had a responsibility.

"And can you fly back after you drop me off upstate and scent check a *new* homicide?" He agreed, and Sunny gave him the Upper West Side address. "Great! I'll pick you up in forty-five minutes," she said. After a quick drive across the George Washington Bridge into Northern New Jersey, they would pick up the Appalachian Mountains to conceal their flight in the ridges and valleys.

Camille asked Marshall to call upstate to make arrangements for Sunny's visit. Camille's father, sister, and a few others were cleaning and painting the center for its summer opening. He wished he could help as he had always done.

Chapter Thirty-nine

The Haudenosaunee cultural center would soon open for the summer. Ariwiio and his vice president, Lyle Smith, dusted and cleaned artifacts. Seventy-three-year-old Lyle rarely appeared at the center without his *gustoweh*. The handful of feathers atop the headdress fluttered as he went about the business of preparing the center for its opening day.

The center was nothing fancy, more resembling a house converted to cultural center. Ariwiio was in the backroom cleaning and rearranging wampum belts when he saw Sunny walk through the front door. Their smiles greeted each other, but Lyle, sitting at the front desk, waylaid the poor woman, even though Ariwiio had told Lyle that the detective slash novelist was on a tight schedule. Ariwiio appreciated her help in getting answers and closure for his son.

In the front room were the sellable items of the center. Paintings, jewelry, books, and bumper stickers filled the area. Ariwiio half-watched and listened as Lyle introduced himself. Ariwiio could see that the bumper stickers on a revolving display rack caught her attention. The display was filled with bumper stickers reading: *We want our country back!*, *Colonialism: The Ultimate Organized Crime*, *Native Pride*, *Everyone is illegal on stolen land*, *No Indigenous Sports Mascots*. She pointed at the last one.

"I played basketball in high school in Oklahoma. We had a Native logo. The players fought to remove the logo but the staff stuck with *tradition*." She air-quoted the word before jotting notes in her composition pad, glancing several times at the bumper sticker display.

"Some get it; most don't," Lyle replied. "Native Americans don't use African Americans, Asian Americans, or European Americans as mascots."

Ariwiio observed that there was no discussion or argument this time about Lyle's use of the term European American instead of white. He noticed that the younger generations had fewer hang-ups. One time, on an airplane flight Lyle and Ariwiio took to DC, Lyle got into a huge argument with another passenger. The heated back and forth threatened to turn the flight around. Lyle tried to explain to the inebriated man how the term had been passed down through his family. Native Americans, Lyle argued, were the original Americans—Indigenous Americans, American Americans, and everyone else should be logically categorized with their continent of ancestral origin followed by the word American—Asian American, African American, European American, an exit from color. Ariwiio agreed with Lyle's rationale, but to avoid such arguments, allowed people to call themselves what they wished—no matter how superficial or illogical it sounded.

Ariwiio checked his watch. Amber should have arrived by now. She was going to point out the murder site to Sunny, where Camille had allegedly killed a man. Later, Amber would drop the detective off at the police station in the Municipal Complex so she could start gathering records to clear his son's name and hopefully find his...remains.

Sunny thanked Lyle for the tour of this part of the center, then made her smiling way back to Ariwiio.

"I really appreciated the sweat lodge. I wrote my experience down when I got back to Manhattan. I'll include it in the book. I'm sure the boys will have a winning season after that inspiring pep rally."

"It was a pleasure to have a guest." Ariwiio repositioned the wampum belts, then decided he didn't like the outcome. He draped several over his forearm before laying them in a different configuration.

"What are these?" Sunny asked, studying the items draped over Ariwiio's arm.

"They're wampum belts...but not a belt in the strict sense of the word."

He explained how his ancestors originally dyed porcupine quill segments and later shaped purple and white quahog clam shells to make beads. The belt was about the size of a bed pillow with five alternating horizontal stripes—three white, two purple.

"This particular belt is called the Two Row Wampum." He brushed his fingers over the purple stripes. "These two purple stripes represent the Haudenosaunee traveling side by side down the river of life with our new brothers from other continents." Ariwiio touched each white stripe, separating the purple. "We agreed never to interfere in the navigation of each other's vessels, each other's lives down the river of life."

"That's beautiful. I'll include it in my writing. Your people kept their promise to the newcomers."

A car door shut in the parking lot. "That must be Amber. I'll introduce you to Camille's sister. She'll drive you into town."

Fifteen minutes outside of Sunadaga territory, Amber's Subaru Outback hit the faster fifty-five-mile-per-hour zone. It was a quiet two-lane country road with no cell phone service. It would be a good place to use the whistle that Camille carved today. This stretch of road was straight with yellow dashed lines for passing. Pine trees towered on either side.

"Your father filled me in on some of your family history when we sat in front of the most spectacular bonfire at the sweat lodge," Sunny said. "What an experience."

"Pop is all about family and Haudenosaunee culture and traditions. And we're really thankful that you're helping us find out what happened to my brother." Her voice broke. "My father's heart aches."

"I'll do all I can," Sunny replied. "Your father said you and your brother were once traveling together around the nation forming a political action committee."

"That's right. The Indigenous population is only about two percent of the United States. We need to consolidate our strength. We've been ignored from the beginning."

"A PAC is honorable." Sunny loosely equated the PAC to how women had to stick together—consolidate—to demand the right to vote.

"There." Amber pointed to the opposite side of the road. "That's my mother's memorial."

In the shade of pine trees, a stone plaque with writing was surrounded by flowers, shiny reflective balloons, candles, and other items. Sunny couldn't figure out what the other items were from this distance. She presumed, like all roadside memorials, that the items represented things dear to the deceased.

"I'm so sorry," Sunny commiserated as they passed the memorial. "Was it raining or inclement weather when the accident occurred?" The detective in her was at work now.

The memorial was on a *straight* stretch of road—no tricky bends or blind curves.

"The weather was perfect. It was a starry night. Mom was coming home from her weekly quilting club meeting. Her Volvo left the road and hit a tree. No skid marks, nothing," Amber said, her voice filled with emotion, but then she laughed. "That Volvo was mom's pride and joy. She polished and cleaned it all the time. Garaged it every night. Wouldn't let anyone drive it. Not even my dad."

Sunny humorously thought of KD and his precious Vette. No way could she drive it.

Amber reached over and removed a small photo album from the glove compartment. "It's my father's. This was before digital pictures. He told me to help with the family story, so I brought along some old pictures." She handed the album to Sunny. Sunny placed her notebook on the dashboard and opened the picture album.

In one picture, Amber was the image of her mother, a beautiful woman with long, dark, shiny hair, soft but confident eyes, and flawless skin. Camille posed with a lacrosse stick, flashing the victory sign, a big ring on his finger glinting in the sunlight. The photos showed a younger and younger family as Sunny paged through the album. Camille was once a plump little fella.

"What a beautiful family. I'm sure you miss your mother and brother," Sunny empathized, closing the album and placing it back in the glove compartment. Sunny didn't know how to discreetly ask the next question, so she just put it out there. She was only curious. "Who is the woman in the picture with Camille?" She quickly added, "It's for the book."

"Camille was actually engaged once, but when he went to prison and disappeared without a trace, she waited and waited, then married someone else. We all had to move on with our lives."

The speed zone slowed as they approached the city limit. Amber made a sharp left turn, and Sunny's notebook slid to the floor, loose pages scattering.

"Oh, look at me!" Sunny called out, her hands busy at work, grasping at the floating sheets. Amber caught a couple pages with her right hand. She held them for Sunny.

"Where did you get this?" Amber's voice sounded quite firm and suspicious.

Sunny stuffed some of the wayward notes back into the notebook. She reached for the sheets Amber extended to her. It was the sheet that Camille had drawn on, a depiction of the Manhattan street grid he'd used to explain his flight plan to Sunny. Why would Amber ask about a New York City street sketch?

As Sunny reached for the sheet, Amber flipped it completely over. Sunny saw that someone had drawn a picture. That someone must've been Camille.

The unique design obviously meant something to both Amber and Camille. Sunny had to think fast. Camille didn't want his family to know he was alive, exposing them to harboring a fugitive.

"Someone at my police precinct must have been doodling." Sunny quickly stuffed the sheet into the notebook. She glanced at Amber, whose eyes batted excessively as she steered the Subaru through the city streets.

Back in cell service reach, Sunny's phone chimed with a text message from Camille. The message read that there was only one person's scent at the last homicide site, and it didn't match any of the prior scents. This was the skinny woman with the uneven nails. Camille tracked down the actual murderer and left him suspended in a colossal spiderweb for the police to find. He inserted a smiley face. Sunny was sad and angry that another woman lost her life but relieved that their caseload would decrease by one.

Amber stopped the car in front of the Municipal Complex, which contained a courthouse and a police station.

She pointed down the street. Very mechanical and monotone, unlike her earlier friendliness, Amber said, "A few blocks down past the fire station is where they claimed Camille…" She didn't finish the thought.

Sunny thanked her for the ride, got out of the car, and ascended the police station steps. She reached into her pocket to make sure she still had the whistle Camille had carved for her. Only he could hear the frequency.

Chapter Forty

Sergey hung back from Amber's Subaru much farther than he would have in New York City, where the traffic was so thick a couple car lengths would do. He applied the brakes at some kind of...he didn't know what this was on the side of the road. Shiny balloons. Flowers. He squinted to see the inscription. He couldn't sit here long. The Subaru was almost out of sight.

Oh! This is where her mother was killed in a vengeful bogus car accident, which led to contracting him once cooler heads prevailed. Emotions could get one caught.

His Jeep rolled forward. He sped up until he caught sight of the Subaru's taillights again and the two women in silhouette in the sunlight.

That second woman was getting in the way. Who was she? A tourist? A news reporter? She was at the bonfire and went into that dome-shaped...hut...with all the drum noise and chanting. Sergey didn't want any more collateral damage. Seeing the old airport waitress rolled away with a sheet pulled up over her face wasn't what he was paid for. Plus, it could widen and intensify investigations. But he would kill the second woman if she kept getting in his way.

The Subaru driver would be the first mother he was contracted to knowingly kill. Collateral damage didn't count. Then he thought of his own mother...rather the picture of her. He had never seen her, touched her. Had he missed anything as a child by not having a mother around? So many questions.

The Subaru's brake lights snapped him from his reverie. He pulled to the side of the road and retrieved his binoculars. The passenger got out and walked confidently into the police station. Police station? Sergey wasn't going into town to risk being caught on security cameras. He lowered the binoculars. The Jeep did a U-turn on the grassy shoulder.

He had to do some thinking, a recalculation to possibly include the interfering second woman. Attaching C-4 explosives under the car would do the trick. Take out both of them if need be. He couldn't miss paydays and end up homeless on the streets of New York City, people stepping over him like so much garbage.

Through the Subaru's rearview mirror, Amber watched the woman mount the steps to the police station. Who had her father allowed into their lives? It already felt like someone was following her. Now this. Did this woman have something to do with it? Only Camille knew about her new US flag idea. Camille was the family artist who painted her idea onto canvas. The detective, or whoever she was, swung open the police station door. *Doodling?* The flag US flag on the detective's paper was a pencil draft with erasure marks. Amber called her father.

"Pop, are you sure you know who this Detective McGraw is?"

"Huh." There was a long pause of the unexpected. "Well, Marshall vouches for her." His voice turned worried. "Are you okay? First, you talk about eagles following you. Now this."

She exhaled heavily. "Maybe I need more rest, but there's so much work to get done." But she was going to keep an eye on Detective McGraw.

As usual, Amber slowed as she approached her mother's roadside memorial. So many mysterious occurrences had happened on and off the territory. She contemplated postponing her next PAC trip to Nebraska. The Winnebago, one of the Ho-Chunk tribes of Wisconsin, was forced to relocate eleven times finally to Nebraska so that *settlers*—she despised the bonfire of euphemisms— could move onto the tribe's homeland. Invaders, encroachers, commandeers, thieves, or squatters would better describe many *settlers*.

Leaving her mother's memorial, she thought of her brother again. It was her idea to redesign the US flag, but again, he was the artist in the family. Their people were the discoverers of this land, the original owners for millennia. They ensured the immigrants' survival, but the US only recognized the first thirteen colonies with thirteen red and white stripes. Later, fifty stars were added to represent the fifty states. A handful of US *state* governments displayed Indigenous symbols on their state flags. Amber believed that the US ignored Indigenous people's advanced civilizations and contributions.

Her idea was a powwow drum embedded among the red and white stripes to represent the thousands of years of Indigenous life on this soil. Camille was to use only red, white, and blue in designing the powwow drum.

Amber hurried home. She needed to help her daughter with her homework and then turn to some accounting work she brought home.

Chapter Forty-one

Back in Manhattan that Saturday evening following her ride with Amber to the police station, Sunny and her bag of burgers made it through security at 100 Centre Street in lower Manhattan. One guard asked where she had gotten the delicious-smelling burgers. He was also going to buy himself a bag of wavy potato chips as Sunny had done.

The building at 100 Centre Street housed the New York City criminal court and the office of Assistant District Attorney Greg Ross. The normally bustling building was dead this evening. Sunny took the elevator up. Neither of them had time for a real dinner, so a bag of burgers had to suffice.

Greg's office number was painted on the opaque glass of a shiny wood door. She rapped her knuckles softly on the wood and heard him say come in.

Sitting behind a huge metal desk covered with legal pads, documents, and a laptop, Greg smiled warmly. Sunny had watched too many *Blue Bloods* and *Law and Order* episodes. She expected an ADA's office to be a little more...interiorly decorated. His chairs didn't match. Three large gray metal...not oak...filing cabinets completed the eyesore. But the place did have a window. Behind him hung his Yale diploma.

"And I was ragging on you about your job dominating your life. Look at me," Greg said, waving his arm over the mess on his desk. "A fellow ADA broke her leg while water skiing." Sunny winced. "Now I have to bone up on her cases in the event she doesn't make it back on crutches."

He reared back in his big black vinyl chair and eyed the bag. "Smells delicious," he said, pointing at the bag.

Sunny started doling out dinner. "I thought that guard downstairs was going to confiscate all the burgers for himself. His mouth was really watering." She slid Greg's fries, burger, and a can of 7-Up across the desk into the space he had cleared. Sunny tore open her bag of wavy potato chips and crunched on a few.

Greg loosened his dark blue red-striped tie before taking a large bite from his burger. "I promise you and I will have a real dinner when this is over," he said in a burger-muffled voice. "So, did our serial killers strike again?"

Sunny couldn't tell him that Camille didn't match the scent at the third murder site of the skinny woman with the two previous murders and her assault site. Even so, panic and terror in the city rose with each unresolved case. Pressure on KD and Sunny from City Hall and One Police Plaza rose exponentially. The NYPD task force would be fully up to speed any minute now. The FBI was already set.

"Everything's in Forensics' hands right now," she answered. "It's summer and homicides are at their height in the city." She took a swig of Coke from the can. "There's a huge backlog at NYPD Forensics," she said, shaking her head. "But we've shifted some of the work to the FBI."

Just then, her cell phone chimed with a message. She glanced at her greasy fingers and grabbed a napkin.

"Oh," she grunted, reading the message. When she looked up from her phone, Greg was chewing and gazing at her with a quizzical look on his face. "The ME," she said, turning the phone display toward him. She could now share the news without revealing Camille. "The third victim was a prostitute. Drug overdose. Her neck bruises were old, probably from her pimp. We'll turn the case back over to local precinct detectives. They already have her pimp in custody."

Although the homicide wasn't tied to her current cases, it was never satisfying in any fashion to lose a life...no matter who it was. He appreciated the update.

His desk phone rang. He peeked at the display. He started chewing faster and swallowed with some effort. "My boss." Greg hurriedly said, "I got a fantastic job offer from a Los Angeles firm. Let's do dinner so we can talk."

Sunny nodded as Greg lifted the headset. She left Greg to his extra workload. She was exhausted from the full day of back-and-forth flight, skimming the treetops of the Appalachians to Sunadaga territory, the cultural center, the local police station, soaring down the Hudson River on the back of a falcon under the stars, 100 Centre Street, and then home. She already had a thought about Los Angeles.

Chapter Forty-two

Saturday night. Jennifer had already let Tuffy out to roam the city streets. Now, he was back rubbing his cheek against Sunny's legs as she sat on her bed, massaging her tired eyes with the back of one hand while talking with her mother on the phone with the other. It was Sunny's turn to listen to Margarette McGraw go on and on about being lonely with no grandchildren to boot. Sunny had agreed with her sister not to tell their mother about the red bruise on Jennifer's forehead.

"And I still can't get anything out of that police department," her mother complained. "I need to know who killed your father. Until then, I don't feel safe."

We all want complete closure, Sunny thought, part of her mind on the irregularities she found in Camille's mother's so-called accident report. If what she found was true...

"I hear in the news about all those murders in New York City. You girls should come back to Oklahoma City."

Because there are no murders in OKC, Sunny countered in her mind. *I lost my father there! Remember?*

A scraping noise at her bedroom window grabbed Sunny's attention. Tuffy darted to the open window, followed by Sunny. Her mother was still droning on about the mean streets of New York City.

She pulled back the drapes to see a pigeon at the open window scraping the screen with its beak. What happened next startled her. Tuffy and the pigeon started vocalizing back and forth. Camille? Then she remembered his communing with the skunk near the sweat lodge. Sunny quickly said goodnight to her mom.

"What are you two talking about?" she asked the pigeon.

"Tuffy thinks it's cool that the two of you travel the city," the pigeon said. "And he's so glad he doesn't have to eat out of garbage cans anymore."

Sunny focused on Tuffy. "You do eat well. Now get outta here while I talk to this pig with wings." She pointed to the pigeon. NYC pigeons were infamous for eating anything and everything, then shittin' white streaks all over the cityscape as thanks.

"Hey! I *resemble* that remark," Camille said, flapping his wings in mock hurt feelings. Then his voice grew wistful. "All these visits to the territory with you are making me homesick. I'm going to make a quick visit tonight—fly over the old territory. Hey! How would I look as a bat?" he suddenly joked, strutting on the windowsill while making screechy bat sounds.

Sunny smiled. "You be careful." Then her tone turned serious. "I'm sorry to have to tell you this." She paused. Sunny knew this was going to hurt. "But there're irregularities surrounding your mother's death."

A voice came from the other side of the door. "Are you still talking to mom?" Jennifer asked, coming down the hall. "Let me say goodnight to her."

In a flash, Camille took wing. Sunny would share her troubling findings tomorrow.

Forty-five minutes later, Sunny's ringing cell phone caught her lying across her bed, a little drool at the corner of her mouth. Her bedside clock displayed midnight. She had fallen asleep in her street clothes. It was KD.

"Sounds like I woke you up."

"I must have nodded off. What's up?" She wiped the drool away with a tissue.

"I got a call from the FBI," KD began breathlessly.

"The FBI? Tell me we're not getting kicked off the case just yet."

"Hang on," KD said, forestalling her rant. "Remember we turned over that Big Gulp cup to the FBI, the one you fished out of that nasty corner garbage can." He chuckled. "Guess what?"

She heard satisfaction in his voice. "C'mon, KD. No twenty questions, please. What?"

"Oh, okay. You're no fun. They verified Aaron Thomas's DNA match on Christine Lowry."

Sunny shook the cobwebs in her head. "Let's cuff his ass tonight!"

Aaron wouldn't cooperate with the detectives. He clammed up and lawyered up, demanding a public defender. He spent the night at Central Booking being processed.

Several hours ago on Sunny's apartment windowsill, Camille told her how he longed to be closer to his family. Once he saw the lights go out that Saturday night in his father's and sister's houses, he flew on bat wings over one of his boyhood haunts on Sunadaga territory.

Twin Lakes shimmered under the moonlight. He remembered canoeing, swimming, and fishing on the waters and, in winter, playing snowsnake on its frozen surfaces. The kids still slid the javelin-like "snake" across the lakes just as their ancestors had done for millennia to deliver messages to the other side. The lakes, shaped like an hourglass with a wooden footbridge over the narrow center, lay still tonight, mirror shiny as Camille performed an aerial dance. His bat wings allowed for sharp and abrupt maneuvers in the night air show. He wondered how Sunny would like this rollercoaster ride on the back of a large bat.

After a frolicking, chirping, triple spin, the touch-sensitive Merkel cells on his wings detected a change in air pressure from an object ahead in the dark, descending at a forty-five-degree angle. Camille switched to echolocation, a radar-like system bats used in total darkness to locate flying insects and to avoid crashing into immovable objects such as cave walls. Bats could "see" in the dark. He rotated his ears toward the rapidly approaching object then emitted ultrasonic sound waves and waited for the return signal like waves bouncing back from the shore.

A split second later, the sound waves changed direction. *What the hell?*

He was expecting perhaps an owl, another creature capable of skillfully navigating the night sky. Then he heard a faint whirring sound, like that of a jet engine.

His advanced echolocation started assembling a picture in his head. This was no owl! It was a hawk. But hawks weren't night flyers, so why was a hawk on a collision course with him? He didn't need to ask any more questions.

Flashes of fire emanated from the menace above, accompanied by a spitting machinegun sound. The serene Twin Lake waters below splashed violently as hot bullets from a silenced weapon tore through its quiet, gleaming moonlit surface.

Camille was going to perish in the cool waters of his boyhood haunt if he didn't act fast. He folded his leathery wings tightly around his body and plummeted from the sky, but the hawk followed, closing the gap.

Attempting an evasive roll to blunt the inevitable collision, Camille braced himself. The severe but glancing blow to his head nearly knocked him unconscious. He was falling, falling, the shimmering lake waters getting closer. His opponent possessed no animal scent, only metallic qualities.

Regaining enough consciousness, Camille took the offensive. He concentrated, shifting to additional powers.

War mode!

In preparation for battle, he quickly adjusted his size to meet his larger opponent. By the time he was a few inches above the water's surface, the transformation was complete. Muscles like bridge cable steel, skin like impenetrable armor, he unfolded his enormous wings, breaking his fall. The hawk was immediately behind him. The touch-sensitive Merkel bat receptors were in total alarm at the closeness of the danger.

In a maneuver worthy of an ace fighter pilot, Camille performed an aerial loop the loop which left him behind his foe. He thrust his head forward, sinking his war-mode hardened fangs into the hawk's back. The creature made no distressed sounds. Camille released his mighty jaw muscles to plan his next move, but the hawk whirred off into the dark night as quickly as it had arrived.

Was someone out to kill him? After his mother's death, the family couldn't survive another loss.

His head still smarted from the hard blow. He flew to a nearby pine tree to hang upside down in a roosting position until he caught his breath and was able to fly back to New York City.

Chapter
Forty-three

Noon the next day, Aaron Thomas was driven up from Central Booking, where he had spent the night in a jail cell. A uniform officer now stood guard over Aaron inside the Twenty-third Precinct Interrogation Room 3. With relief that the DNA match from the Big Gulp cup was a huge break in the murder cases, Sunny had slept like a log last night.

As KD entered the interrogation room, the uni left them to their suspect. Aaron slouched in his chair. With Lieutenant Sanchez, Sunny reluctantly stood in the Observation Room on the other side of the interrogation room one-way window. Once there was a DNA match, the Loo pulled her back to ensure her personal interest didn't derail the investigation at this point. The city couldn't afford to blow the case. Women couldn't afford the NYPD to blow this case.

"Does it still smell pissy in those Central Booking jail cells, Mr. Thomas?" KD prodded. With some suspects, detectives attempted to needle them into spilling the beans by getting them upset, off-balance, and angry.

Aaron Thomas's bloodshot eyes narrowed to malevolent slits. KD might have hit a nerve. Aaron sat forward, placed his enormous wrestler's arms on the table, and interlocked his fingers. He looked as cocky as he had on the city street, sucking on his red Big Gulp. He flexed his huge biceps, dancing them alternately. The athlete in Sunny suspected performance enhancing drugs were the source of the man's freakishly bulging muscles.

"Where's my lawyer?" Aaron demanded. He had invoked the L-word last night.

"We contacted Legal Aid already," KD said. "Your lawyer will be here soon."

Sunny stepped closer to the glass, momentarily fogging it as KD took a seat directly across from the man who might have straddled her in the park Monday night. She was boiling inside. It was a good idea to separate her from this...this.... She balled her fist tightly and gnashed her teeth.

"Again, why am I here?" Aaron asked, suddenly leaning his hulk menacingly forward toward KD. The man started talking without his lawyer present.

The detective first grade didn't flinch. "It's what we told you last night when we cuffed your ass," KD growled. "Assault, attempted rape, rape, and murder."

Aaron threw himself to the back of the chair and smacked his lips. "I didn't do it."

From a folder KD had brought in with him, he extracted a document of DNA sequencing. He flipped the page onto the table like a frisbee. It spun and nearly fell into Aaron's lap before KD reached and slammed his hand atop the page. Aaron's eyes finally fell from KD to the document.

"What's this?" Aaron asked.

"It's you."

Aaron lifted the page and studied the stripe-filled columns. "Where did this come from?" he asked calmly.

Ask to see his chest, Sunny anxiously willed to KD from behind the window. She shifted from foot to foot. That night, she had clawed someone in the chest. She needed to know.

"Are you going to be okay?" Lieutenant Sanchez asked his agitated rookie detective. "I don't want to have to pull you completely from these cases."

Sunny held up her hands resignedly. "I'm good, boss." This man held her career in his hands. She needed to do this professionally, by the book.

"Aaron, that page is your DNA from the crime scenes along the Hudson River Greenway." KD flipped a second page toward Aaron. "And this is DNA from your Big Gulp." KD fixed the man with a stare. "They're identical." KD tilted his head to the side, toying with the hulk. "And DNA don't lie!" KD singsonged while tauntingly tossing his shaved head side to side.

Just then, the interrogation room door flew open. A young woman stepped confidently inside.

"I'm Mr. Thomas' attorney. I need to talk to my client," she announced with a scowl. "This interview is over."

As KD completed paperwork for Aaron Thomas' interrogation, Sunny made a quick visit to MH Construction. She could hear Camille pounding the boxing heavy bag as she ascended the stairs. He caught sight of her and stopped punching. He wore a bright white workout tank top and black sweatpants. His smile was broad, glad to see her. But what she had to tell him would be no smiling matter.

"I hear you got a lot done yesterday upstate," Camille said, wiping glistening perspiration from his neck and shoulders with a white towel. He held his handsome smile, his sparkling teeth peeking past ample lips.

As Sunny stepped closer, she noticed a bruise on Camille's forehead. "What did you do? Hit yourself?" She pointed at the heavy bag gloves he wore.

"The weirdest thing happened to me last night as I flew the territory," he said, sliding the heavy bag gloves off his hands. "I got into a battle with, I don't know what, some kind of advanced weapon." He shrugged and spread his eyebrows in confusion. "I think it was trying to kill me." He rubbed the head bruise and winced. "I switched to war mode in the nick of time."

Sunny stood with a huge, confused frown on her face. "And you say you don't know what it was?"

"Beats me," he shrugged. "Didn't seem like anything natural."

"Keep ice on it," she advised. She pointed at the chairs. "Can we sit down and talk?" she said, her voice sounding dour.

"Sure."

She followed him, and they sat across from each other. The towel was draped around his neck as he continued to wipe perspiration off. He breathed in huge audible gulps.

"I learned a lot about your life, your Sunadaga culture, and I have records from your arrest."

"Then why the sad face? Am I going to have to stay a fugitive?"

Sunny cleared her throat. "I was also able to get the accident report from the night of your mother's accident." She paused, struggling to continue.

"And what?" Camille said slowly with apprehension in his tone.

Sunny looked him straight in the eyes. "It was *no* accident."

Camille's mouth fell open, and his eyes widened. He sat back in the chair bolt straight. Sunny wished she didn't have to deliver this horrific information.

"Your sister was telling me how much your mother cherished and pampered her Volvo."

Still stunned, Camille nodded his head. "Her pride and joy. Cleaned. Polished. Not a scratch on it."

Sunny watched him try to process the horrific subject, his brow furrowed. She continued with the utmost empathy.

"Camille, I have the accident report and pictures at my apartment. It was not a *single* car accident. I sent the report and pictures to a friend in the NYPD Automotive Collision Investigation Unit. I described your mother's love of her car. Your mother wouldn't have allowed the dents they saw under the Volvo's trunk. The dents are consistent with the bumper of a modified Hummer caught on EZ-Pass a few minutes after...she was run off the road."

"*What?* Why?" he shouted. He jerked the towel from his neck and aggressively wiped his face.

Sunny reached across and held his trembling hand. "I don't know why. The name Excorp was on the side of the Hummer. Does that mean anything to you?"

"Yes," Camille said with spite. "That corporation harassed the Sunadaga to sell some of our territory. Said they wanted to build a research facility on the land and provide local jobs. My father said its offer caused a lot of hate and discontent at council meetings. There are homes and wildlife on that land. Our ancestral cemetery is on that land. My mother..." His voice trailed off.

Sunny was suddenly making the connections with the accident records. Excorp's CEO was Larry Exford. And Exford was the surname of the man Camille was convicted of killing.

Her cell phone chimed with a text from KD. Aaron Thomas and his attorney were ready to continue the interrogation.

"Tonight, I'll scour the records trying to make more sense of it all." She rose quickly. His large chest was heaving hard and fast in anger. "Please don't do anything you'll regret." She leaned and embraced him warmly. "I'm so sorry."

Following Sunny's distressing revelation that his mother's death was no accident, Camille tossed restlessly all Sunday night. He searched Excorp Industries' website for its location. Monday morning, he shifted and took flight to lower Manhattan, searching for Larry Exford.

Camille chose the kestrel for its ability to hover like a helicopter. The bird was of the falcon family but not as large or as fast as the Peregrine falcon. The kestrel could hover with a steady head, focusing on his prey. His prey today was seated at the head of an executive conference table.

Camille last saw the short, fat, round man slamming his limousine door shut outside the Sunadaga Administration Building after the Sunadaga rebuffed his final monetary offer to purchase land in the southeast of their territory.

Everyone at the conference table finally stopped to view the strange bird hovering twenty-two stories above the busy Manhattan streets. Wings outstretched, occasionally flapping to correct his position in the wind, Camille's steady eyes never left Larry Exford. No matter the turbulent gust of the bird's wind-battered body, his head was steady as a Go Pro camera fixed on his prey.

"I had better not find out you're responsible for my mother's death, you son of a bitch!" Camille fumed, gliding closer to the skyscraper's glass window. He felt like going war mode, crashing through the glass, grabbing Larry Exford's fat ass, flying as high as he could, and dropping him to the traffic-congested asphalt. But he swiveled his wings to back away from the glass.

"There will be justice!" Camille promised. He folded his wings and dropped out of the sky like a dive-bombing jet plane.

Back at MH Construction, Camille was still feeling vengeful of Larry Exford, CEO of Excorp Industries. But Sunny had warned him to do nothing he'll regret. First, they had to be certain Excorp Industries was responsible for Camille's mother's death.

Fortunately, Camille had a distraction for the moment. Too busy, Marshall needed Camille to attend a face-to-face construction bid down in Tribeca. It was a remodeling job that shouldn't take too long to bid. Marshall handled all new groundbreaking construction bids.

Camille donned his trusty shades, pulled down his cap brim, locked the shop door, and rode the rocking, rattling, Number 1 train to Franklin Street into the heart of Tribeca.

The triangle below Canal Street—Tribeca—was a lower West Side Manhattan neighborhood of pricey offices, expensive apartments, shops for the moneyed crowd. Camille stepped out of the hot, noisy, subterranean subway tunnel into the elegance. He had heard that Taylor Swift lived near. He hoped the singer, her adoring fans, and accompanying police on crowd control were nowhere near. Fortunately, the street was relatively quiet by New York City standards.

Franklin was a one-way street east. He walked the few blocks to the bakery and after uncomfortably removing the shades, introduced himself to the owner. The bakery had been in the owner's family for over fifty years and now they were selling and retiring. Camille strolled through the large establishment occasionally jotting down what load bearing walls needed to be removed and replaced with steel I-beams in order to open the space for the new highend women's boutique. The smell of bakery goods reminded him of the breads, cakes, and pies baked in his family's oven on Sunadaga territory.

Doing a doubletake, Camille observed a young

couple sitting by the sidewalk window enjoying lattes, croissants, and each other's company. But he had work to do. He finally made his way behind the counter. The pecan pie tarts caught his eye...and his stomach. He would buy three to take back to the shop. One for him. One for Marshall. And one for Sunny.

As he examined the wall structure behind the counter, tapping it with his knuckles to get a feel for depth, an authoritative voice boomed behind him.

"Can we get two of the Boston Creams, please."

Camille turned. On the other side of the display stood two NYPD uniform officers. Camille almost froze, trying mightily not to appear startled. He wasn't wearing his ever-present shades. Today he was going back to prison for certain, back to the gangs, the monotony, the racism, the guard brutality. He wouldn't ever see his family again as a free man. He just knew it. But then a counter girl rang up her customer and helped the police. Maybe only detectives memorized mugshots. He breathed a little easier. He occasionally glanced in the polices' direction but not directly at them for fear of looking suspicious.

Twenty minutes later with three pecan tarts in hand and the bid pad tucked under his arm, Camille exited the to-be boutique. He had barely completed his turn west on the sidewalk when he heard the chilling scream.

"Help! My baby is in the car!" A half block down at the daycare Camille passed on his way to the bakery, a woman was frantically and unsuccessfully pulling at the car door to save her baby. The car engine roared as the thief threw the Audi into gear.

Oh my God! Camille quickly searched the street for police and other people. All was quiet except for the woman's bloodcurdling screams. He dove to the street pavement between two parked cars sliding his pad and tarts beneath one car.

All senses red alert now, he felt his heart racing and

his skin tightening with muscles and dilated veins as the internal transformation supercharged his strength to war mode. He chose to appear as human as possible, not a charging rhino, not a rampaging bull in case security cameras were recording.

The Audi bowled in Camille's direction. Laying on his side beneath the park car's gas tank, Camille readied his fists. On a nature TV show, he had seen a pistol shrimp hiding under a coral to escape a hungry eel. The shrimp's one huge, specialized claw snapped closed with such force it sent forth a pressure wave knocking the eel unconscious. The pistol shrimp had given Camille an idea that he now used fighting crime.

The four interlocking rings of Audi's brand grew larger as the car sped closer. Camille tightened his fists. If he smashed the windshield with a massive pressure wave to stop the driver, the sharp glass shards could injure the infant, or worse. Instead, he focused on the four rings in the car's front grill. Knocking out the cooling radiator, oil pan, and electronics at the engine's front would disable the fleeing car.

With lightning speed he punched the air, one, two, with both fist. The air missiles exploded the underside of the rushing car. A plume of steam suddenly rose and an oil slick spread beneath the wounded beast killing it in his tracks.

The distraught mother jerked the rear car door open to retrieve her wailing baby. For a moment, Camille smiled triumphantly from beneath the parked car. But he needed to get out of here. He body rolled to his pad and tarts and dashed across the street to the subway tunnel.

Larry Exford, CEO of Excorp Industries, angrily swept his arm across his mahogany executive desk. Documents went sailing into the air. His laptop spun to the edge of the desk.

"A bat?" he shouted at his chief scientist, Martin Kramer.

Martin Kramer headed Excorp Industries' Secret Projects Unit, a department of Excorp's Autonomous and Robotic Systems Division. Martin flinched at his boss's outburst. The rail-thin man pushed his wire-rimmed glasses up the bridge of his nose.

"Yes, sir, Mr. Exford. Our robohawk's onboard camera recorded the entire skirmish," the scientist explained. "It's all right here," he continued, flipping open the laptop he had tucked under his arm. "Unfortunately, we lost connection with the robot and it went fully autonomous. Excorp's programmers created algorithms that allows our robots to learn by trial and error. The machine quickly teaches itself to—"

Larry Exford waved off his rambling scientist. "I don't give a shit about your recordings. I only care about results!" the CEO demanded, striking his desk with his fist. The existence of Excorp Industries was at stake. His corporation competed to supply the US military-industrial complex with its next generation of robotic soldiers for warfare. The super soldier replacing humans would make warfare much easier. Advancements in artificial intelligence—AI, and robotics would allow war from the comfort of one's desk. The robohawk was but one version of soldier, which included Excorp's humanlike robots, dogs— the list was endless.

Larry Exford wanted to know was Camille Smoke actually dead, not just missing, or would he have to finish the job. He had paid a pretty penny to get his hands on Camille Smoke's pile of jail clothes to capture the man's scent. Money could buy anything. The Indian's…Native American's…whatever…scent was loaded into the hawk's systems. Larry Exford could kill two birds with one stone: test Excorp's new, most advanced productions and get revenge for his son's death.

All the airborne desk documents finally drifted onto the plush carpet. Larry Exford leaned back in the black leather executive chair and steepled his fingers in thought. He was not going to be reliant on the Chinese or anyone for rare earth elements needed for US military advancement...and Excorp's bottom line. Not when the elements were right in his backyard, or more precisely, upstate New York on some freakin' reservation.

Martin Kramer scurried around the office mumbling scientific gobbledygook while gathering the wayward documents from the carpet.

"Let them stay there!" the CEO barked. "You and your department fix this problem." He shook his head in agitation. "A goddamned bat," he muttered. He could see the collapse of his company if his competition landed the lucrative government contracts instead of him. He wanted that entire Indian family dead. He had paid a mint to the Russian mob.

Chapter Forty-four

If Sunny could reach from the observation room through the interrogation room window to choke Aaron Thomas, she probably would. Screw a promotion. *This asshole and his wilin' crew tried to kill me.* Lieutenant Sanchez and ADA Greg Ross flanked her. She needed to keep her head. She had been warned about her temper on past cases. She and Greg still hadn't had that dinner or the LA talk. She was too busy...and avoiding him.

KD confidently entered the interrogation room. Aaron Thomas's attorney, Kathy Crosby, was seated next to her client. Aaron's cockiness was still springing eternal.

"Where's your sidekick?" Aaron's voice was salacious. "That looker." He smacked his lips the way he always did. The lewd gesture even got his attorney's attention, who gave him the hand signal to tone it down.

"Mr. Thomas," KD began, taking a seat across from the pair. "You're pretty fresh and cheeky for someone facing

261

prison time." KD leaned his head, feigning looking under the table. "I bet the other inmates would love to *meet* you."

Aaron's expression fell. He squirmed in his seat. "I didn't do it, I told you!" Aaron's voice boomed off the gray cinderblocks.

"Aaron, we're beyond that," KD counter, unperturbed. "Remember? We have your DNA from under one victim's fingernails and more of your DNA at other crime scenes. All's a match with your Big Gulp cup."

KD retrieved a picture from his folder and placed it before Aaron and his attorney. It was a chest picture of Aaron taken during his strip search at Central Booking last night. Fingernail scratch marks ran down his muscular left shoulder to his chest. Sunny sighed loudly, her forehead almost touching the one-way window. They hadn't told her about the fingernail DNA match. *It was probably a good idea*, she seethed.

"Aaron, you can make this hard, or you can make this easy. It's all up to you." KD held his arms out, palms forward. He paused to let the words sink in. "Right now, you're looking at a life sentence." KD confidently eased himself into his chair while eyeing Aaron.

Aaron sat up straight and glanced at his attorney. The musclebound man closed his eyes and massaged his temples.

"Our records show that your family is well-off but not rich, Aaron, like the others you were with those nights. Their parents are friends with the mayor and other high muckamucks. They'll bring in a team of hot-shot lawyers to defend them, probably plead affluenza." KD snickered. By affluenza, he meant a person who was deemed ill due to too much wealth. The defense had been tried before. "They'll throw you under the bus."

Aaron started nervously wiping his mouth. His brown forehead now glistened with sweat.

KD set the hook. "The first to cooperate gets the juicy deal."

Aaron leaned to his attorney. They whispered an exchange. Attorney Crosby nodded acceptance, and KD waved to the interrogation room window for ADA Greg Ross to enter and cement the deal. Sunny marched to follow the ADA, but Lieutenant Sanchez grabbed her by the arm, stopping her in her tracks.

Aaron Thomas gave his confession of all the wrestling frat boys' off-campus booze, cocaine, and steroid use. They had no respect for women. Women were there to serve men. KD grabbed the garbage can as Aaron Thomas got sick, puking.

Chapter Forty-five

With Aaron Thomas' confession, the case strengthened. DNA at Christine Lowry's rape and murder scene included Aaron's saliva on her breast, other suspects' skin cells under her fingernails, and pubic hairs. Aaron named all the other wrestling team members involved in the brutal and deadly crimes.

The detectives hit the road to round up the team, rich kids full of drugs, alcohol, steroids, and privilege.

Two suspects were handcuffed right in their classrooms, one in physics lab, the other in history class. The last, Luke Chambers, was on the run, his Porsche missing from its Manhattan condo parking spot. An APB, all-points bulletin, was issued for his arrest.

At the precinct, Sunny searched DMV records for the Porsche's license plate and then the EZ-Pass toll system and city automatic plate readers for Luke's travel.

"I see where he went through the Battery Tunnel. He's on the move." She sighed. The tunnel connected Manhattan and Brooklyn.

"I think I got something, too," KD said, leaning into his laptop. "I can't get any pings from his cell phone. Must have turned it off. But I see credit card usage." He turned the display so Sunny could see it. "Gas, liquor store, pizza. Judging from these timestamps, he's headed east out on Long Island."

"What's out there for him?"

"Don't know."

Lieutenant Sanchez leaned out of his office. "Jackson. McGraw. I just got off the phone with Suffolk County police. The APB may have netted our suspect. He's in Riverhead at a vacation home owned by the Chambers." The Loo shook his head woefully. "We have another problem, though. Our boy Luke has taken an eleven-year-old girl hostage."

Shit! With that guy's state of mind, what had he done to the little girl? Sunny raged inside.

"In ten minutes, I'll have a chopper waiting for you two at the Wall Street heliport," Lieutenant Sanchez announced. "Head there now! I'll have ADA Ross there as well. He may have to make a deal with this bastard."

"Mr. Chambers is probably still in Manhattan," KD affirmed. "I'll have a patrol car, lights flashing, get him to the heliport also. He may be useful in hostage negotiation with his son."

The NYPD helicopter sat idling on the heliport. Its twin turbine engines whined as the four rotor blades on top spun, creating enough downwash to blow Sunny's hair over her face.

Greg squinted as dust and debris swirled around them. He leaned toward Sunny. "Are you avoiding me? You haven't said one word."

Sunny used the noisy chopper blades to conceal their conversation—no way she wanted to talk inside the helicopter.

"Greg, I'm not going to LA," she said bluntly.

"Can we at least discuss it first?"

"I'm sorry. That's your career. Mine is here. And I'm not having a long-distance relationship either." Greg certainly wasn't her real estate salesman ex-boyfriend who she in the end suspected would have asked her to leave the life she loved, one that made a real difference in the world. It was a life that also honored her father.

He started to debate further, but the pilot was beckoning all to climb aboard.

On the sly from her pocket, Sunny fished out the whistle Camille gave her. She blew a silent alarm. She stepped into the helicopter behind ADA Greg Ross and Mr. Chambers. KD brought up the rear.

"KD, you rascal," the woman pilot said from behind dark aviator shades.

KD introduced Laura Perry. "Is this your new ride?" KD asked, surveying the chopper's interior, patting the seats in appreciation. "It looks different from the last time."

"I'm told you folks needed to get to Riverhead in a hurry. That Bell 412 chopper we were in a year ago charging above Interstate 95 in Jersey after your triple murder suspect can't outrun this new Bell 429." She laughed. "It's like, should we take the family SUV or your Vette?"

KD laughed along with Laura. "Do you miss your Apache?" he asked. He shared with the other passengers how Laura flew Apache helicopters in Afghanistan.

"I miss my Hellfire missiles," she guffawed. Laura checked that everyone had their seatbelts fastened. "Hang on to your underwear for about twenty-five minutes."

With that, the turbine engines roared, and the G-forces glued them to the seat. The chopper lifted and steeply banked to the east.

Once they had reached cruising airspeed, Mr. Chambers finally broke his silence and his face of stone. "I'm so sorry." He shook his head. "How did I not know?"

"Mr. Chambers," KD began, "my experience is these hostage situations rarely end well." He let it hang in the air for a moment. "Prepare yourself, sir."

The chopper interior went quiet, the drone of the turbines filling the void.

With a single bounce twenty minutes after takeoff, Laura Perry set the Bell 429 down at the far end of Long Island in Indian Island County Park in the city of Riverhead. Sunny and her ex-boyfriend had once passed through Riverhead on the way to the North Fork and a fancy three-fork dinner party. Riverhead got its name from the fact that the Peconic River—situated at the convergence of the famous Long Island *forks*—gets its start here. Suffolk County police shuttled the NYPD detectives and two others to the Chambers' vacation home five minutes away.

Upon arrival at the Chambers property, Sunny had a hard time believing she was looking at a vacation home— brilliant flower beds, mulch-surrounded trees, freshly mowed lawn, not a single weed in sight. The sea blue vacation home was probably three times the size of her childhood home in Oklahoma City. She could almost smell the money.

Emergency Service Unit had the property surrounded. A distraught couple, presumably the eleven-year-old's parents, embraced out in the street. ESU personnel dressed in all black crouched near their black trucks, automatic weapons, and battering rams ready. KD and Sunny approached a man with ESU emblazoned on his back and a bullhorn to his mouth, having a conversation with Luke Chambers, who was somewhere inside near a window at the front of the house, out of sight.

"Release the child, Luke," the husky ESU captain demanded into the bullhorn. At the sight of the NYPD detectives, the ESU officer introduced himself as Leonard Palmer. KD quickly described how he planned to swap positions with the captive eleven-year-old girl. He took the bullhorn.

"Luke, this is Detective Jackson. You know me. Let the little girl go and take me instead." KD handed the bullhorn back and began disarming himself.

There came sick, sadistic laughter from the house. "I don't want any *men*. I always choose *women*." There was a long pause. "Send in gorgeous Detective McGraw," he drawled salaciously.

ADA Greg Ross shook his head vigorously. But before he or KD objected, Sunny volunteered. "I'm going in. That little girl must be terrified." She started removing her weapons.

"No! We can't do this," the ESU captain countered. "We need experience in there." He beckoned for an Emergency Services Unit female officer to join them. He again raised the bullhorn to his mouth. "We'll swap one of our female ESU officers for the little girl."

The response was immediate. "I'll kill this little bitch if you don't send in McGraw," Luke spat.

Everyone looked at Sunny. The decision was forced. "Make him prove the child is still alive," she said, removing her holster.

KD put the bullhorn back to his mouth. "Luke, *prove* to us that the girl is still alive."

"I don't have to prove shit!" The man cackled, sounding demonic as if in some altered state of mind. But moments later, the frightened child's head appeared in the window, gray duct tape over her mouth. With one hand, Luke held her neck tightly from behind. Sunny knew the terrifying feeling of hands around one's neck. Luke's other hand pressed the gun against the child's temple.

Sunny took the bullhorn. "Luke, I'm coming in." ESU and KD gave Sunny instructions to maneuver Luke near a window for a sniper head shot. She marched forward with her hands high.

Chapter Forty-six

"Let the child go, Son," Mr. Chambers' amplified voice came through the bullhorn from behind Sunny on the lawn. "Let's end this whole thing right now. Release the child. No detective exchange." There was quiet. "Why are you doing this? Shaming the family? We've given you everything."

The living room curtain moved slightly, Luke's hand pushing the curtain. ESU personnel raised their long guns, but the squad leader waved them off. The deadly gun barrels lowered.

"Yes, Dad, you gave me every-*thing*."

"Then why are you doing this?"

"You never got it, did you?" Luke yelled.

"Got what, Son?"

Luke's voice was sad, garbled, slurring. "I never could measure up to Howard Jr." He sounded ready to cry.

Father and son went back and forth as Sunny stepped closer to the house on the exquisitely manicured lawn. In the exchange with his father, Luke admitted removing his brother's wristwatch to feel closer, more accomplished, and gifted like his big brother, upon whom his parents lavished praise. Sunny flashed to Luke's meager display of trophies among Howard Jr.'s on the huge fireplace mantle in the mansion. Luke couldn't compete with his big brother.

During the instructions, Sunny was also told that ESU would rush in at shots fired from inside the vacation home. Halfway to the house she removed her Kevlar vest.

"Remove the gun that's in your boot," Luke shouted angrily.

Sunny complied. She was going in defenseless to tangle with a desperate, nothing-to-lose, WWF-like man, jacked up out of his mind on alcohol, cocaine, steroids, and who knew what else.

After ascending the three steps to the porch, Sunny waited for Luke's next move. The front door cracked open.

"Any funny business and this little bitch's brain is all over the living room," came from behind the door.

Sunny raised her hands in the air to prove she wasn't going to try anything. She slowly dropped her right hand to open the screen door and then pushed open the main door.

Just then, a hummingbird, its wings buzzing, flew past Sunny and Luke and into the house. "Hurry up and shut the goddamn door," Luke shouted, spit flying from his mouth. "You're letting in all kinds of shit."

The living room wasn't Chateau *Westdale* in Millbrook, but it was nonetheless lavish. She didn't know furniture manufacturer names, but she could see that all the furniture, sofa, and several recliners all matched.

Luke stood in the center with one gun pointed at Sunny and another tucked in his waistband. His eyes were bloodshot and droopy. He didn't look all there. He swayed on his feet. His huge biceps strained against a short-sleeve shirt. On the coffee table were two lines of cocaine, a syringe, and a bottle of vodka. A pizza box was on the floor with a half-eaten pepperoni pizza. The man was soaring. The little girl was nowhere in sight.

"Where's the girl?" *You piece of shit!* Sunny felt like screaming. But then Sunny caught sight of two bare feet as she allowed her eyes to scan the place. Behind Luke was a dining room. The little girl was on the floor with her feet poking out from behind a partition wall.

Luke smiled demonically, then momentarily pointed the gun at the child to indicate her location. "She's right there."

"You promised to exchange her for me."

"I did?" He cocked his head, toying with her.

"Luke, she's just a child. Let her go, please." Sunny now played to his fantasy. "You have me now, a grown woman who knows how to please a man. That little girl can do nothing for you."

Luke stared at Sunny for a moment. Sunny could practically read what was happening behind those bloodshot eyes in his drug-altered head. He started nodding his head. He grabbed his crotch with his free hand. *Bingo,* Sunny thought.

"Yeah…yeah, I do have a grown woman now," he replied, his words soaked with carnal desire. He looked Sunny up and down anew. "But I need to restrain you first," he said as he backed to the living room table, not taking his eyes off Sunny. He grabbed a roll of gray duct tape.

"Lay down on your stomach and cross your arms and legs," he commanded. Sunny lay on the plush blue carpet as he searched and secured her. "What is this?" he asked of Camille's carving.

"A whistle my uncle carved," she quickly lied. She hoped that hummingbird was Camille. She had no idea how to get out of there alive.

Luke hurled the whistle aside, bouncing it on the carpet. He dragged a groaning, restrained Sunny against the wall to a sitting position.

Luke tucked the second weapon in his waistband, then grabbed the child by her hair, dragging her like a sack of potatoes into the living room. Mouth taped, the little girl squealed in fear, terror in her young brown eyes.

The girl's distraught parents had told law authorities that their daughter's name was Jasmine. The child's skinny arms and legs were bound with gray duct tape. Her eyes were damp and red-rimmed from crying. Her tiny legs trembled. Sunny wanted to comfort the terrified child in an embrace, but she, too, was bound. On the floor, back against the wall, Sunny twisted and pulled, testing the tape's strength to free her hands. It was no use.

"Sweetie, it's going to be all right," Sunny directed at the quaking child. Jasmine's bony legs shook uncontrollably. On the inside leg of the child's white shorts, Sunny noticed blood. *That freakin' pervert! He molested her. Give me one chance to kill you!*

Sunny exploded. *"What did you do to her?"*

"You want to get some tape on your big loudmouth, too?" Luke threatened. "She fell off her bike as I grabbed her off the street."

"Luke, let her go, please. That was the deal. You got me now."

"So I lied." He laughed and shrugged his musclebound shoulders. "I got both of you now." The man's huge frame wavered, drugs and alcohol in command.

"Don't make this worse than it already is. The ADA is outside. We can make a deal. Let the child go," Sunny pleaded. "She's terrified."

Luke was quiet for a moment, then he stepped to the trembling girl and tore off the child's taped leg restraint but left her arms and mouth bound. He marched the stumbling frail child to the door, opened it, and pushed her in the back onto the porch, where she tumbled down the steps and hit her head on the ground, with no arms to break her fall. Sunny heard the child's parents cry out in anguish and relief. She took a deep breath. Now, how would she get out of there alive?

"Why did a big muscular guy like you ask for little old me to come in here, Luke?" She was trying to get in his head now.

He sniffled, thinking. He eyed the lines of cocaine, then walked away to face Sunny, towering menacingly over her.

"Men dominate women. That's the natural order. Always has been," he said matter-of-factly. "I'm going to have a little fun with you." He leaned his head to the side, ogling Sunny up and down.

Sunny pressed herself harder against the wall, turning her head to the side, away from the monster. *He's going to finish what he failed to do in the dark park along the Hudson,* she thought, her mind racing for a solution.

She needed to buy some time to figure out how to subdue this violent, crazed brute of a man.

"May I have some water, please?" She licked her lips in feigned thirst. "I'm so thirsty." Sunny was trying to get Luke to move past the window to give ESU a shot at him.

Luke slowly lowered the gun. He looked confused. Then he suddenly jerked the gun back at her head. "No!" he shouted and backed away a few steps.

She was going to die. She always knew it would be in the line of duty like her father. But not ignominiously tied on a floor. Small talk wasn't going to work with this man. Before the bullet exploded her head, she owed it to Christine, to Christine's baby, to Elaine to hear it straight from Luke's mouth.

"Why did you have to kill them?"

Standing ten feet away and looking down at Sunny, Luke was getting more agitated. "Will you shut the fuck up?" He grabbed his head with both hands. "I can't think."

But Sunny kept up the pressure. Maybe he would make a mistake in her favor. She had no other option.

Something soft and furry brushed against her hands taped behind her back. Camille? Had the whistle really worked? She turned her attention back to the madman.

"In Aaron Thomas's statement, he says you wouldn't stop kicking and punching Elaine as she lay dying in the alley. You lost your watch there."

Luke cackled contemptuously. "That freak! That was a man dressed as a woman!" His huge shoulders shook in a disgusted shutter.

He briefly squeezed his eyes shut, then opened them and glanced again at the lines of cocaine on the table. Then he scowled and shook his head scornfully. "Aaron Thomas. I knew we shouldn't have let him into our circle. But that other *real* woman..." He meant Christine. He started nodding in satisfaction. He licked his lips and seemed to snap out of a dream. "I don't know what happened to that first woman." He was unknowingly speaking of Sunny. "*Something*...something grabbed me and hurled me through the air. Something very strong," he admitted. "I don't know..."

So he was positively there that fateful night, helping to choke the life out of her. Reflexively, she thought of springing up and beating the shit out of the creep now that her hands were free behind her back. But her legs were still hobbled. Through her peripheral vision, Sunny saw a chipmunk scurry behind Luke and into the dining room.

"Was that...*something*...that grabbed you that night...furry?" She needed to distract him.

Luke froze. Stared at her for a long moment. "How do you know that?" He took a quick, aggressive step toward her with the semi-automatic aimed at her head.

Sunny braced for the bullet impact, squeezing her eyes shut, her heart a jackhammer. But something in her just didn't care anymore.

Noise in the kitchen stole Luke's attention. Glass smashed on the floor in there.

"Come out with your hands up," Luke spun, shouted, and pulled the second gun from his waistband. One gun was aimed at Sunny, the other toward the kitchen as he slid sideways, his head on a swivel for action from either direction. "I'll shoot this bitch if you don't come out with your hands up." The kitchen went silent.

Luke eased to the dining room and took a quick peek into the kitchen so as not to get shot in the face. "Whadda hell?" he screeched, stumbling backward, shaking his head vigorously. "A big ass wolf!"

Chapter Forty-seven

As Luke spun to run from what he called a wolf on the other side of the partition wall, he blindly fired several shots in that direction and then slipped to the carpet, face first, as he lost traction in his haste. Sunny saw her chance. A hummingbird. A chipmunk. A wolf. Camille. She tore the tape from her legs and, in a split-second, dove on top of the prone man's muscular back, choking him with all her might, trying to cut off blood flow to his brain. From his fallen position, he gagged and attempted to aim the semiautomatic behind himself. Sunny ducked and weaved her head, frustrating his aim. His big body lay on the .38 Colt revolver in his waistband.

She tried to reach the revolver but couldn't wedge her hand past their combined weight. The semiautomatic swung toward her head again, and she ducked in the other direction to avoid a headshot.

After the shots were fired, ESU would be crashing the door down any second now, but not soon enough. She was on her own for the moment against this crazed brute. Grunting and gagging, Luke made it to all fours with Sunny still clinging to his back. More struggling, he made it to his feet. She wrapped her legs around his waist and leaned back, straining for added choking leverage caused make him to lose his balance. Luke staggered backward, gurgling. Both his hands free now, he grabbed the revolver from his waistband. Both gun barrels flailed, seeking their target. But reaching behind himself only threw the huge man further off-balance.

Wrestling in the ring was his advantage, but this was no ring with referee and rules. The drugs and alcohol brain fog, and ironically, the guns, Sunny believed played to her advantage. Guns weren't used in a wrestling ring. He was clumsy—out of his element. Her guerrilla strategy had to prevail, or else she was a dead woman.

The duo staggered backward into the fireplace mantle. Priceless antique heirlooms went flying as Luke's huge arms swept, seeking support to regain his footing. Sunny's shoulder crashed into the stone mantel, sending an excruciating message to her brain that she might have broken it. She couldn't continue to choke the delirious man.

They bounced off the stone mantle and spun to the center of the living room. Her choking grip was slipping, her numb shoulder giving out. She needed a miracle to see tomorrow.

And then it hit her. In a move made infamous by Tyson fighting Holyfield, with all the strength she had left, she pulled herself forward as they whirled in their deadly dance in the center of the thick blue carpet. She opened her mouth wide and chomped down on Luke's ear. A warm, bloody chunk of the cartilage-filled appendage rolled over her tongue. AIDS...she didn't care. Hepatitis...she didn't care. She might survive those. Bullets to her head.... She spat the warm, crunchy, bloody mess onto the carpet.

He howled and lurched to the side, falling into the lines of cocaine, splintering the coffee table. Sunny somehow hung on as her bad shoulder slammed into the table, again sending hot lightning up and down her spine.

But, in the heap of splintered wood, she was able to reach around Luke with her non-shooting left hand for the revolver he had dropped in the crash.

Apparently sensing his opportunity, Luke reacted violently to Sunny loosening her choke hold around his neck as she reached for the revolver. In a burst of drunken, high, disoriented energy, he rolled away from Sunny toward the fireplace at the same time firing the semiautomatic aimlessly, windowpanes shattering. Then the room went quiet as he got his bearing again. Finally, his wild, crazy eyes locked on hers. He raised the semiautomatic to fire, to take her out.

His roll to the fireplace had given right-handed Sunny enough time to adjust to shooting with her left hand using the clumsy revolver. *The weapon recoil would cause severe pain, but so be it.* This was life or death.

Before Luke could squeeze the trigger of the automatic again, Sunny's gun exploded with one round above Luke's right eye. Her right hand would have put the bullet between his eyes, even with a revolver. He jerked backward but seemed to absorb the round like a bull elephant. Two more shots into Luke's face sent the hulking wrestler flat on his back.

Sunny lowered the revolver, white smoke curling from the barrel, and rolled onto her good side. Her other shoulder hurt like hell.

Doors in the front and back of the vacation home burst open with battering rams. She heard law enforcement rush in, shouting, KD with them.

Rolling onto her back and squeezing her eyes closed, Sunny grimaced at the shoulder pain. "KD, we did it! KD, we did it!" she repeated over and over.

279

Exhausted and out of breath, she opened her eyes, scanning all the grim ESU faces looking down at her. She massaged her shoulder. She struggled up on one elbow, clutching her possibly broken shoulder. Her breathing was labored. A hummingbird flitted through the house.

On one knee, KD helped Sunny to a sitting position. "You did good, partner," he said, looking around the demolished living room. "I like how you've decorated the place," he joked. "What is it? Early McGraw-esque?" She smiled through the pain. He lifted Sunny to her feet and to a waiting ambulance.

Chapter Forty-eight

Several days after Sunny shot Luke Chambers to death, the Miss Ellis Island ferryboat rocked on the choppy waters of New York Bay below Manhattan. Sunny preferred the open-air top deck of the triple-deck ferry for its panoramic view. In public, Camille made certain his braid was well tucked under his dark blue cap, its brim pulled low, with dark wraparound shades completing his concealment.

Sunny had taken a few days off, popping Tylenol, soaking in hot baths, and sleeping. Fortunately, her shoulder wasn't broken. Today, she wanted to visit Ellis Island, something she'd been promising herself since moving to New York. Camille was game. They also planned to go jogging along the Hudson River Greenway during this administrative leave.

Squawking, conniving seagulls patrolled overhead chasing the ferryboat, waiting for generous tourist food offerings, or, for the unsuspecting, to turn their attention away for a moment only to see their snacks fly away in the mouths of hungry gulls the size of chickens on Uncle Joe's farm.

On the top deck aluminum bench seat, Camille, on the sly, leaned toward Sunny until their shoulders touched. She didn't pull away.

"I was ready to pounce on Luke Chambers after you two crashed into that stone fireplace, injuring his shoulder. I tried to keep my furry wolf back hidden below the windowsill." Camille described how he crouched low in the dining room, carefully watching Sunny's advantage slipping away.

"Chewing the duct tape from my hands and then creating that noise distraction in the kitchen surely saved my life. Luke came stumbling into the living room, and I saw my chance. I have you to thank...again."

"I did what I could under the circumstances. You already have enough trouble trying to explain the gorilla fur." He laughed. "But I would have turned myself over to authorities and gone back to prison to keep you alive."

"That's so sweet," Sunny said, momentarily laying her head against his broad shoulder.

"But then you got a taste for *ear*, and that turned the table." They both burst out laughing but then subdued their fun when other passengers looked their way. Camille didn't need attention.

The Statue of Liberty was in the background. Sunny twisted in her seat to see Lady Liberty. She mentioned visiting Lady Liberty some other day when they had more time. Today, she wanted to see what her ancestors experienced as they sailed to the New World.

"I can just imagine them on these very waters," Sunny commented, surveying New York Bay, squinting as the brilliant sunshine reflected off the water. "But you never think like this, right? Your ancestors discovered this land thousands of years ago. The rest of us got here only a few minutes ago relative to your ancestors. This means little to you, doesn't it?"

Camille smiled at her concern and curiosity. "There were intermarriages, and I'm sure some of my relatives came through this harbor. I have some curiosity. Indigenous people say we've been here 'forever.' Not all our European surnames," Camille continued, "were due to force assimilation."

His mind flashed to the horrid Indian boarding schools where Native kids were ripped from their loving parent's arms and stripped of their names, dress, culture, and traditions.

She must have picked up on his quiet deliberation. "Are you okay?" She reached for his hand.

"I'm good. Thank you," he reassured.

Sunny changed the subject as the ferryboat closed in on Ellis Island.

"I ran Excorp past my old college chemistry professor. Told him how the corporation is heavy into genetics, artificial intelligence, and robotics for the military. He thinks Excorp interest in that particular region of Sunadaga territory is all about rare earth elements essential to the corporation's business."

"And that's the reason they killed my mother?" Camille's jaw muscles worked as he contemplated avenging his mother's death. Greed once again had no conscience.

Sunny squeezed his hand. "Please don't do anything rash, Camille. Let me finish investigating. Let's not make things worse." She tugged at his hand. "Promise me!"

He wasn't going to mention how he hovered twenty-two stories above the city streets at Excorp's headquarters. No one inside knew who he was so that particular rash moment didn't count. He solemnly nodded that he'd allow the investigation to finish.

A half mile northeast of the Statue of Liberty, Miss Ellis Island ferryboat steered to dock at the Ellis Island

Immigration Museum. The ferry jostled and rocked on the waves, bumping the boat against the dock. From the third deck of the ferry, they had an unobstructed view. The red brick building had white limestone trim. Four spires rose four stories into the sky.

Camille tentatively took her hand, and they weaved their way down the stairs and off the ferry. With limited time, they had agreed in advance to hit the high spots and not linger too long. That evening, they had to pack the saddlebags for a flight tonight to the upstate powwow.

On the main floor, they strolled behind a tour group that was admiring and snapping pictures of an exhibit of historic dusty suitcases and trunks piled high behind a chest-high glass enclosure. Early immigrants brought their most valued possessions across the ocean in suitcases.

They eavesdropped on a tour guide. "Most arrived in third class," she said, "or steerage, some called it." The tour guide wore green pants, a safari coat, and a Smoky Bear hat. "A thousand people crammed into the dirty bottom of the steamship for two weeks with little food, fresh air, or sunlight." Some in the tour group looked repulsed, along with Sunny, who shuttered. The tour group meandered to the next exhibit.

Sunny whispered to Camille, "My former chemistry professor studied the topography of the land Excorp wanted. There's a stream running through it and out of Sunadaga territory. The professor wants us to collect water and soil samples tonight in that area for analysis."

"We can do that. I know where we can *steal* an old farm truck to get there." She looked askance at him as he winked.

Deeper into the Main Floor signs beckoned with: *The Peopling of America 1550-1890*, the era before Ellis Island became a processing station. They broke away from the tour at times, tugging each other in different directions, observing the myriad exhibits. He enjoyed being with her.

"When is your Internal Affairs interrogation?" Camille asked as they approached a huge Western Hemisphere map that illustrated the "Against Their Wills" Atlantic African slave trade and another map the European migration. A panel of text referred to Europeans who were forced to America, the Native Americans who were forced to plantations in the Caribbean, and the largest forced migration, African slaves chained cheek by jowl in the belly of the slave ships for months.

"How do you know about Internal Affairs?" she asked.

"I watch TV. I like *Blue Bloods* and *Chicago PD*." His face spread into a wide grin. "I know that following any cop-involved shooting, you folks are interrogated. I also know you have to see a shrink. Maybe you can tell them about all the strange animals that only *you* have seen."

That cracked her up. She bent forward, laughing, and told him to stop. She took a deep composing breath and stood contemplatively for a moment to continue reading the "Against Their Wills" display. Her head tilted to one side. She pointed at the word European. "There were plenty of my Irish ancestors in there," she finally said, her voice painfully wistful.

Camille looked from the display and then to Sunny, her head still leaning in thought. He allowed her the moment, interlocking their fingers tighter.

"The English dehumanized my ancestors, called them *savages* too," she muttered. "And they took my ancestor's land." Camille nodded his agreement.

After ten more minutes of exhibits hand-in-hand, they took the stairs to the second floor. Signs indicated they were in the Registry Room.

The space was enormous, cavernous. The Registry Room echoed with many tourist voices. Sunny spun, taking it all in. The incredible room of vaulted ceilings once greeted millions of immigrants escaping poverty, religious intolerance, and tyranny.

"Can you believe this place?" She was amazed, eyes wide.

"It is impressive." Camille pointed to another tour group. "Let's listen in."

"This area was once filled with what resembled rows of cattle pens," the tour guide said, "then later filled with long wooden benches." He went on about how the immigrants slowly wound their way to the Inspection Desk, where they endured lengthy interviews. Those in good health with their papers in order exited via the Stairs of Separation, which he pointed out behind the Inspection Desk. "At the bottom of the stairs is the Kissing Post," the guide continued. That got Camille's attention and gave him an idea.

Sunny leaned close to him. "I just thought about something you said on the way here."

"What's that?"

"You said *you're* going to be *in* the powwow, not *at* the powwow."

"That's correct. Follow all the attention this evening directed into the woods." He gave her another wink. She looked confused. With a huge, knowing smile, he turned and listened to the guide. Sunny playfully jerked at his arm for keeping her in suspense.

Her cell phone chimed with a new text message. She read it. A smile rose. "I met Gina Duncan at Club Posh. She's throwing a benefit at the club to give Elaine a proper and dignified burial. Elaine doesn't have to be buried in an unmarked mass grave."

"That's wonderful," Camille remarked.

"I want you to come with me," she said from Camille's side, leaning against him. "Come as Brooklyn the Yorkie." She laughed.

Camille barked, panted with his tongue out, nodding yes. Next, he pointed to the Stairs of Separation just to the right as the tour guide descended the stairs to leave the museum.

"We better be going," he said.

They slowly descended the stairs as the guide described how elated immigrants met their loved ones at the Kissing Post, a spot now marked by a gold plaque on the wall. Camille allowed the crowd to move forward before he and Sunny read the plaque describing how immigrants were reunited with friends and relatives with abundant kisses.

The tour moved on, and no one else followed down the stairs. This was Camille's chance. "You and Greg still seeing each other?"

"He's a friend. That's all," she replied, grabbing his arm with both hands. "He just landed a job in LA. I have no interest in LA or a long-distance romance."

"Good."

The tour group was dispersing. The Kissing Post plaque hung on the wall next to them. Facing her, he took both of her hands, looking into those brown eyes with green flecks. Ever since that fateful night along the Hudson River Greenway, he saw something in her eyes when they sat in the tall oak tree. Strong. Courageous. Caring. Attractive. She possessed the qualities he admired.

"This is going to be complex," he whispered.

She nodded, her eyes gleaming. "I'm good at complex."

"But I'm a fugitive *and* a freak of nature. And I don't know how all this superpower, shifter stuff ends." He pulled her closer.

"We'll have to take it one step at a time."

He placed the sweetest, tenderest kiss on her lips.

Then the stair door above jerked open. A bunch of laughing, frolicking kids descended with their parents and tour guide in tow.

Chapter Forty-nine

The tall aromatic pine trees thirty yards behind Sunny and his father offered the best spot for Camille to observe and hear them talking. In the evening's golden twilight, Sunny and Ariwiio sat in metal folding chairs overlooking the powwow circle. Next to them, a gigantic, four-peaked, brilliant white canvas marquee food tent stood. Its triangle-shaped, white banner flags snapped in the breeze, while inside the tent, cooks stirred and tasted traditional Native dishes.

As the sun set, Camille simultaneously snorted and stomped one hoof to the ground a few times, garnering the attention of his fellow Sunadaga. Sunny twisted in her seat to view the powerful whitetail buck with an impressive antler rack standing between the pine trees not far away. Her smile told Camille that she recognized him. Just follow everyone's attention he had told her. Camille rotated his ears forward to hear their conversation.

"I've never seen that buck round here," Ariwiio remarked. "Must have migrated from another area."

"Have any ever migrated from New York City?" Sunny quipped.

"Huh?" Ariwiio's brow furrowed in confusion.

"My attempt at humor," she admitted, smiling at Camille in the tree shadows.

Longing once again to participate in a powwow, Camille watched the Sunadaga dance in a circle to coax beloved Mother Earth to do the same in her graceful circle around Elder Brother—the sun. For the Sunadaga, to stop dancing was to stop life. In the woods, Camille started bobbing his antlers in rhythm with the rumbling powwow drum.

Five minutes later, the big drum quieted. From the loudspeaker a man's airy chant, rhythmic trills, warbling heights and dips filled the powwow ground. This signaled the start of the Smoke Dance. In the dark woods, Camille aimed his ears to hear his father again.

"I used to Smoke Dance," Ariwiio told Sunny, pointing to the powwow ground, "until I sustained a shin wound in the Army. I started Camille Smoke Dancing when he was four years old," he said wistfully. He quickly explained the Smoke Dance's origin of needing to create vigorous movement to force smoke through the longhouse roof smoke hole.

"That's some fancy footwork," Sunny pointed out, intently watching the powwow.

On the darkening powwow ground, men dressed in full, colorful, flashy regalia performed dizzying swirls. Their feet were a blur. Their energetic moves were not for the unfit. The Sunadaga singer drummers, their bodies rocking to the steady beat, their drumsticks crashing on the taut deer skin, bent earnestly over the big powwow drum. Camille rocked to the beat, his antlers wavering side to side. The drum's hard downbeat connected with the dynamic dancers, their moves in perfect harmony. Later, the women, including Amber, swirled in billowing overdresses of elaborate beadwork. Their arms were outstretched. They wore leggings above their moccasin-covered feet which were a flash of activity.

Ten minutes later, Amber was still breathing hard from the Smoke Dance. Her bead dress clicked as she brought Ariwiio and Sunny fry bread on paper plates. No powwow was complete without the fried dough treat. Camille ached to hug his sister.

"You were so graceful and athletic out there. And I just love your dress," Sunny complimented Amber, eyeing the elaborate beadwork embroidery of symbols.

"Thanks. It's my mother's dress." Amber paused. She seemed ready to cry, but then described that the hissing and clicking of the dress were due to hundreds of multicolored shiny beads lovingly laced into the dress, mostly during the long cold winter months. When in the powwow circle, the dress sparkled under the lights, glistening and clicking in time with the sacred drum.

"This is so much good material for the book. Much more than I bargained for," Camille heard Sunny say, both his ears pointing at her. Amber waved at someone under the tent. "Amber, when you get time, let's further discuss the PAC that you and Camille were developing. I want to include some details in the book." Amber agreed before joining friends under the food tent.

In twenty minutes, the sun had set. A string of light bulbs around the powwow grounds fought the night. The drum quieted for only a moment. Now the beat was slow, a far cry from the throbbing Smoke Dance tempo.

"Go join," Ariwiio urged Sunny, pointing to the now-forming circle of dancers. "This is a Social Dance. It's for everybody, Native or not. For millennia, we've asked immigrants to join us. You can wear anything: baseball caps, shorts, jeans. My shin is sore today, or I would join you." He massaged his leg. "All you do is step, tap, step, tap the ball of your foot on the ground, as easy as walking."

Sunny took Ariwiio up on the opportunity to actually be a part of the Sunadaga Nation—if only for a moment. She joined the circle.

The powwow ground lighting created long, deep shadows. The drum and chants were hypnotic. In the circle, men's ankle bells jingled, deer hooves clattered, horn rattles clicked, and women's beaded dresses hissed with each step. It was mesmerizing.

In five minutes, Sunny had the Social Dance moves down pat. She even added flourish with shoulder swings that complemented her steps. She was startled from her trance when someone tapped her on the shoulder from behind.

The man's face was heavily painted, and he wore a feathered headdress, a *gustoweh*. His head was bowed, the feathers hiding much of his painted face. The lights above threw shadows over his facial features. Suede streamers ran down the side of his buckskin trousers. He wore a dark blue, ribbon shirt. Something about the man's build was familiar.

"Is that you?" she whispered, craning her neck for a closer look, trying to see the man's face under his bowed head.

When the man smiled briefly, she knew for certain it was Camille. Her mouth fell open. He was taking quite the risk of being found out, but she knew he had to be here, with his family, with his people.

"I just couldn't resist. Only a few minutes," he whispered. "I'm missing my old life." They danced two full revolutions of the powwow circle.

Sunny was smiling ear-to-ear, feet dancing to the powerful beat. But then she slowed. "Your father just stood up. He's staring our way." They danced to the drum for another half circle.

"In ten minutes, meet me in the woods where I was. We can quietly borrow old man Swamp's farm truck.

Everybody borrows it to haul firewood. We can drive to the edge of the territory for the water and soil samples."

Camille discreetly exited the powwow circle, his head low, face hidden.

Chapter Fifty

With the vials of soil and water samples safely stored in the saddlebag on the floor of the old truck, Sunny marveled at the full moon rising on the horizon. They sat on an outcrop of rock at the edge of the Sunadaga territory, forty-five minutes from the powwow ground. Chirping crickets, croaking frogs, and a hooting owl somewhere in the distance broke the quiet of the cool night. She could get used to this.

Camille swung his large arm around her shoulders and pulled her closer. She ran her hands under his braid and wrapped her arm around his strong waist.

Camille still wore his full regalia from the powwow circle. His face was painted traditionally. The feathers in his *gustoweh* fluttered with each wind gust. His eyes shone in the moonlight.

"You're helping me solve my mother's death," Camille said quietly. "So maybe I can help you solve your father's death."

Sunny thought for a moment. *How could he help with her father's unsolved case?* Which of his powers could get to the bottom of her loss?

"Thank you. I'm going to keep that in mind." A definitive answer wouldn't bring her father back, but it would allow a measure of closure. She leaned her head against Camille's shoulder while watching the full moon inch higher above the treetops.

Sunny was ready to spend more time with this incredible man. What had started out as gratitude for saving her life was growing into something else between them. She wanted to help him out of the shadows. Camille needed to be free, free as the breeze, free as a flying bird, free as a dolphin spinning above the Hudson River.

She would soon have the ME report on the man Camille supposedly murdered. With that last piece of the puzzle, she could start to free him. She looked up into his handsome moonlit face behind the face paint.

First, his eyes smiled, then the corners of his mouth turned up. Hesitantly, he leaned to kiss her with the warmest kiss on the lips, then pulled back, his teeth gleaming as he looked into her eyes. They both moved forward, but then Sunny's phone rang, interrupting the moment.

It was her Loo. "Hey, what's up?"

"Our team just caught the next case."

"Already?"

"It's summer in the city, rookie," Lieutenant Sanchez cracked. "I already called KD. Again, congratulations on solving the Hudson River Greenway cases. I've nominated you for the Police Combat Cross for your act of heroism against an armed adversary."

She knew going into law enforcement that her time wouldn't be her own. The Job demanded first dibs, and in a small way, this was how she made the world a little better place to live in, and, to honor her father.

She never gave it a second thought about saving the terrified child from Luke Chambers. She and Camille would have to saddle up and, on falcon wings, get back to New York City immediately. But not before she turned back to Camille with a big smile.

"Where were we?"

About the Authors

Dwight Peace(Salaam), Donnie Tehonatake Fadden, and Dave Kanietakeron Fadden all reside in New York state with their families. When not engaged in storytelling(written or oral), they spend their time painting, crafting, working on cars, reading novels, or enjoying their families and pets.

www.ingramcontent.com/pod-product-compliance
Lightning Source LLC
Chambersburg PA
CBHW062126170626
46813CB00002B/580